"ASTONISHING. MARVELOUS! JUST SIMPLY GRAND. SYLVIA ASHTON-WARNER IS ONE OF THE GREAT PROSE STYLISTS OF OUR DAY."

—*Chicago Daily News*

Readers of the superb bestsellers Teacher *and* Spinster *know the singular spell Sylvia Ashton-Warner weaves. Here, in this marvelously fresh creation, she brings to life her most stunningly vibrant heroine—Tarl, a lovely woman fiercely determined to live as she and not the world chooses; a loving mother set on raising her children in her own independent and wondrous way.*

"Full of spirit and the fire of genius . . . original, affecting and unforgettable, the story opens strange vistas into the human spirit."

—*Columbus Dispatch*

D0971472

Books by Sylvia Ashton-Warner

- SPINSTER
- INCENSE TO IDOLS
- TEACHER
- BELL CALL
- GREENSTONE

- Published by Bantam Books, Inc.

SYLVIA ASHTON-WARNER
BELL CALL

BANTAM BOOKS
TORONTO · NEW YORK · LONDON

BELL CALL

A Bantam Book / published by arrangement with
Simon and Schuster, Inc.

PRINTING HISTORY

Simon and Schuster edition published December 1964
2nd printing . . . March 1965
Bantam edition published June 1967

All the characters in this book are fictitious.

Published simultaneously in the United States and Canada

Bantam Books are published by Bantam Books, Inc., a subsidiary
of Grosset & Dunlap, Inc. Its trade-mark, consisting of the words
"Bantam Books" and the portrayal of a bantam, is registered in the
United States Patent Office and in other countries. Marca Registrada.
Bantam Books, Inc., 271 Madison Avenue, New York, N.Y. 10016.

PRINTED IN THE UNITED STATES OF AMERICA

To my country
NEW ZEALAND

That one who spoke of "the little loaves and fishes
of poetry" hoped, doubtless, to feed multitudes
from this rapt act. I have no such wishes.
Ploughing my furrow in empty latitudes
this practice becomes an exercise for fingers
that would weave deftly a trap for strangers;
a little net for reality to enter and
there be known. It is myself I seek,
and something permanent from the casual week
that filters away relentlessly as sand
in the lady's hour-glass ...

—Louis Johnson, New Zealand

ONE

❧❧❧❧❧❧

Ploughing my furrow in empty latitudes . . .
—LOUIS JOHNSON

❧ THURSDAY EVENING turns out to be cold and windy although it is nearly spring. Funereal clouds have buried the moon so that the trees sway and groan in deprivation—tall many-armed male bodies in the night of womanlessness. From his chair by the fire in the music room Daniel is at one with them knowing exactly the meaning of womanlessness. Like theirs his love is moon-dead too and shrouded in distant clouds.

"You're not at work?" from the Head on his way back to school, where he keeps abreast in the evening. Surprised.

Dan makes the gesture of at least lowering his paper but seems to have no answer.

The sound of keys in the headmaster's pocket, as his fingers move in inquiry. "Aren't you going back to work?" Then with feeling, "By gee you've got a nice blaze here."

Dan reaches for his smokes and begins reflectively rolling. "Will I never learn not to answer the bloody phone?"

Later as the Head moves off up the hall laughing, Dan calls after him, "Turn on the outside light, Ric." She'll never find her way through the trees in the darkness.

He hears Ric's steps crossing the veranda and down the front steps, then along the concrete path until they fade in the rushing of the trees. But later he doesn't hear hers coming. Just a soft knock on the door, dead on seven, the time arranged, soft and rueful like the voice on the phone. Something with padded feet. He slippers up the hall to the door.

"I came to ask for something. I hope you don't mind."

She's lithe, like some furred animal adept at slipping in and out of shadows, snatching food and dashing off in danger. She's small, she wears some jersey thing with contoured stripes like parallel shadows of branches. She's got marvelous eyes. They're dark, spilling with pathos. They're large, they're luminous, they collect all the stars from the outside light and toss them back at you. He's surprised to see two children who follow her in from the night . . . he thought she said her business was "private, very important" to herself. None of the three has a coat but none is shivering. "They wanted to come so I brought them." Take it or leave it.

Sits on the arm of the big chair, not in it, and the children curl down by the fire. A girl about nine, a boy about seven, slight, dark, sensitive.

"There are some books in that cupboard for you children. All sorts of . . ."

Swiftly from the parent, "They don't need anything, thanks. They're all right." The children, who were rising, settle down again and give themselves up entirely to the light of the flames, as one gives himself up to the moment, with no morning or night, no before or after, with no horizons whatever. Their moment is in a vacuum of nothing.

Thirty-odd. Unkempt-looking really. Long black hair tied with something yellow round the head. White face, shadowed cheeks, no make-up, and these large, luminous and brown eyes, hopeful yet fearful, like an animal dangerously seeking food. She's not upright enough about the shoulders, they're humbly rounded, only the hold of the head has defiance. Or bravado it might be, or desperation. And this striped jersey on the top over matadors too baggy to give a man much, leaving the lower legs bare: slim, browned, haired and bare. Worn flat shoes, a fashion or two old. Although the eyes slip away from Dan's they bravely return again. Ah, that's it. It's not defiance, bravado or desperation that emanates from her but a straight-out bravery. All told, in this woman from the night there could be nothing further from the portrait of his wife behind her in its curly-wooded gold frame, that other who comes from the night.

The "private, very important" thing she's come about boils down to the merest trivia as he had feared it would. Help, of course. People never really don't want something. It's the impulse behind all our actions. How to market some paintings of

4

hers, overseas agents and such, did he know of some rich collector of originals? Things anyone could do under their own power. He did at her age.

It comes out as she talks that there are four children, the two younger ones home with the father—he's interested to hear there's a father—that she sleeps between these younger two and paints when they are sleeping. "Oh-h-h . . ." hand pressed to cheek, "the job I have getting out of bed without disturbing them. Just one leg out and one of them wakes."

He leans back and rolls a smoke as she talks. And it is she who talks. It's her line of thought that dominates, not his, the man's. She has not uttered the courtesy, "How are you?" and does not once refer to Dan or his work. Here is no follower of a man. Here is no material for a harmonious man-woman relationship. Or a woman-woman relationship, as far as that goes. No relationship at all, unless it could be with children—the last resort of the lonely. Also, as she talks, it is revealed to him that she's spent little of her life's quota of passion at all. One might well be afraid of these people. It's there all right but . . . it's there in her all right, you can see it in her eyes, but the pallor of her face is not that of the overlived, overspent, the bankrupt in feeling. It's the pallor of one under the strain of all those who determine to walk counter to the common. It's the pallor of one who still believes that just about everything matters. There is nothing in her of the relaxation of the children, their submission to timelessness. But there is in her the passion to be what they are—bubbles on the Everlasting Now. In the same room as the dark firelit grand she seems out of place in civilization. Whereas everyone knows that it is more profitable and certainly less uncomfortable to appear to be part of it.

"We don't send our children to school until they want to go. The symbiosis between mother and child should not be broken until the child himself breaks it. We mean our children to live their own lives in accordance with their original nature." Pause. "Ramona started school when she was nine but only because she wanted to. She said, 'Oh I'll go I suppose.' But Bennie hasn't said that yet." Then carelessly, "We got round the law by traveling overseas. We were always visitors."

He doesn't make coffee . . . the irritation. She doesn't reply to what little he says, she indicates no admiration of him and his work and shows no signs whatever of having fallen in love with him as most women should on sight. Above all there is no awe or respect at all in her manner toward him but rather a familiarity. All told, it seems that what she really wants of him is not the trivial advice she professed to have come for, but his audience value; a confirmation of what she is. Besides he doesn't like legs frankly haired; nice women shave them. Lustrous silk stockings are the least of the tributes he expects from women who meet him.

Although she does have a soft voice and a certain humility. . . .

"What," asks the Head on his way home at nine, "made her think you wanted to see children in the evening?"

"They wanted to come so she brought them. What I wanted didn't occur to her."

Daniel recounts the conversation on the Prackets' attitude to schooling while Ric turns his hands this way and that before the secret embers, like turning thoughts over in mind, and says, "Praise God that's not my problem."

"No. They're three schools away."

"They're . . . beg your pardon?"

"Three schools away." Enunciated with clarity, although Dan is sure Ric heard in the first place.

"Three schools? Oh, they're three schools away? I see." Pause . . . then he veers from the subject. "You've got no work done tonight, I suppose."

"Don't talk about it."

Some weeks later the white face and the eyes at the door again. In the evening at seven as he is on his way to work along the green veranda, here they are padding silently up the steps. "I've got something to ask you, Mr. Francis. I couldn't get you on the phone so I just came. I hope you don't mind?" Her luminous eyes lift to his in masterly pathos. Still the jungle stripes on top, the soiled pants and the yellow scarf round her head. They've walked in the darkness up the playground and through the watching trees. "I saw your outside light on."

"How pleasant to see you, Mrs. Pracket. How are you?"

Back to the music room all over again. After a couple of hours as she rises to go, "But what I *really* came for . . . I wonder if you'd give me something to read. Lend me something. I can't go to the library with four children and when my husband is home it's closed. My aunt won't mind them for longer than twenty minutes."

"The term 'lending books' is synonymous with 'throwing them away.' I no longer throw away my books."

With respect, "All right then."

But he does lend her an overseas magazine with reproductions of a French woman artist. "Or a Chinese?"

"*Thank* you," reverence.

To the Head on his way home at nine from school, where he has been writing up the committee minutes and sorting and storing the art supplies, "I didn't give her any more advice although she asked for it. She did the exact opposite to what I advised last time and ran into the very trouble I warned her she would. And another thing, by God, I knew better than to offer the children occupation this time. They simply sat and listened to everything that was said."

The Head's smile was gone. "By gee I'm glad it's not my problem."

"I gave her some wine though. I was pleased with her word 'symbiosis' and with the way she used it. Besides she's a variation. We must always devoutly thank God in this country for the slightest variation. But I'm still furious about my rejected advice."

Ric stirs uneasily. Pockets a hand and you hear key on key. "And you've done no work?"

Dan reaches for his smokes. "Why ask advice? Something to do the opposite from?"

"Well I must get home. I've got an enormous week. Three meetings at . . ."

"What infuriates me is that I never give advice anyway."

". . . at night and a visiting school. Are these your letters on the stool? I'll take them."

"Infuriates me."

All this and much more from Mrs. Pracket as spring slides into summer.

Most Saturdays Dan collects Angela and the babies from the farm in the heart of the country at the foot of the high blue ranges, driving the twenty-five miles along the estuaries and back again twice, making a solid hundred, and hilariously and intimately the two of them toss off these days together in and out of the babies and usually to the roar of the motor mower. Urgently, snatchingly, they live them. But now, on occasion, Tarl Pracket appears, neither of them knowing why. The first time she comes without the children and spends the entire day. A very cold new-spring day with a touch of the antarctic on it.

"I've got to talk to you," on his doorstep in the morning soon after he has returned with Angela. "It's urgent," pacing the length of the old schoolhouse. "I must have a long deep talk with you," suddenly pulling up in front of him in the music room. "I'm desperate. I want you to tell me some Maori pa* where I can go with the children. You must know many, don't you?" Weaving her way through Angela's babies, "We're not happy in civilized places," taking up her glass from the fridge in the kitchen and taking a sip of civilized wine, "I want the children to grow up in primitive simplicity, to live their lives as they should," gasping from the veranda to the kitchen in her worn raincoat and back to the veranda again to breathe in the cold wild air. "We prefer the Maoris and their natural values." Another flight outside and back to base in the music room where a large fire blazes behind a guard. A sip of her wine, "I've got to get away from that hovel." Puts down glass a moment, "I've got to get away from suburbia. I can't breathe surrounded by Victorian tradition." Moans and presses a cheek with a hand in a way Dan has come to know, "I must find a place just right for me. Oh-h-h . . . I must have freedom." Until finally, late afternoon, as he prepares to drive Angela home, "I feel a bit better. I might last a bit longer." At which they are obliged to leave her sitting on the step, knees to chin, brooding.

"What disgraceful behavior from a woman," from Angela as they swing out upon the road. "All that performance in front of the children. Where's her control, Daddy? Where's her feminine dignity? To plunge into your house and behave like that."

Angela is a willowy-wandy girl swaying all ways, taller than Tarl Pracket and more like Dan than her mother. She's all fair hair tossing, white teeth laughing and blue eyes sparking. She jumps at sudden noises and touches people easily. Her hands reach out swiftly in the gestures of love as one finds in women who live with kisses from the dawn right round to the next, who breathe kisses and tears like air. Kisses from Rod, kisses from her children and many a kiss for her father. These girls with husbands and annual babies . . . could they count their kisses? Are they even aware of them? Hands reach quickly from girls like Angela to touch some part of another and tears play suddenly, willingly as spring and summer showers . . . all from a built-in sympathy. But after a day of Tarl Pracket, feeding her with hot scones and coffee to little apparent avail, Angela's laughing, touching and eye-sparking have closed up somewhat and there's only hair-tossing left; waving fair hair down her back and summer-sky eyes.

---

* pa: Maori village

"Did I put that lettuce on board for you, Ange?"

"Coming into the house like that. She needs discipline."

"I only remember putting in the silver beet. Did . . ."

"Behaving like that. Her husband must be weak."

". . . you put the lettuce in? I gave one to Mrs. Pracket, I remember. Gosh I must say she lapped up the civilization today. The fire and the scones and the wine and so on. And the overseas papers."

"It's you she's after, Daddy." A toss of the long fair hair tied behind and a spark in the lively eyes. "Yes I put in the lettuce."

"Ay? Oh you did?"

"It's plain as plain she's after you."

"Oh, *don't*. The thought of it knots my guts."

"Your attention at any price."

"Oh stop it. It's you, Ange. I know I'm irresistible and all that but you're nearer her age and you've got small children too. Isn't it always Saturday she comes now when she knows you're here?"

"When she was at my place she was asking questions about you all the time."

"Oh?"

"You heard me."

"Anyway I do thank you for being kind to her. And all that."

"Mother would have done it had she lived." A blue summer tear, brief. "I was sorry for her anyway. Four little children." The tear has already dropped somewhere, on the top of the baby's head. "By the way, *did* you know this? She told me that when they first returned to New Zealand they lived in Hallibut's orchard next door. Just over your fence. All last summer," sensationally, "in a tent in the trees. Just over your fence."

"Hell."

"And what about this, Daddy? They've left that hovel on the mountain behind the muddy cowyard now and have rented a cottage on the inner harbor just below your land."

"*Ay?*"

"Work that out."

"I didn't even see them over the fence last summer."

"But she saw you."

"Oh."

"Think that over."

At the close of another Saturday he is watching Angela gathering her young about her before setting out for home. Is there any more poignant and beautiful picture beneath the protecting

9

heavens than the female animal collecting its young, radiating from the parent center, rising in graded levels? Does she see this, he wonders, she so ever-present? I do . . . for I am "she."

"Come to Mummie, little Brucey. Mary—are you coming, Mary? Daddy, will you hold the baby a minute? Now have I *got* everyone? Have I got everything? Oh Daddy, don't let me forget those vegetables. Goodbye, Tarl. See you again."

A rueful gaze . . .

"Goodbye, Mrs. Pracket," from Dan. "Make yourself at home. Put some more wood on the fire." He doesn't say, "Come with us for a run."

It is not until they are well on the way to Rod's place, sweeping and curling along flower-lit roads striped with shadows from rearing trees like a sleeping jungle animal, or sometimes like the shadows of parallel bars across a pondering prisoner, a wondering remembering prisoner . . . that he says, above the engine and the children's voices, "We've got to be careful, y'know, Ange, with people like her. She's got hold of something. She's got some qualities that aa . . . they don't occur in the mediocre. This impression she gives of being ready at any moment to take big risks rapidly, that's one of them. Her vague designs, they bear the mark of grandeur. We've always, all of us, got these longings for freedom, barely discernible. It's just that most of us are less frank about them. And her aims—they're high. She's got this contempt for contingencies while the mass is concerned with detail."

Tenderly, "You'd defend anybody, Daddy." A pause. "You spoil people."

"Kaapar song me," from Bruce wrapped round his neck like a scarf.

"See how you're spoiling that boy? Trying to drive with a boy round your neck and a baby swinging on your beard. Every single, solitary person you meet you spoil, including me. Gosh what a teacher you were." She unwinds Brucey from his neck. "And you're going to spoil Tarl. But it's all right, I understand. There's little I don't know of the. . . I mean, I know artists. I've picked up their ways. I haven't lived with you most of my life for nothing. I'll try to see it your way."

"Your mother used to talk like that, Ange. She could follow another's thought. And she could catch alight from another's feeling. Not everyone can. Mrs. Pracket can't."

"I'll do my best to be kind to her."

"I believe it. You've got just the same grand permissiveness for all that she had."

"If only Tarl would comb her hair, Daddy. Is that too much to expect? Surely she could at least change her clothes once in a while and—and it wouldn't hurt her to stand upright. Well, it wouldn't interfere with her . . . what did you call it? Combing her hair wouldn't hurt her 'mark of grandeur.' Oh never mind, I'll be kind."

So far the Pracket story does no more than pass over Dan like . . . no. I was going to say like short showers over the countryside laying the dust, glistening the leaves and cooling the breathless flowers which dry out at once in the following sun. No, it's more like a draught from the antarctic coughed up over the lower Tasman Sea with an edge of breaking ice. Which will cease altogether when they take off to a Maori pa. So that when Angela and Dan run into the whole family on Election Day one benign Saturday morning on the beach below his land the impact is no more than dust deep. Tarl Pracket must be feeling a little better as she said she did that cold day in spring, since, far from retreating to Maoridom to wallow about in freedom, here she still is with her husband in the heart of civilization, renting quite a pretty hovel below his land.

It turns out that not only does Tarl Pracket not mean to vote but also that she didn't even know it was Election Day, from which point she and Angela blaze at each other with passion. "There's no future," claims Mrs. Pracket. "Only the present is real."

Dan is quite content to leave her to Angela, having long since repudiated argument, especially with women, let alone one with a cause. And Gavin Pracket extricates himself with a smile and goes off to vote before joining a working bee at Ramona's school.

"Well," sparks Angela, "if that's how you feel about the future I can see why you don't vote. But I bet if you found yourself in a country where the people had no rights you'd realize the privilege of voting fast enough. You seem to forget that it's only on account of the law that you and the kids can walk the country roads in safety. And what about the control of food and disease, not to mention education? And what about the social security you take advantage of and the child allowance you draw? How could we remain civilized? All that about freedom and no-mind, no future and the Everlasting Now . . . it might have been all right in the Stone Age. Things were different then. The pace of living for one. What you don't seem

11

to register is that we're living in the Space Age now. No one can hide themselves away. Fallout will find us all, in or out of caves. You're just burying your head in the ..."

"Our heads would be better in the sand."

Angela appeals to her father, "What do you say to a thing like that, Daddy?" But he knows better than to answer. "Honestly," she continued, "would you really prefer to be back in the Stone Age?"

Grandly Tarl Pracket commits herself, declaring she certainly would, and quotes poetry Dan has never heard. But Angela's feet remain on the ground. "Well there's still a few countries about like that. Why come to this one?"

But for some reason she doesn't answer.

From the car Dan risks, "Whether we would be better off in the Stone Age than in the present one is hardly, I suggest, an issue. We *are* in this age *now*. And no man can live outside his era."

Tarl is in fine form. "The whole twentieth century is out of its era. Man does not belong here." Both these girls love argument.

"Come on, Ange," from Dan, "we must make a move."

"Oh *please* don't go," from Tarl. "*Do* stay. I never have visitors. No one ever comes to see me."

Angela, "We've got to go and vote."

For all that they end up in the cottage for tea, submerged by the two lots of children. Going in the door they all step carefully over a circular design in sand, shells, leaves and flowers composed by one of the children. Much sweeter than anything from a toy shop. And in the gentle hostess you'd never recognize the woman who strode up and down the house a month ago demanding oblivion in a Maori pa, while the reciprocal trust and respect between her and the four children is a lesson for anyone.

Driving Angela back to the school to vote, where the Head is returning officer, "It wasn't so absolutely frightfully dirty or untidy in that cottage, Ange."

"Daddy. You didn't see out the back. I had to take Mary to the toilet."

"Of course, some people, they just don't see the material."

"I've never, *ever* seen such ..."

"When the inner eye is occupied with vision it can't—there's nothing tangible, physical to them. They ..."

"And not voting. Daddy, she *must* be mad."

"If she has any acquaintance with reason I agree it is accidental. But I think she ... I've got to be careful in case I'm mistaken. I think she's got in her hands a vast universal truth concerning the freedom of the mind. Moreover she has either the courage, stubbornness, desperation or inspiration to stand by what she believes, an unlikely thing in New Zealand. It remains to be seen how she operates it."

The school is moving toward the end-of-year break-up function before the six weeks' summer holidays and Tarl Pracket brings Angela along since none of the row of cars lined up beneath the trees at the farm will go. Tarl's choice of clothes might look all right in the shadows of a jungle or against the sand of a beach but side by side with the glamour of Angela . . . "I had to wear this old skirt. I couldn't get the hem of that dress right. No one has given me a dress for a long time. Only strides." The comparison is outright sad, the streaking untended hair against Angela's sheen and earrings. And she brings Ramona and Benjamin.

When it gets back to the Head that the two Pracket children were so enchanted with the school and the many Maori children on the roll that they decided to attend here directly after the holidays, even Benjamin himself, he stops praising God it is not his problem and says only, "It'll be interesting to see what comes of it."

"I shouldn't be telling you this, Daddy, but . . ."

"That's a very good opening sentence." At which she laughs and sways this way and that. He is driving them home one Saturday through the breezes drifting absently from the west over the Tasman Sea so that the taffeta tops of the gums sway to and fro like Angela.

Angela stops laughing. "D'you know what she did? She sat down in the music room and fed that great boy of two-and-a-half from herself. More than once. He'd just leap upon her and she'd whip up that striped top and—can you believe it? Wouldn't you *think* . . . I mean . . ."

"Did you keep the door of your mother's room shut?"

"There was no need to. The whole four children are most undestructive. Never fight or cry or break things or anything like that. Not like other kids. Not like my own. And when both want a thing you hear them say—and you won't believe *this*— 'You have it.' And they are sincere about it. And I will say she's taught them how to eat quietly. No one knows more than I do how hard that is. But her kids don't mix, y'know. Dessida was too shy to play with Mary. And Mary's a born mixer."

Mary herself adds, "Dessida was shy to come in. I told her not to be shy to come in but she was shy to come in."

Later, "But Daddy, oh I can see it is you she's after."

"No, it's you."

Into the shadow of a glade and out in the sun again, then through one of these deep cuttings of scarlet clay layered in yellow. "If only she'd straighten her shoulders, Daddy, don't you think? And put on a pretty dress, even a little make-up. She's so slim. She's got so much. I've never seen such magnificent eyes. She could still be a knock-out and keep her 'universal truth' in her hands."

The road sweeps round the top of an estuary here and the tide is out. Down the marshy valley the blue of the sea is distant. Dan's thoughts dwell on the far shining water and when he speaks again it is about something else. "I don't think the Head really believes they are coming to his school. Today she says they are but tomorrow . . . no. This wind from the west blowing from the Tasman . . . it'll be blowing from the Pacific by morning."

"I've come to say goodbye."

It is Tarl Pracket and the whole four children right down to Dessida and Homer, on the eve of the summer holidays. She has the heavy Homer on her hip and leans awry to take his weight. With no sound whatever they have materialized in their beautiful touching grouping on the grass beside him where he is swearing over the rotary mower sharpening and oiling the thing. "Hullo, how are you?"

With reckless finality, "We're going away tomorrow for good." The wind has changed from the Tasman to the Pacific. Then her voice lowers ruefully, "I've brought all the children with me so Gavin can scrub out the cottage." Lower, more rueful still, "He's not in a very good mood." It's Saturday and there's no Angela here, which doesn't mean he needs Mrs. Pracket in her place.

"I don't like this district, Mr. Francis. We're going right up north and we're not coming back." In low swift prose he hears how Gavin Pracket has resigned his job at the college, send-off function, present and all, and how they're all going to find a place "just right for me"; some secluded spot, some forgotten overlooked Maori pa where they'll live in primitive simplicity, where there are no more respectabilities, Victorian traditions, conformities or appointments and where the children are out of reach of school buses; no more law, No One In Charge and where the children can merge with nature. And Gavin can . . .

"There's no such thing," carelessly, "as a forgotten Maori village where there is no schooling for the children. Beyond the reach of buses the child is expected to be enrolled at the Correspondence School. There's not an overlooked child in the country."

Irrelevantly but with fire, "Schools are Institutions of Force with Someone In Charge."

"Besides, Gavin, I hear, is an excellent teacher."

"I don't approve of teaching. He should be selling matches."

"I don't argue."

Later when he's made the tea because Angela would, because her mother would have, with the children full blast on civilization all over the house and grounds, never breaking or taking or quarreling, however, "But what I really came for . . . could I store a couple of suitcases here? We won't have room in the car. I may pick them up some day."

"There's not room in the house for a mousetrap more."

"Not under some bed? It's only rubbish. Behind some door?"

"I'm not a storer really. Not of suitcases."

"The garage would do."

"Have you seen the garage?"

"Well could I leave the guitar here?"

"Leave anything behind but the music."

"Oh-h . . . how lovely." The hint of a smile but behind a hand. Up goes the baby on her hip again and her eyes lift to his in wistful vision. The sun is low now, stretching its long tree-shadows through the trunks making a pattern of bars on the lawn, and the smell of cut grass is sad. The dark irises of her eyes are set in flawless white, incomparably dramatic and in them as she looks up at him is this thing to be seen so terribly in the young—hope. And her voice is soft with faith. "Tomorrow we'll be with nature where there's no one at all In Charge. Freedom . . . oh-h-h."

She continues in the rounding up of her young, than which there is no lovelier sight in nature. "Come on, Dessida." The four-year-old with the long dark hair throws her arms passionately round her mother's slight legs. "Where is Bennie?" Up the tree. "Ramona?" Skips like a fairy down the steps, all but taking flight, her long hair wafting. Then she turns to him, her body at an angle from the unnecessary weight of the boy on her hip, "Nothing can harm us in the Everlasting Now." Along the path a bit then back to him with pathos. "There are obstacles, always obstacles, but I will overcome them. I'll find security in the Now. The magnificent Do-Nothing." Through the watching trees, the young assimilating her mood, gamboling about her like a flock of tender animals, across the empty playground to their dusty little car at the gate.

Through the gate, into the car and off to Shangri-La.

⚜ MIDSUMMER AND PEACE.

With the school firmly closed, comprehensively locked and every child and teacher gone, Angela wholly engaged on the farm, the Head and his family away at the Lakes and the Pracket family presumably at Shangri-La, Dan's domain is quiet awhile. Only echoes and phantoms arrive and depart on the steps of the shaded veranda or beneath the outside light, only the paper boy and milkman down at the gate.

Earnestly, morning and evening, he makes his way along the veranda to settle down self-consciously at his table as though work were the answer to life and the only alternative to pain, as if there were answers to these. As though writing were worth it anyway, or any other effort for that matter to a man without a wife; never learning the lessons taught by the moon that women learn in half the time. Poor old Dan at the end of the veranda toiling among his phrases. Way back in youth before I died to the scent of anesthetic and freesias he never thought of toiling.

Here he is during these summer weeks of silence engaged in taking himself seriously as well as all these other shadows like love and death and beauty and life and even the talk of truth, not to say that most nebulous of all concepts, that condition of the greatest complexity such as no logician would even attempt to analyze—freedom of the mind . . . as if these abstractions really mattered. The moon and I would tell him differently. The high moon has watched them for eons and eons and I for the years of youth, and we both remain unimpressed. Whatever the drama she witnesses below she remains exactly the same: cold, calm, white, indifferent as she strolls the star-sown roads.

Dan used to be a teacher living from bell to bell so that when he hears them now he still is constrained to answer. When they go he goes. Even though he's no longer a teacher but only a man now he still goes to work when the bells are calling. As for this school bell right next to him—he himself rang it until a year ago when he gave up that job, when he stopped teaching the children in the school and sank to writing of them. But he still lives in the old schoolhouse. Everyone knows but does not say so that he should have moved out by now but the practical organization of building a house of his own . . . so far, it is beyond him. And the new headmaster, Mr. Richmond, lets him stay until he has built his own, being a man who habitually "lets," he himself renting a place behind.

This historied old house he lives and writes in alone, rooming all ways like afterthoughts, added to absently over the years like writing its own house diary, is actually set in the school grounds with the hundreds of children swirling and noising barely fifty yards away with no fence or hedge between. Through the trunks of the towering trees planted sixty years ago he sees them through the door; hears their voices, watches them playing and answers the bell when they do. So bred is he to this condition that I doubt he could do without it. Which could be the real reason the Head lets him stay, though neither of them has mentioned it.

He works satisfactorily enough by day through the rollicking of the children nearby and their outbursts of singing in class though they do pin him down to reality. But in the evening, long after the buses have taken them home, when of their calling, carousing and caroling there is not an echo left, after he has put out the milk bottle way down at the gate, has collected from there the evening paper and has eaten a meal reading it, when he has walked up the hall and turned on the outside light and has made his solitary way along the veranda barred with the stripes of the shadows upon it from the old-time reaching roses to his table in the library . . . then reality is cleanly rubbed from the blackboard and imagery is chalked upon it.

Midsummer and peace.

The only bell now that calls to work is the one in mind in the library when he summons his creatures to him. The only sound he hears above the birds by day and the tapping of the moths on the pane in the evening is the whirring of the wings of his spirit. Waking in the early mornings he sees them in mind flapping ridiculously against the high ceiling, their flimsy feathers fluttering. He and his spirit alone together in the sentimental solitude . . . the kind of thought that disgusts his critics and that would nauseate me myself were there feeling of any kind this side of the grave.

In the equilibrium of days and nights however he does find the track to the other world of fluid imagery that more realistically I'd call the imagination. As stealthily as a truant schoolboy he climbs through the wires fencing off the unreal from the real to the domain of imagery where, sneaking its barefoot ways, he outwits what he calls his teacher, pain. He crosses this border between reality and the exhilarating territory of the imagination —an estate vast, unboundaried, its horizons the eye-blue mountains—to raid his memories, snare his phantoms and spend the hours in the past. Down forgotten sunlit ways he digresses shamelessly far from his anxious present to dally and philander in romantic shadows by unforgettable streams.

To win once more the pleasant oblivion from the accent of life upon him. No longer does he wash or dress in the morning but goes straight from bed to work evading the civilized routines that scatter the riches from sleep. Preserved, unbroken from pillow to table are the fragile inhabitants of the mind let loose during the night; they continue to breathe on paper. He hears their voices and sees their faces as clearly as those of reality. There come to him increasing and nameless flights of time when their passionately lived drama is the one reality of life, making the world called "real" the shadow. Ecstatic and dangerous reversal. There's no room for the monster, pain, during these midsummer weeks obsessed. Is it morning or evening, day or night . . . when is he, who is he . . . where?

During these unrecorded evenings and days of peace in his treed retreat he wins the battle for surcease on the acres of the mind. No longer does he find himself dueling with the hungry living monster of pain which cannot be eased by others. Pouring him out in anguished talk does not defeat this monster for, in such passing relief—in giving sorrow words—he eats sufferer and listener alike, the only tangible result being that two agonize now in place of one. Besides he returns soon after and once again come the knives and numbness physically within. What is this talk of "sharing pain"? It's no more than spreading pain. Pain must be dealt with alone in his lair and since in the first place he was born of some interest the only answer is another interest. Counter interest with interest, passion with passion, obsession with equal obsession . . . or so he tells himself.

Writing in the library with his door open one evening there are times when he has in mind a girl not unlike me, his wife, when something makes him look up and see the original, a phantom in the shadows of the veranda. He can just make out this red coat of mine over something white at the throat, the black of my hair fusing with night and my star-pale face. As always when I come my blue eyes are pleading for life, to return to the womb of his mind and endure among his heartbeats. But he knows better than to speak or approach me or turn on the outside light. I'll vanish, his love from the night. If he so much as speaks my name, Macushla, there'll be no one on the veranda. Only the presence of the mighty trees wooing the pale moon.

The peace of a long midsummer. In the music room on his way to work or returning wearily from it he sometimes confers with me in my portrait on the wall, a brilliantly colored oil painting by a sister of his when I was seventeen. To this day she insists it was never more than a practice painting trying out a new technique and she never had the chance to finish it. Which could well be true, however accidentally, since when he took it from her that day the paint was still frankly wet and even got smudged in places on the long journey home from the capital. I recall a howling wet day, a genuine Wellington southerly, and he had it wrapped in newspaper. I was with him that day in the car. Prophetically the painting was never finished since my life was never finished. Indeed it had barely begun.

Not so much "poor old Dan toiling among his phrases." With his belief in the importance of all states of life—its joys, griefs, crises and its sensibility to love—with his ration of apportioned feeling not wholly used and his persisting capacity to hope, it's truer to say "poor *young* Dan." A man must spend all that he is before I'd call him old, so that looking down upon his spent heart in the red of the fallen leaves rapidly discharging its life he feels like the moon. Blenched and bloodless like the moon before I'd call him old. But man is not like the moon. Expended passion leaves something behind in a man you'll never find in the moon. You'll never read compassion and understanding in that high pallid face, not as you do in man.

It's all very well for you, moon, to ignore human passion. Eons ago you could not have ignored it in your own cosmic passion. In your travail of being formed by some collision of fiery galaxies you knew heat one time yourself. All very well your cold face now, supercilious moon.

⚜ A SUN-SHED Sunday afternoon. School reopens tomorrow morning after six weeks of silence.

His door open upon the summer and here comes this fantail Mary is fond of flying this way and that, erratically, like a somewhat inconsequent human. Maybe there's the lure of a dream on his mind and he seeks the perfect life as Dan and I confidently sought it when we fell in love, and which we did know for a year. Maybe this bird is after a place "just right" for him as Tarl Pracket said she was, and suddenly thinks he has found it in the reflection of the garden in the window pane on the drowsy veranda, for he flies bang into it, headlong, beak-on, only to be knocked back hard to reality as Dan and I were. Shangri-La he thought he saw but struck fact instead.

Unevenly and with no doubt a bad headache he flies away, as Dan follows him with his eyes, knowing exactly how he feels. But does he see something else? Is that someone moving . . . coming? Does he hear soft sounds? Don't tell me these are the Prackets, the human seekers of Shangri-La. Have they returned to civilization? Is the dream in the pipe smoked out? Have they too banged their heads on what was mere reflection? Sure enough here comes this little flock of ibex back into his private domain. Not that he knows what an ibex is; he thinks it's an animal but he might be wrong. Which is exactly the feeling he has about Prackets. He thinks they're something but he might be wrong.

The male parent is not with them of course. In the animal world you don't see much of the male in the rearing of the young. His instincts tend to lie elsewhere, in the direction of racial preservation which we lightly term sex. It's the female whose strongest instincts are for the safety of the brood, rather than for the retention of the male as they are on the human level. Were it not for this clause in the human contract the race would have died out long ago.

They flock up the path beneath the trees, the mother with Homer on hip, Dessida close to her legs and Benjamin and Ramona eddying outwards in perfect symbiosis. How beautiful the female looks in the center of her young radiating from her in natural gradation, the youngest a part of her, the next near to her and the others spiralling out on the summer grass. In the modern image of woman, the lean lone siren designing herself for sex, you don't see these gestures and patterns of tenderness, this meaning in her eyes—never feel the primeval dynamism that wends its way up his path. Does the Space Age woman prolong sex a little unseasonably or would she look better, more naturally adjusted, with children about her loins and legs, her appearance in frank disarray? Nature never meant her allurement of the male to continue indefinitely, out of season. In the first place man doesn't earn it, this extended season of seduction. And in the second place I doubt if he wants it. All this bounty of the gesturing of love directed to the inconstant male who, after all, seeks little more than the expression of himself; the natural direction of a woman's love at this time of life is to the arriving children. Embraces, kisses, touches and tears bloom to the full among children being as part of a mother as breathing. It is a domestic personal love, a central love, an enduring love, a starting point which, as she matures, turns automatically outward upon others. Without this beginning point, the love for one's children or of children in one's care, a woman seldom comes to universal love.

Soft-footed, silent-tongued, glancing alertly this way and that, both fearful and hopeful, as though they might find food of a kind, could they skilfully avoid the danger. But what kind of food do they seek at his place? Understanding, approval or reflected glory, or the juicy fruits of civilization won by another's labor? She can't be after companionship, surely for he has shown that cupboard closed. Don't tell me it's his time and attention again, or even his audience value. He's run out of that commodity. Or is it water she wants—a drink of inspiration?

What is this danger she anticipates making hazardous the approach to his lair? Criticism, conformity, authority? It might be something as light as advice, even though asked for, which with its overtones of persuasion and force can be insupportably heavy. It might even be the forbidding mold in which his face is cast, his beard and his stooping height. God knows he is fierce-looking enough to the toughest in the jungle, which most of the time he's grateful for and even engineers.

As they pause at the bottom of the steps he turns down the page before him. The parent puts down the baby on his two bare feet, who climbs the steps as scout, patters confidently along the veranda through the door round the table and looks up in his face with a smile. An excellent child from any angle, with his mother's eloquent eyes.

"Good day, Homer. Back from Shangri-La?"

"Yes," a smile.

"Can you say, 'I'm back from Shangri-La'?"

"Yes. I'm back from Shangri-la." No baby talk from the baby.

At which the rest, ears cocked and scenting a congenial climate, follow up and along, the whole lot barefoot and brown. At last Tarl Pracket has exchanged those permanent baggy pants for something that gives a man a chance. Tight white things, what d'you call them? . . . clinging to the thighs to below the knee leaving the lower leg bare. She still wears on top this cover with stripes, as any ibex would moving in and out of sun and shadow beneath the swishing foliage, and the same bright yellow round her head holding the long hair in place, but the thigh gear remains successful. It's a fact men keep from women that the first thing they look for is thighs, and breasts only next, whereas the face comes a frank last. Women would spend much less on their faces if they only knew this. Not that this face is expensive; no longer hollowed and white but filled out and browned with freedom, it hasn't any paint. On the whole the impression is of someone from a people centuries removed, of a character materialized from Candide perhaps . . . Peruvian, Egyptian or Inca.

"I can see you're busy."

"Hullo. How are you all?"

"We'll only stay a minute."

"Well well, here are the Prackets."

"Just one minute." Padding furtively along the veranda she and the ibexlets all have smiles for him, yet there is conscious courage in her greeting, if it is a greeting. She never herself voices the question, How are you?

"How pleasant to see you, Mrs. Pracket." He forgets to rise.

"I had to come . . . I had to."

"I thought you'd all vanished forever. I pictured you all in forested ravines or roving the tussocky plains. I saw you peering above dangerous cliffs down upon the ocean below or watering by shaded streams." Pauses a moment to admire his own words, then, "Hullo Ramona, Benjamin, Dessida." Soft hullos in return. "Come in," to the mother. "Tell me, how are you?"

"Oh-h-h . . ." long breathed-out relief, creeps in over step, past the armchair he keeps for visitors and sits, legs spread-eagled, on the bed.

"Sit in the chair. It's more comfortable." A reluctant glance, then does so. Ah . . . a false step. Of course she doesn't like chairs, these symbols of civilization, and is not accustomed to them. Pressure from him, bad. But he still finds paper and pencils for the whole four children which he shouldn't do either, maybe. Will he never learn these children are not supposed to need occupation, trained as they are in spiritual serenity? Habit of thought dies hard especially in a former teacher. But they receive it joyfully enough settling down on the bare floor to draw, making all sorts of soft little sounds.

"Oh-h-h . . ." again. Then, "We've had a wonderful time. Right to the tip of the island, to Spirit's Bay and we drove the entire length of the ninety-mile beach but, I don't know, I . . . here I am back again. I had to come back . . . I *had* to. We didn't find a place just right for me. And Gavin said, Come over to the East Coast. But oh-h, every time I pictured the East Coast I'd feel faint. I'd suffer a physiological and psychological upheaval. I'd collapse into soft long shuddering moans." She holds her stomach, "I'd become physically ill. I'd actually have to hold my stomach like this. Besides," rather carelessly recovering, "the children have decided to attend this school."

He looks all over the place for matches which turn out to be in his hand, then he lights the cigarette he has rolled and takes hours putting the match in the ashtray. Poor old Head with his "Praise God that's not my problem." At last he thinks of something to say which turns out to be "Oh?"

"The children thought the break-up ceremony last year simply wonderful. All that Maori singing and the play and the oratory contest. They fell in love with the Maori children. Even Bennie made an offer to attend this school. Ramona has bought a grammar and is learning the language. *And* . . . d'you know where we are now? Next door to you at the Hallibuts'. Just over your fence. Two rooms."

God, what will Angela say?

Later, with some lager under the umbrella tree, "Please call me Tarl." A pause and a glance then, "These barriers we build about us . . . between us."

"I'm weak on that sort of thing."

He gets two solid hours of the Prackets. The children have the run of his civilization, painting and drawing with the materials Angela keeps here for her children, cracking nuts on the red-room floor, climbing unresisted all over the parent, push-chair, doll's pram, running round eating apples from the trees, always asking first, indeed asking for everything first, there's no snatching among them. They whisper in their mother's ear what they want next, and she relays it to Dan. "I wonder if Dessida could have . . ." and so on. "D'you mind?" Until the time comes when he says to her, "There's just one thing I can't stand, Mrs. Pracket —apple-eating near me. One of my infirmities." Which she receives with genuine respect and at once whispers suggestions to the children.

There's something else he can't stand either but which he does not mention, although he turns his head when he comes upon it: this great male of nearly three in trousers feeding from her in the music room. "I hope you don't mind," eyes supplicating, "some people don't approve." Benjamin up a tree surveys his and nature's acres until, walking to the dividing fence and passing his vegetable garden, "But what I really came for . . . I hope you don't mind," ever so humbly. "Could I have some of these carrots?"

"Yes, do."

"And a cabbage? I must put some vegetables on for the children. I've been married ten years and I've never had a garden. Gavin has never given us a home."

"Take this cabbage. Some silver beet?" very proudly.

"*Thank* you."

"How pleasant to be asked outright. Most people protest when you offer them something. Oh, can you spare it? Oh I mustn't. It might make you short, and such. Actually, the taker gives more than the giver. He gives the giver the joy of giving, a greater one than receiving. We're very behind in the art of receiving, our society. Did you get those plums, children?"

She swings Homer on her hip. "Dessida? Come on, Ramona. Where are you, Bennie?" And off they flock beneath the chestnut tree toward the dividing fence. With practiced agility they all climb over and their voices fade out in the orchard next door.

Dan ambles back to the house and sets about cleaning up after them. So she didn't find her Shangri-La. She thought she saw it through the glass like Mary's pet fantail but it proved no more than a dream; a reflection of the summer only.

When he returns to his table, however, and turns up the page there are only words with no meaning. He gets up again, puts away the children's papers, settles down and again examines what he's written. But they're still only words on paper. No brilliant boundless territory of the imagination flashes open before him and he's lost the track that leads there.

TWO

Give unto Caesar that which is Caesar's.
—NEW TESTAMENT

❧ FEBRUARY'S A WONDERFUL time in New Zealand. With the heat and the stillness and vibrating color it feels like a pause in life. One can be excused for thinking in nebulous intangible terms like The Everlasting Now. Not that anybody does that I know of excepting Tarl Pracket in and out of February, and she says so on occasion. The rest of us just accept the beauties of the land and the bewitching oceans and give in peaceably to lassitudes.

Overseas visitors say we are silly to start school in February when the mind and body call aloud for the roadsides and the beaches. Teachers do too. But there are ways of getting round most things and in this lazy month you often see classes outside, visiting other schools, making expeditions to beauty spots and seeing their country together. Teachers take their children over new ships in port to get to know the visitors, to the forest reserves and the orchards and to the beach to swim. All of which is recorded as learning of a kind, a pleasant February kind.

Even the bells call *sotto voce,* iron tongues in iron cheeks, calling all over the land turning up for the year ahead. Their tone is desultory, however, since they feel the mood themselves. Come to school, they ring, come and tune up too. Come to school and get into gear. Use this first hot slow month to recover the feeling for paper and books you've forgotten at the Lakes or on the distant mountains. Sharpen your pencils as you will later your minds, fill your pens at least and reacquaint yourselves with the air of a classroom. Reassemble all your senses, children, to direct, channel and exercise them for the year's work ahead. Get the feeling of the course again in order that when summer has had her turn and has had to relinquish her temperatures to the cooler ones of March you can leap from the mark like a runner with the sight of the tape ahead, soundly organized. Ringing across the drowsy paddocks and down the treed roads, ring, ring, ring a-ling. Come to school, children. Come and prepare to learn. For there's much to know of your culture that you won't find otherwise. A nation stands or falls by its culture or marks fatal time.

To be fair, young Benjamin did answer the bell one day last year at the former school but Ramona, not the school, made him unwelcome, Ramona having several vital reasons for keeping ahead of him—not the least of them his being their mother's favored child. She signed the whole attempt with a bad attack of asthma that night and their mother with a fainting turn. So that the following morning when Benjamin went out bravely enough to the roadside to get on the school bus again and when his mother had a nerve storm right there at the bus stop and Ramona pointedly left him behind, he signed the whole affair himself in his own little-boy way; he ducked back into the house and hid and hasn't been to school since.

Not that he was without education of a kind, of a Pracket kind I'll say. His parents cheerfully gave him all the access he wanted to the correspondence following, which he tried to read: the formal reminders from the school described by Tarl as "terrible, crude, threatening documents," communications from the Education Board as "The Brandishing of Authority by Those in Charge," and the summons to attend Court, "Legal Duress." But none of it persuaded him to change his mind and respond to the call of the bell.

Yet, believe it or not, when the bell calls on the first day here he actually turns up at school. I don't know how. Dan sees it for himself as he walks outside before beginning work. Dan hasn't gone straight from bed to table this morning after the Pracket visit yesterday; moreover you are inclined to be caught up in the general feeling of rebirth on a school's opening morning. On go a clean shirt and proper trousers after a bath and a trim of his beard, making at least a compromise with respectability. It's hard to avoid making this attempt to be decent when the Head passes by to school at eight in a glamorous tie and new shirt, never growing up from his enchantment at the opening of school, though the bell doesn't call till nine.

Dan lurks by the dahlias beneath the gum tree. Is that Benjamin? By God it is. Hardly recognizable in uniform and sandals. He looks at the child anxiously with the eyes of his mother; for the moment he *is* his mother, which is the infirmity of a writer. Not that he needs to be, I'm sure. She'll be peering from behind some tree in the Halibut orchard next door.

Benjamin is following Ramona furtively in the way he follows his mother when she leads them on strange ground, which is often enough. Fancy having to follow Ramona when he knows she doesn't want him. He must be taking it hard. He's walking just like his mother too, though he doesn't as a rule: head forward a little, shoulders crouched in defense and with short nervous steps, clumsily in his unfamiliar sandals, not feeling the joyful security of the good earth beneath his feet, beneath his new stiff soles. No, Dan doesn't see how he can last long there, and when he inquires of the Head as he passes through at five on his way home from school he replies evenly, "Oh yes, he came. But he went home at lunch time and failed to return. He began his education at nine and completed it at twelve. Which is exactly what he did at the first school."

"What about Ramona?"

But he's obviously thinking of something else, the enrollments this morning, the accommodations and supplies or the qualities of the parents who brought new children, their school-support value. "What about . . . beg your pardon?"

"Ramona."

"Ramona . . . Oh, what about Ramona, did you say? Oh, she settled in very well. Head up, full of confidence, a crowd of children around her. But she knows school." And nothing else. He never lasts long on this subject, Ric, if you bring him to it at all. Examining Dan's face, "Anything wrong with you?"

"N-no. Only that my accountant rang me up about my taxes." Not a joke but the Head's voice lifts high in laughter.

Dan hears there's an exchange of letters between the Head and the new parent, each on a very high level and ever so decorously put, hers about how Benjamin is "not yet ready for formal education"—although how she gets "formal education" on one first morning at school in February belongs to her own personal kind of reasoning—and his about how can a child negotiate new situations in future life when he is allowed to withdraw from these early ones without sympathetic help. But it is strictly no longer Dan's business and he keeps well clear. Or tries to.

One afternoon the very next week as summer dreams away in the garden like a breathless woman of much color and fragrance and packed with untold secrets he senses another presence. Does he or does he not hear anything as he works at his table in the library? He believes he does. A shadow across the curtain and gone again.

"Daniel . . ." so humbly from the veranda. Yes, there's Benjamin again on the steps. From the schoolrooms nearby just beyond the totara lift the crow and the call of the infants at work.

"Oh. Mrs. Pracket. How pleasant to see you. How are you?"

"Oh-h-h. Look, we won't stay more than a minute. Just *one minute*. Are we disturbing you? I absolutely *need* to spend a moment in the garden. To get away from all that next door. You should hear Mrs. Hallibut on her illnesses." Gasps and holds her forehead. "No culture there at all." There is at school.

She settles down on his step, knees drawn up to chin and her arms clasped around them. The whole thing over again but now she is one of Ric's school parents with a more solid footing and parents are important to the Head. It's rather a privilege to be one of his parents, you hear round the district. Unwittingly they assume the glamour of his work and are part of his widening family. Wine and so on follows, tea on the lawn and hours of civilization.

"Don't tell me," from Angela on Saturday, "they've settled in next door. Gosh that's close. What's the next move? Over the fence in here? Why not? Plenty of room, plenty of beds made up." She passes him a quite definite cup of tea. "I don't like the look of it, Daddy."

"Ay, you don't?"

"I don't want you to think I'm thinking things or anything like that but . . . you know how animals they circle their prey, round and round sniffing, closer in and closer before they . . . I mean . . ."

There's amusement in Dan's eyes, long and gray as the ninety-mile beach, "I'm not as attractive as that."

He shouldn't have told Angela about Homer defecating on the blue-room floor. "Why don't they go and live with animals if that's what they want to be? Too darn lazy to train her kids."

"She said, 'Happiness is more important than cleanliness.' "

"I wish she'd said it to me."

"I'd no idea what to answer."

"*I'd* have known what to answer." Angela goes in for these

swinging flowering skirts in summer, not unlike the flowered roadsides, just the thing for a long waist and long legs, and as she sways and gesticulates about the kitchen like the trees in a sudden gale the skirt does too. Lashing round the kitchen in words and in person, all sorts of sparks are flying like petals and leaves, vivid in the autumn, and the fair hair tosses like a mane. It often occurs to Dan that he himself wouldn't like to find himself on the wrong side of Angela. "I'd have said, I'd say, 'You mean *your* happiness is more important that anyone else's.' That's what I'd say." Youth doesn't fear, as Dan does, to hit the nail on the head or have a good smash at it anyway. Hit or miss, does it matter? "She's getting too close to you, Daddy. I don't like the look of it. You should have put your foot down from the word go."

"I simply don't know how to. All I know is—and I mean this —I know she's a far better person than I am. I've got about six or seven faces whereas she has only two or three."

"That's what I'd have . . . what did you say? Tarl better than you? *Really* . . . Daddy."

I suppose Dan could put his foot down if only he knew which foot and where to put it. But there's no place so far in the half-light of his passivity for the firm putting down of a foot. The flock of ibex still swarms expectantly over the fence when they're not at the beach or the Bay or roaming the soft blue mountains identifying themselves with them, paddling hidden creeks where the fern dips in the water and rolling in thigh-deep grasses, at all times loaded with civilized cream buns, fish and chips or anything else from the shops which the children fancy and which involves no work from themselves. "Do you get any painting done, Tarl?"

"I can't with the children and . . . oh, my state of mind. I'm . . . Painting needs a studio and a model. I need conditions just right for me. The conditions over *there*—no tap, no sink—with *children*. Trying to strain rice down the hand basin. One gas ring for cooking. Seventeen people in the house all using the one toilet. D'you know what they did this morning? They cut down a beautiful shrub in full bloom that I'd just been admiring, to make way for a tomato bed. Oh-h-h . . ."

"Still, you don't have to stay there this lovely weather."

"We're out of the place by ten o'clock. Every morning. And we find such wonderful places. Little secret creeks way up the mountain, the children were in heaven. And long wild walks round the estuaries. And we met the most wonderful Maori

31

who'd been to jail twice and who thinks just the same as we do. Bennie simply adores him." A sip of her wine, luxuriously. "I take a positive stand about housekeeping. I refuse to allow myself to enter into any form of it. If you climb onto the housekeeping treadmill while you've got little children you'll end up either a strict parent, which is spiritual death to them, or you'll end up put away. *Housework* . . . a stupid, futile waste of time. What a disgrace to oneself to be *busy*. 'Busy' . . . that horrible word. That fungus in society. The children need their freedom. Who am I to deprive them of their native inheritance just for the sake of a clean house? Housework is a tragedy. I choose the earth."

Until later, "But what I really came for . . ." sort of crisis air . . . "could I leave the children with you while I go to the doctor? No one else will mind them."

"But that's *time*," with sudden feeling. "You're asking for my time. I never give my *time*."

She glows to have aroused him. "All right then," softly, "never mind."

"Just one minute. No more."

"It's all right," weakly, "in the afternoon but some people come in the morning.

"Oh-h-h . . ." all sympathy.

"Just as I'm settling down."

"Can't you send them away?"

"I'd lose face with God."

Utter amazement at the Christian ethic. "*I* would send them away." Settles down knees to chin on the step. Until very much later standing center stage in the library, "But what I *really* came for . . . do you know of a house we could live in? A home. We've always been wanderers but I feel the need of a home now for the children. It's all Gavin's fault. He's always had a good job, but . . ."

"God damn it, don't blame anyone in my presence."

Again she glows to have roused him. Her large luminous eyes lift to his. "I feel at last I can settled down but only in this district." She gazes at the sea of treetops rolling away skyward, "It's a very beautiful corner. Pastoral."

He lives to regret what he told her about visitors in the morning. From now on she comes in the morning. "Bennie likes the trees over here." Never mind the school over there. And sure enough here is Benjamin up his favorite tree from which he can see all the other children at school while they can't see him.

"Bennie spends hours at a time in a tree. Look at the way his bare feet curl round the bough like a bird's . . . his pure at-oneness with the tree, his symbiosis with nature. Bennie's not ready for school. He's a poet and needs his solitude."

Is this her Shangri-La? His secluded domain of sun and shadow, of birds and butterflies, of storms and introspective rain-wraiths; the spare rooms with the beds made up, the music and the books, the oils and originals on the walls and the incoming overseas papers; the coffee, tea, fresh scones and wine, and in particular his audience value? Angela is inclined to think so. Why is it that although originality is a thing we constantly clamor for, we constantly quarrel with it?

⚜ A JOY COMES to a writer when he achieves his goal . . . union of the creature he is himself with the creatures of his mind, a joy that equals the fulfillment in love and does at times surpass it, being less earthbound. An unpremeditated fusion that blows when it will since no creatures are more uncatchable than these in the fluid world of the imagination; these fragile ephemeral beings in the short brilliance of their chaotic lives. Yet caught and held they must be and, in the heat of union, recorded on sheets of paper. For the joy has become a drug; once known, forever needed. A drug that makes reality endurable, that can even allay the clamoring of the physical man for his birthright of physical union. An elixir indeed, luring him in the face of failure and fatigue to return yet again to the labor of his table. He wins this thing or else.

But this sought state calls for equilibrium in the lower regions, and Daniel often can't find it these days in the contagious unrest from next door. The flights and returns from Shangri-La whenever the bells are calling . . . they all start here and they all end here, yet he doesn't do anything about it. There's something about it he secretly likes.

As the autumn dreams away he finds himself more and more often losing his way to the imagery of the mind and for longer periods of time. Increasingly, before the onslaughts of his neighbors he loses hold of his work and his work of him. Weeks go by at a time when he does not know the joy for which he labors, never achieves the elixir he craves . . . a scented product he could smell all day without waiting for the boronia in spring and the few remaining freesias. "It's the hardest thing in the world," he tells Angela one Saturday, "to keep my mind on my work with these Prackets over the fence. Well, no . . . not quite the hardest. I do know a harder. To keep my mind off my memories."

"To *think*," from Angela with heat and flash, "that with all the thought you give to the health of other people's minds and . . . and . . . you can't protect your own. That's—that's the joke of all time."

"Funny thing y'know."

"It's never any trouble," from Tarl one morning airily, "visiting with a family. People take one look at the children and open their doors and you're inside the house with all the children before they know what's happened."

"That's a funny thing too, y'know."

Her lovely eyes narrow somewhat in inquiry but he says no more.

He always thought as he sat on his favorite canvas chair on the veranda, his sort of halfway house to work, or coming from it, reflecting on the vagaries of life, the stories of the past the trees tell, listening to the birds working out their problems and discussing their feathery headaches, and to the sound of the children arriving—taking in the temper of the morning in general —that he sat in utter privacy, but he's of two minds about that now. He's got neighbors next door with eyes. Nor does it help to recall that for six months they lived in the orchard over the fence when he knew nothing about it. He takes a new look at all this seclusion he once thought he had and at the trees between. An impenetrable curtain when in leaf but already many of the leaves have fallen and the lawns increasingly reddened and yellowed, so that on occasion he inadvertently sees the dusty little car cruising hopefully down the Hallibut lane appearing and disappearing amid the foliage as they take off to the beach or bush or some home-hunting expedition. In later autumn and into early spring he'll be fair game sitting here. What an invitation! A man relaxing in a chair reflecting on his own. A sitting duck, no less. Who could resist it? Could he himself, let alone the Prackets?

"What I mean is, Daddy . . . I don't want you to think I'm thinking things or anything like that but . . ."

"What?"

"This sounds awful I know. I shouldn't be saying it but . . ."

"You're simply marvelous on opening sentences. I'm dying to know what you shouldn't be saying."

Laugh, toss and flash of eyes, then, "But you know how animals they circle their prey, sniffing, watching, round and round before they dash in to the kill. Those first six months in the orchard, then the move to the hovel on the hill, then the cottage below your land and *now* next door. *Well*. I shouldn't be saying it really. I mean I . . ."

Yet he's usually glad enough initially to see her, receiving her with an effervescence to be greatly rued later. The coming of any woman cannot be to him other than a matter for celebration at any time, besides, to see her white face light up when she finds him and her eyes widen with joy . . . well it's fearfully good for any man's ego. Moreover and after all she at least hails from the world of reality, however disrupting that is, whereas the people he entertains on paper belong in the mists of the mind, phantoms only of the imagination, an elusive slippery company who come or don't come at will.

Until, as the hours plod by, "woman" as such deteriorates to "woman in particular" and turns out to be Tarl, regardless. There's no mistaking it. "I liked your use of that Auden poem in your last book." She is sitting on the bed in the library, legs spread-eagled, although an inviting armchair waits nearby for guests.

"Auden? I didn't use Auden."

"Yes you did."

"I know what I've used in the books I've written."

"But you did."

"You're not right, Tarl."

"I *am* right. I know I'm right."

"I don't argue."

"But I know. I always just *know* things."

"Aa . . . very well. Just leave it your way."

"You lend me that book for a couple of days and I'll prove I'm right."

Down comes a first edition from the shelf he never lends from, in order to prove her wrong. "I must have it back in two days. I grieve for my books in their absence."

The awful rage she leaves in her wake, the consequences of which she escapes herself. She quite merrily climbs the fence with his book. To Jim, a crony of his at the Bay, "She leaves my ego in such a mess. And she . . . which is worse . . . leaves my writing mechanism in a worse mess because of the wine I drink with her. I like to work with my mind exactly as God made it."

"I always seem to have something to ask. You must get tired of my requests."

"Oh no. I might as well hear them."

"I always seem to be in some extremity when I come over here. But I just *have* to come. I must have a little rapport to survive."

"I'd rather you came in your crises," magnanimously. But everyone likes sensation.

She certainly comes in her crises. Striding the length of the alarmed old house or crouching on a doorstep knee to chin softly railing at society, at the dehumanization of human nature in the "doltish" world about her, vomiting her hatred of law and order and of anybody In Charge, with many an analysis of their domestic state. "Our happiest times used to be when we were altogether. Alone. Weeks on end in the tent on the beach living on pipis and milk, or out on the open road in the car heading nowhere and singing. Singing like mad. But it's all different now. He's never with us now." People, Dan notes, use the words "always" and "never" too loosely. "We never have the whole family outings now. He teaches all day and . . ." Oh, he's back at the college after all that send-offing? ". . . and comes home late and prepares work all the evening. D'you know what he does on a Saturday? The Saturdays when we always got together and went to some lovely wild place? *Labors*. He labors on the road with gangs. After all he taught me about the shame of being 'busy.' All this lofty talk to justify himself about getting us a home. Saving up. What has our family come to— saving up?" The dark eyes above the knees brood ahead upon something he does not see. "He gives no time to the children."

Or if it's raining, sitting on the bed in the library, her legs shockingly agape, "I must . . . honestly, Daniel . . ." He reels at the use of his intimate name, the bloody cheek of it. "I really must get away from the countenance of the Philistine. Have you noticed how ugly it is? The whole history of joylessness in the features, recording their stricken childhoods, the hatreds of their disciplined youth persisting and passed on to the children, recreating their hatred, oh-h-h . . ." Hand to forehead, "I'll have to get away. Next week, tomorrow, at once." A wild glance through the window at the distant horizons as though flying there this moment were possible, "I must find a place that's just right for me. Oh, I must have freedom."

Beneath the umbrella tree sipping wine. The tree in autumn is an enormous tent covered in a million red berries. Children and birds love it. Children climb up from the inside to thrust their sudden heads through the top excitedly calling, "Look at me." And the birds are on top anyway gracefully pecking from right and left, their slim supple necks extending, reducing. "But," asks Angela practically, "can Benjamin read?" A cigarette. "I mean . . . *read*." He can climb at least. He is running up, on all fours, through the center of the tree in a way to put an opossum to shame. "Look at me," when he reaches the top.

"I think so. He says he can. He sits with the paper sometimes. And he read all the threatening documents we got from that other school where he went for a day. And all this brandishing of authority on paper we get from the Education Board these days. And from the Child Welfare and the court. And he spells out the headlines in the paper when we've had a case. He spells most gracefully. And all what the magistrate said. And we help him so he can understand and appreciate the situation. Gavin explains to him very carefully that if he doesn't go to school he'll be taken from us. He knows words now like 'terrible crude threatening documents,' 'the brandishing of authority by Those In Charge,' 'extreme legal duress' and 'the sword of Caesar.' He's quite getting on with his reading."

She puts down her glass on the old garden table, and her eyes light dangerously. "As if education had anything to do with the earth's simple ways. The Self is above education. Children should learn only what they want to. Schools are Institutions of Force with Someone In Charge. Schools are cages designed by technicians to fit into a minimum of space the maximum number of children, to bring them to the efficiency of machines in order to win some problematical race . . . to—to shape them for the future. *Future* is only a word. Words are words and nothing else, Gavin said in London when he was at the peak of his grace. Only the present is real." The two smaller children, Dessida and Homer, roll and pull all over her and she continues above their heads:

"There should be no government at all, and certainly no laws. Laws are force. I don't believe in force. We've had all we need since time began without the interference of laws. We wouldn't be needing any social security were we free. When the mind is right the body is right . . . there wouldn't be any illness." Airily, "There'd be no need of social services."

She's warming up now. "There should be no need of civilization. We should all be running round free." Some people, notes

Dan, use the word "should" with too much abandon. "We need no government to teach us how to live. We lose too many precious years with other Folks In Charge. Shaping futures for us that never come. Time won't wait for these futures: these classrooms, offices, routines . . . all the strife you find in cities. We should grasp the present here and now and do all the things we want to. All the things we longed to do in childhood. In a cave we'd need no government . . . only the good earth, a fire, children, womanly tasks and a man. We don't need states with their politics and wars and their crippling institutions. We don't need diversions. All we want is independence and men, real men. Strong men, tender men, not technicians concerned with procedure and progress. All we need is freedom . . . since time began."

"You mean," from Angela, "*you* don't need all that. You yourself. But as a matter of fact *I* do. I like, and I'm sure I like, the future. All those other things you say . . . diversions and procedure and progress and I . . . I'll tell you what I like most of all . . . and that you like too if you'd admit it. I like the Child Allowance. And there'd be none of that without a government. And that's that." But Tarl is suddenly engaged in attending to the wants of her children.

Until the "I feel better now. I'll be able to carry on a little longer," and the "What I *really* came for . . ." part, which turns out to be more vegetables, carefully cultivated in a civilized way with much back-bending and treated with scientific fertilizer worked on by technicians, and until finally she swings the heavy Homer on her narrow hip, urgently summons the rest of her brood. "Dessida? Ramona, where are you?" And to a tree, "Come on, Bennie," and off they flock pad-footed, tenderly united, under the trees and over the fence to "their place."

But one does come to know her wonderful feeling for children. Whatever her state of mind, embittered, chaotic or merely sad, she's as accessible to them as a mother cat, or a mother ibex if you like: gentle, attentive, sympathetic, indulgent and patient beyond telling, which is her great secret beauty. It is something that validates her out-of-step credo and that Angela herself takes note of. "Others," says Tarl ruefully one morning, crouched knee to chin on the autumn step, her eyes visionary as they gaze at the unseen ahead, "others produce their verbal argument when trying to defeat me but I produce my children. And say nothing. I have no need to. They are my argument, my final word." "I must say," admits Angela with a toss of her hair, "I do agree that she knows her subject. On the rearing of children, Daddy, and on childbirth . . . well, you should hear her. She gave me a wonderful lecture the other day at my place."

And sometimes when conditions are "just right" for her, and they often are at his place, she warms to this subject of hers, childbirth and the rearing of children, revealing close study and experience, using terms an aesthete is unaccustomed to: permissive parenting, tenderness taboos, anger reaction, exteriorize, calamity suggestion and horror trauma, bringing home to him his own awful ignorance. And during her talkings on the veranda, under the tree, on the lawn, in the library or on the favorite chair by the fridge in the kitchen—a chair ever sought by all —or crouched knees to chin on the step, he comes to know her contempt expressions: suburbia, effusion, dehumanization, enslavement, bourgeois, busy, spirit annihilators and the ever-recurring epithet "stupid." And he cannot avoid learning her favorite words: rapport, do nothing, kindred spirit, soul mate, whim, moment, emancipation, symbiosis and the Everlasting Now. To say nothing of her favorite of all: freedom, which bursts to the surface whatever her mood.

Moreover, as the autumn temperatures drop and the rain moves in, in a grand take-over bid for the season, she takes to wearing some thin brown frock in drably figured print that someone has charitably given her, and she actually buys with Pracket money, just like any other woman, a raincoat of yellow which she never takes off . . . and "never" *is* the word this time. Only rubber, but the effect of this yellow on the brown of her eyes and on her black streaking hair . . . it so arrests him as she looks up at him from the chair by the fridge that his guards come down a moment and he releases his only compliment, "That coat . . . your eyes . . ."

Apologetically, "I had to buy it to keep off the rain." But you can see she's been accustomed to compliments.

One morning towards the end of autumn, when the changing colors of the leaves convince him agonizingly of the impermanence of man and his work, when he is full of unrest at the loss of equilibrium, a craven victim of deprivation and starved of the drug of his personal elixir, he is standing at the top of the steps in the thin-blooded sunlight while Tarl stands at the bottom, her young gambolling about her. She is poised like a bird before flight, the brightest yellow bird in the grounds, with Homer on hip. From the nearby playground rise and fall the lift, laugh and shout of the infants before the call of the bell; a sound he lives with contentedly enough as long as he need not answer, which no doubt is what Benjamin is feeling swaying aloft on a tree.

"I've come to say goodbye," is her reason today, and two hours she's taken to say it. Here is another grand bid for Shangri-La, some hypothetical house they've found up the mountain out of reach of school buses and from which Benjamin can be theoretically enrolled at the Correspondence School . . . there being all sorts of ways of evading the law for one who grimly means it. From all of which he gathers, but does not ask, that the wheels of the law are turning again with revived purpose, to somehow get Bennie to school.

It's this pathos of the human creature with its load of dream that is ever Dan's downfall. To see a dream, any dream, struggling madly for birth supplies the momentum for most of his work. What is man without a dream? What would make him go? The clear large eyes stagger with the load of one as her slight body staggers beneath the weight of Homer, who has two strong legs of his own and, moreover, loves to use them. As she looks up at him supplicatingly from the bottom of the steps, the black hair carving the yellow of the coat, compulsively he slips into talking, into the dangerous pressure of advice. "Tarl . . . do you mean to teach Benjamin anything yourself? Are you going to let him grow up, Tarl, to turn on you and ask, 'Where are my skills and abilities? I have the brains, I know it, but where is the habit of learning, the desire to complete something and the concentration to fulfill it? Why can't I work like other people? My life is extraordinarily empty.'" He pauses apprehensively.

Her eyes light with glorious vision and her pale face takes on a glow. "When I get away from this soul-searing suburbia, way up there on the mountain where things are just right for me, I'll teach him all the cultures. Painting, music, reading, poetry, all . . . all of them." No mention of books, painting materials or a piano but the offspring listen enraptured. She must have forgotten for the moment that she despises possessions.

"Some of these cultures," warily, "one cultivates early." He nearly said "one must cultivate early," but refrained in time from using "must." He's got to tread so carefully. This raw mind can't stand any force whatever, not the lightest touch of suggestion. He's learned this if nothing else. His whole engagement with her for a year has been an admirable exercise in withholding pressure from others, yet at times he feels the truth can be as light as it can be heavy with an eternal weightlessness.

40

"Especially the crafts involving muscular control, as in a musical instrument . . . mind-muscle coordination. Not only that. It's the habit of attitude towards a thing one cultivates earliest . . . to become a need like breathing. With the need ensured the rest follows."

But he's touched on her precious theory. "If the mind is free *all* will follow." Airily contradicting her intention to teach him. "His learning will come of itself in time, *from* Bennie himself. It already is. When he wants to learn further he'll ask to be taught." With fire in her voice, "The free mind is capable of *anything.*"

It takes him a moment to control his fury at being contradicted by someone younger, at having the best of his thought kicked aside. The insolence of the thing. Then he produces suavely, "Your answers are too clever for me."

Ashamed, "Oh I shouldn't."

She turns to sway along the path beneath the weight of Homer, who loves walking and running anyway. "Come on, Bennie," to his eyrie in the tree. "Dessida?" Ramona is at school.

"But," he says with effort in an attempt to hide his rage, "what about these leaves that are falling? You won't see the replacement by the blossom in spring."

A tenderness halts her flight and in her white face is a marveling that anyone should care whether she saw anything or not. Anything at all between a flower and a fact. Not that she looks at the trees even now, although he mentioned them emotionally. It is Dan she looks up at, large, bearded and fiercesome, ruling his domain from the top of the steps, looks up at him with a childlike quality, vulnerably wholehearted with nothing of the feeling of the "have-not" to the "have." Then her gaze drops downward in that way he knows, pondering profoundly. "I'll be back sometime to see them."

They hurry away eagerly until, as they near the Old Man Totara, the great solid native pine with sixty years in his sap, he calls after her again, "What about Ramona? She loves this school. How can she get to school with no bus?" A pause in the flight. "And what about Gavin? How can he get to college?" After all he is the breadwinner, or the pipis-and-milk-winner if you like.

Surprise and annoyance at this crash to earthy detail; detail . . . ever the enemy of the dreamer. Dreams wobble, brought down to earth. "They can both come down in the car."

"Too far for a child every day . . . waiting for her father after college."

Sudden grand lift of the head, "We'll all ... *all* ... go on Correspondence." No mention of who will earn the bread. A few more urgent steps, then another pause and a glance back to him. With conscious martyrdom, "It's so hard to give each what he wants."

He descends from his spurious pulpit and moves along the path a little too. "Gavin knows you're going?"

Restlessly, irritably, "No. He told us to wait till the weekend to give him time to make sure the house is available. And to inquire how long it will be before the buses do go that far. And to help us move but ..." impatiently ... "the children want to go today, Daniel. *Now*. They're all very excited." Her eyes holding all of the autumn in them lift to him, "A wonderful house, Daniel. No Hallibuts. And a stove and a bench and a sink, can you believe it? And a tap and hot water. But you should see outside. Not a house within sight. Acres and acres of fields with bush on the hills surrounding. I'll be able to paint up there. Hours, days, weeks of peace with nothing whatever to do, oh-h-h ..."

"Come on, Mummie," from Dessida tugging at the yellow coat.

Homer on hip looks earnestly from her face to Dan's well above them all, taking in everything through all his pores as she adds softly, ruefully, "It's always I who has to look for a home." Eyes downward in dark reflection, "Poor old Gavin. When he comes home tonight he'll find us not here." The charity in her voice is that of the victor for the conquered. He's beginning to learn this taste she has for the situation of Gavin's finding them "not here." The satisfaction of the contrived chase, maybe. But only maybe. You can never think anything for certain about Tarl. But he does suppose how strongly aware of him she must be, unadmittedly and darkly loving him. From which he stubbornly draws his conclusion, "All will be well."

Disapproval ...

"I'll come to see you one day."

Approval. "I'll look for that day."

"Come on, Mummie," from Dessida.

"Come on, Bennie," her battle cry, and off to Shangri-La.

The Head is a tall wide dark man whose wife feeds him fervently and irons his shirts with energy, the Head being that kind of man whom women like to feed and iron for anyway. He's got this way with women which makes us want to serve him, most of us, that is. Frankly, I'd call him a rather subtle slave driver, but no one breathes the word, since, basically, women like to be driven anyway. It could be . . . and was one time . . . our natural state.

Men think he is serious and earnest and are not attracted but women and children know better. Dan knows better too, knows the smiles as they do, the playground smiles caught from hundreds of children, thousands over his lifetime, smiles that are willing, casual and frequent, and the unbelievable patience. But he still thinks to himself that the Head is a little too fond of keys and of locking up behind him, not that it hurts the school; it rather pays in orderliness. Besides he emanates this authentic permissiveness that gets through his own locks easily, so that Dan often gets the impression that his locking and keys are no more than a symbol of something in him other than a love of order.

He passes the old schoolhouse on his way to and from school to the place he rents behind it, as a rule wearing his smile. He invariably dresses with the greatest care, with meticulous attention to his shirts and ties, and always polishes his shoes. From all of which he is a pleasant sight as he appears across the playground beneath the Old Man Totara. He is smiling now as he disengages the hands of several small children who have accompanied him across the playground, and approaches along the path, but reading Dan's mood and face the smile peters out. "You've done no work this morning?"

No answer from the chair on the veranda.

"I take it 'they've' been here."

"They're so fearfully pathetic."

"Must this boy continue to do his truanting in my own home right on the school grounds in full view of the children and staff?"

"They're very pathetic indeed." He looks towards the distant blue mountains. "They do enrage me but still touch me so deeply."

There's the sound of key on key in the pocket of the Head. "Have they gone?"

"Gone? They've gone all right. They've gone for good."

The Head waits.

"Right to the top of the mountain. Couldn't be further. Children, whims, freedom and all. Shangri-La forever."

"I venture to say," evenly, "they'll all be back again. We've heard all this before." He turns from him. "All this interruption to your work, I don't know, I'm sure."

Dan still gazes over the tops of the listening trees to the blue

43

line of Shangri-La. "I can never quite believe this situation, y'know, of a parent fighting God, Man and the Law to keep a child from you. If only she knew you, what you are. Of course it's not really you. It's her concept of education."

Uncomfortably, "Can't we drop this subject?" Then the playground smile reappears. "You know Paddy Tu? He came along and said . . ." and so on, and in no time the two are laughing.

"See what I mean, Ange?"

"I see what you mean. I know it's all very romantic and all that, Shangri-La and everything, but I can't stand by and watch this happening to you. Mother would never have allowed it for a minute."

"It's the sort of thing she'd have done herself."

I don't know that I would have. I never would have become such a perfect woman, had I finished my life. We dead are so misrepresented.

"I think they will be back, Daddy," as she hangs up the receiver.

They are. The owner of the house on the mountain suddenly withdraws permission for the Prackets to live there, giving no reason; also Gavin brings home word that the buses will be reaching as far as that in a matter of weeks. This very night they are back next door.

Is there anything more elusive than the perfect life?

⚜ THROUGHOUT THE AUTUMN he hears nothing from Tarl of the occasional court case over Benjamin's absence from school, a boy getting on for eight now, conducted behind the closed doors of the Children's Court to be adjourned by the magistrate each time to allow the parents to sort themselves out before the law takes definite action. She never mentions them. Not, he's sure, because she's ashamed of them, far from it, but maybe because on her own inner landscape of values they would appear such irrelevant trivia—other than reading material for Benjamin. What has the court got to do with the Everlasting Now or the magnificent Do Nothing? Neither does he hear much of the growing tension between the parents of Benjamin, possibly for the opposite reason, that they dominate too painfully the inner scape. All these maybes and possiblys in relation to Tarl; he supposes a difference in ethic over the fence, a difference in race, a difference in species even.

Yet he gets the impression she is good and he recognizes some rare qualities. For a start she never boasts and is wonderfully free from pride. She is gentle and humble in her ways, when with him, anyway, and whatever the nature of these ways . . . she can think on deep levels when she wants to and soar to the purely poetic. And it seems to him that she strives to know herself, to understand and honor her instincts. She has studied arduously her chosen subject, childbirth and the rearing of children and the potential of the mind when free; also her feeling for children in general, and not just her own, is all but messianic. Above all she can return a book . . . isn't that remarkable? In all, she could be quite inspiring company had she any sort of outer eye . . . an eye for others, for instance. And were her mechanism illumed by love . . . of which he is by no means sure.

It appears to him that she doesn't see our routine sins and faults as we see them in the framework of Christian morality. He doesn't think she's got any morality as our century sees it. With her there's only *normality,* and the only sins she sees are the offenses against that, the only faults a departure from nature. And even though civilization is constantly outraged at normality it remains a refreshing gift to be brought to one's door, greatly outweighing the paltry offerings he manages to spare for her.

Uncomfortably in him the impression that Tarl is good takes and maintains root, but only the impression. The only thing that is more than impression and that nothing so far has shaken is that in spite of her inaccuracies—he would not say "dishonesties"—he thinks he would trust her with anything important . . . anything on the level of a dream or a mood, with the delicacy and fragility of a look, anything, something beyond the capacity of the usual mind. As indeed he would trust cheerfully anyone at all with practically anything who could return a magazine.

The autumn term is nearly over now. Holidays according to the law are due next week—a fortnight's worth. But as a holiday in the academic sense for those who have worked, a regrouping, recuperation and a recovery from hard energy expended, the thrill of the rhythm of labor and rest naturally alternating . . . well, to Tarl and Benjamin, holidays are superfluity. But even superfluities need money in this era, civilized money, and there are all sorts of ways of coming by it to the initiated without the disgrace of work. Dan himself is not yet geared to Tarl's way of coming by it, when there's a holiday in view and he looks up from his table in the blandest innocence when she plunges in one morning, unkempt and futuristic in her black and yellow with the children whirling behind her. "Say no, say no."

"Yes."

"Look, I feel dreadful, but will you buy a picture of mine? You don't have to. Say no if you need to. If you don't I'll have to sell my sewing machine. That would be awful . . . poor little kiddies. They need clothes. I was just going to make them some green velvet pants, a pair of each all round. I've got the material and cotton there and Bennie found the scissors at last under the trees behind the fowl run. Fancy no machine." Closes eyes, presses cheeks. Recovers and takes center stage in the library. "This picture won a prize in a gallery overseas from two hundred others. But I'll have to get it back in a fortnight's time because there's an exhibition coming up in town. It's a chance to get commissions for portraits. I'll buy it back with my Child Allowance. I've been torn by hours of torture this morning coming to this decision. Could I? Should I? It's outside under a tree." The beautiful eyes rest upon him immobilized at his table. "You can always say no."

"How much?"

"Ten guineas."

He reaches behind him for a checkbook and lays it on the table before him. London bank. Wrong. He reaches again but it turns up American. "Wrong again," he murmurs. Mesmerized she watches him reach back yet again. "Damn it, this is Australia." Finally he lands New Zealand, opens it, writes a check, blots it, passes it to her and in it goes to her raincoat pocket. "Now bring in the picture," he says.

Off she scatters out to the trees, the children flying after, while he sits back and rolls a smoke. In time this picture comes in, framed, and she stands it on the armchair, the children hovering anxiously. He doesn't like it at all. The coloring is dull, nothing like what you'd expect from the brush of Tarl. "I did it long ago in a street in Wellington."

He pays it the doubtful tribute of silence, not knowing he's paying for their holiday to come. After they've gone an hour or so he removes it from his sight in the library and hangs it dutifully in the music room—on a wall where Angela, and indeed the Head, would not be likely to notice it, the shaded wall backing the windows. At least it's an original and from an artist he knows, which is what he usually likes.

They don't tell him this time they are going. No tender flock of ibex foots warily through the trees sniffing and peering from left to right to declare they will stay but a minute. Such a gray orthodox occasion as an *authorized* flight has no audience requirements whatever, no dramatic value at all. Only the tremendous overpowering whim is worth the pathetic goodbye: the crisis, the sensational "have to," the "physiological, psychological upheaval." True, Tarl and the children pack their sleeping bags in the dusty excited little car and dash off along the broad highway soaring and swooping over forested ranges to the languorous Lakes district, but he doesn't think it is Shangri-La. He doesn't register associatively the startling magic and want to go himself.

As for Gavin Pracket, the father and breadwinner, he takes for himself no more than the "change" part of a holiday from college in the form of a laboring job with the Ministry of Works, mixing concrete, he's told . . . and Dan is told practically everything . . . and not without energy and pride either, Gavin having a vast respect for his fellow creatures, in particular those who live by their hands. To keep up with the price of his family's freedom, their cream buns, fish and chips and green velvet pants, as well as to save for the home they demand and which they refuse when they see one coming. All so sophisticated, abstract. Dan is so overcome with admiration for them all that he wonders whose side he is on.

But if it crosses anyone's mind that Tarl means to conform to these man-made, calendar-caused, humiliating dates, they are enlightened when the holidays are over. On the very first day of school reopening, as the bells call loudly to all children, Tarl takes flight again so airily right in the teeth of the bell, reeling from the reek of authority in the air, recoiling from the cramp of reason. All over again she packs up the children in the puffing bewildered little car and off they head for an inland town where some alleged "soul mate" lives who has a lovely civilized house and many gorgeous beds. Not to mention the table. That she should whisk off Ramona too who loves her school . . . well there's more sensation that way. No doubt it's a shame that Ramona cries—Tarl is quite rueful about it, almost apologetic—but Pracket whims are powerful phenomena and count no cost whatever. It's nature to blame, not Tarl. It is simply never Tarl. Besides, as she tells Dan before she goes— this is worth a goodbye—"Ramona is very good with the children. I miss her when she's away. She organizes the others at playing school and teaches them all sorts of marvelous things.

Bennie simply loves it." No mention of where Ramona learnt these things that spare her mother and delight the children, but there are unmistakable nuances of gratification in her voice to have flouted authority by proxy.

✤ THE BELL calls and calls for Benjamin but no little boy replies. Each morning at nine it calls for Benjamin till its iron tongue all but falls out, week after yearning week, but no little boy hears.

Dan does not see them for more than a month, and though he has moments of hell over the fate of his first edition he lent her from the shelf he never lends from, he is disturbed by no one more wayward, more willful . . . more *silly*, to be frank . . . than the fantail Mary loves. Little Freddy Fantail. Examining the veranda window pane wondering again whether the picture of the autumn he perceives there is the real thing or not, remembering his sore beak and head, considering whether it is worth another assault. Watching his deliberations Dan wonders too.

As autumn weeks turn over toward winter disturbed only by unruly weather, a septic alarm centered deeply in the hidden organ of the mind, a sepsis which so far he has no more than sensed, ceases to make itself felt so that once more he is able to enter wholly into the fragile life of the imagination where abide his created people. They come more willingly now. With the threatening throbbing absent he is again able to turn his back on reality with safety. He resumes sleeping in the library alongside his work, leaving his bed at daybreak to garner in the imagery released at night.

May is the beginning of winter according to the calendar. It should be cold by now but for some reason or unreason it isn't. In the library he knows the moist temperature of the womb, a damp warmth heavy on the flesh like some cosmic melancholy. And the leaves fall only now which should have fallen weeks ago, twisting all shapes like drying dreams, their colors draining from them. The fruit trees first, then the snowball tree, then the sumac and mock-orange blossom: the planes in the playground, the oak by the gate and the fearfully untidy chestnut. They throw off their clothes like hungry women. Only the pines and firs, camphor and gum control their foliage excesses, concealing what they actually feel. But when he sees the carrion wasps eating the fallen fruit, burrowing like time into woman's flesh to leave them hollow cadavers, then he joins the prevailing theme himself, for the mood abroad is his.

Yet there do come times when, with no obvious provocation, an irrational storm upsets the prevailing calm as forces from the unconscious levels break through to the surface, bringing down trees and sending up rivers in the most wanton delinquency. Power lines broken and main roads blocked are headlined in the papers. Yet suddenly all is still again in static respectability as though the weather had no idea why she did such a thing, or forgets she has done it at all, and if charged with unlawful behavior justifies herself, blames someone else or denies the whole thing. For what does the weather know of logic or of human morality? No more than a tree, no more than a fantail, an animal or a woman.

Even though winter is officially here there is little real evidence of it. Dan tells Jim Prenderghast, "You see the leaves falling at last and think, 'Ah! Now I can pin down winter.' Yet outside there are things pushing up for spring. See those delphiniums? After blooming all spring and summer they carry on cheerfully clean through the winter until the following spring, then make a show of a great burst of energy, pretending that spring means something to them. I ask you: Where exactly *is* winter? In this part of New Zealand anyway."

"No, you never get the dramatic impact of spring here as you do overseas. Spring's an event in the snow countries you never see here."

There's little indication of the elements gathering their forces in the southwestern oceans. Just as to Dan in his humid seclusion there is little sign of the law assembling its forces over the little flock of ibex. All he manages to register in the landscape beside the downcoming leaves is a faint unrest enervating nature, and all he notes in the mindscape is the absence of Tarl next door.

The days and nights are his own now and reality changes character; changes location, one should say. Whereas it belonged to the world about him now it is in the mind. Mind and he are alone in the room sharing another life. His created creatures toughen up and win authenticity, and are jolly good company. He catches their swift emotions as they laugh and talk and weep their way through interweaving drama. Sometimes he talks too, strongly or frivolously as the occasion demands, and often laughs. Dynamic, eloquent souls they are, infinitely confidential, to whom alone he reveals himself for what he really is. To whom alone he elucidates himself.

Honored as legitimate beings they expand and take on form, their bodies all but tangible. With such vigor do they populate the mind that they follow him wherever he goes. Others the shadow, they the substance. Other voices the echo, theirs the true, so that when occasional friends put their heads in the doorway Dan wonders why they show compassion on him in his vivid private world, and makes a very poor show at answering them.

Across the playground in the evening to put out the milk bottle and collect the paper, the inner conversations endure. He picks up the paper all right but forgets and returns to the house with the empty bottle. Through the bell calling Benjamin each morning, through the singing of the children in the classrooms nearby, the occasional motor passing, the school buses arriving and departing, an airplane or two and the endless interchange of the birds, through all the dreamlike sound and movement of the shadowy outside world that others call the real, he lives the extreme concentration in his self-sought solitude.

"Daniel . . ."
A new voice in mind.
"I had to come."
Pause.
"I *had* to."
He doesn't look up.
"This is a Desperate Situation."

No . . . this is not a voice of his own creation, he can tell the difference quite clearly. Elbows on table, fingers through hair, trying to make the difficult journey from the inner world out while his vulnerable affrighted creatures scatter to the four corners of hell.

"Oh well then . . . I can see you don't want me. I'll spend a moment in the garden, do you mind? Just one minute." Soft steps departing.

By God this is Tarl, and in the flesh too. He turns over the exposed sheet and wipes from the edge of his hair a strange hot line of sweat and whispers, "What were you saying, Tarl?"

In she strides past the chair, children whirling after like leaves swept up in a gale, and takes center stage. "It's dreadful . . . *dreadful* . . . over there. You've no idea, Daniel, what we're going through. D'you know what he did this morning? He tried to get Bennie to school by force. *Force* . . . think of it. After all he has taught me of the danger of force on the growing mind of a child. Bennie ran and hid in the bathroom and locked the door. Gavin started taking off the lock but Bennie got out the window and hid in the orchard. I can't stand any more of this. The strife the poor child lives in. I've got to get him away again . . . I've *got* to." A "shuddering moan," hands pressed to cheeks while the children watch spellbound. "Our car won't go. The top of the benzine tank is lost. Homer put sand in the tank. I must get away from that hovel. I want you to take us to some place where we can live as we should. Oh-h-h . . . will you?"

"No."

"This is Desperate."

Reaches for smokes.

"You must know hundreds and hundreds of places where we . . ."

"I'll not take sides in a marriage."

Calm, all so suddenly, "All right then," and collapses on the bed, legs frightfully astride.

"I'll give you some wine," the grand anodyne, and so on for the rest of the morning until Homer runs a nail through his foot and she carries him screaming and bleeding through the house, dripping into the kitchen, where Dan offers an antiseptic dressing. "No, no, *no!*" screams Homer.

"He doesn't want it," from Tarl. "I'll take him home." But he doesn't want home either and she settles down with him rocking and soothing him in the big chair in the music room until at the sound of the bell at noon and the certain approach of the Head they arrive at the "What I really came for" part and the "I feel a little better" sequence and they hurry off under the trees to the fence . . .

"The disadvantage," he complains to Angela on Saturday when he has shut down the roaring rotary mower and has joined her at lunch in the kitchen among the babies, "of being a writer is that you can't avoid seeing everyone's damned side of a question. I'm already on three of these sides, no, four: the school's, the law's, Gavin's and hers."

"Why don't you tell her off?"

"Each side I too thoroughly understand."

"You ought to tell her off. Why don't you?"

"Because everybody does. It's one of the more minor obligations of a writer to prove everybody wrong."

"You've got a different reason every day."

"Each would stand on its own. Besides," lowers his voice, leans towards her and touches her skirted knee, "if ever I did let go, if I ever did, there'd be nothing living left next door."

"Nutteen ne't door," from Bruce.

Winter breaks suddenly, viciously, even with something that looks like spite, if anything so mindless as nature could harbor anything mean. "Viciously" is a word to be withdrawn also with its human overtones. It would be more accurate to say simply that the forces of nature burst their covering as the forces in the unconscious mind at times sweep from them the superimposed confinement, our laboriously built layers of custom, ethic, tradition and the keeping up with appearances. Winter wants to come this way . . . "I simply *had* to . . ." and that's all there is to that. Nature does what she likes, when and how she likes, living frankly with the whole of her mind, a master of the whim technique, the Everlasting Now. Does the weather ever consider us when it is moved to act? No more than Tarl would when touched off by impulse. Protest from the rest of us neither Tarl nor the weather would hear. What's the good of calling Tarl mad as society likes to do? Might as well call nature mad while you are about it or say animals are off their heads. The truth is more likely to be, if one had the stamina to face it, that in breaking the layers of restraint she's the least mad of us all. Or would be were she still in control, which is something that remains to be seen. "I'm the only sane one," she claims. "It's the rest of them who are ill."

Winter comes at last, very late for the bell. Not that mornings can't still be lovely on occasion, but you never want to trust a morning. There's no more treacherous a beautiful woman than a sweet morning in winter. She'll stab you in the back by noon. If you plan to go down to the land on the inner harbor with a spade and a tree or two, a thermos and some bread . . . if Angela wishes to walk with the little ones along the soft beach there . . . then catch this woman in the morning while there's still a smile on her face. Go while the weather's fine. She'll be howling with rage before the day is out and blaming everyone else. On her terms there'll be no afternoon.

Dan can be excused for wondering by now what the father thinks of the drawn-out Pracket dilemma and what manner of man he is. As far as he knows he's a human being who completed a university course, presupposing a certain ambition which is a major distinction between animals and men. He takes the greatest care not to ask, but legitimately enough recalls one bland summer morning a year ago on Election Day when Tarl lay beside her husband on the sand on the inner harbor tenderly stroking his hair while he admired Angela's ankles flowing out from beneath a flowered skirt. "Gavin and I," she said at that time, "decided to educate our children in our own way, without any force whatever. He would teach them himself to university standards and they could go on from there."

It's just that Dan sees nothing of this teaching up to any standard unless you call the "do nothing" and "be free" an excusion form of lessons. All he can do is bear in mind the originality of their concepts and recognize a certain nobility in trying to carry them through.

"I see," says an English friend of his called Felix, "nothing original or noble in their behavior. It looks exactly like selfishness to me. And laziness in her. Don't you agree?"

"It's hard to tell the difference, but I . . ."

"She's the laziest and most selfish person I've ever heard of."

". . . but I suspect there is a difference." He looks out the window at the camphor tree shuddering in a storm; in a "physiological and psychological upheaval."

Winter gets more out of hand than ever, not to mention his flock of ibex. "Get out of that piano," Dan roars one day, but she's delighted to have roused him emotionally and, quietly withdrawing the children, glows to herself in secret, watching him with respectful awe. A week or so later, crouched on his doorstep with a glass of wine, "All this don't, don't, don't for children. There shouldn't be anything in a house that children can't have. Who am I to instill millions and millions of don'ts in the slavish care of *things*? It spoils children's childhoods. It is soul-searing, spirit-annihilating. Don'ts frustrate children's freedoms. All they want is freedom."

"Freedom is a word that would not suffer from a careful definition."

But she looks at him with pity, then turns to attend to Dessida, who is whispering in her ear for something she wants. "Dessida wants to know if she can have some more of that colored dough that Angela mixed on Saturday."

"That stuff goes bad. It got put out."

"Why," from Angela the following Saturday, "doesn't she say these things to me? Aren't you allowed a grand piano be-

cause the Pracket kids might stroll in and want to get inside it?"
Angela is pregnant again and the pink of her cheeks has turned
pale. "Aren't you supposed to have anything at all if her kids
can't have it? Or are you supposed to give them open slather,
baby and all? Right, left and center?"

"Just let any Pracket touch my keyboard and you'll see what
I'm supposed to give, by God."

"Good for you."

"I've just about had a gut full, y'know."

"It's time you gave her once round."

There's silence for a moment, then Dan says, "I've got to be
fair, of course. I've got to say this. That all the time they've
been coming I've had my gramophone open. Record on, needle
. . . and never once has that baby boy of hers touched it. It's
marvelous, really."

"Oh I blush. It's the first thing I've got to shut and put away
when my boys are round."

"Oh I didn't mean that. I didn't mean to . . . to . . ."

"I can take it. There's much more tone in her family than
there is in mine."

Felix says, "Y'know that hovel on the hill they rented . . .
that belonged to a little old widow? I had this from the friend
of the widow. It had sprung chairs and a chesterfield. The kids
were encouraged to jump on them as much as they could until
they were utterly smashed, then they threw them into the bush
with whoops of derision. She told this herself, Mrs. Pracket, to
this friend. Fearfully proud of it. And many of her pots got
tossed out too."

"D'you know what I'm going to do, Fee? I'm going to put
up a list on a prominent wall. 'Don'ts for visitors: Don't eat
apples in my hearing. Don't eat them in my sight. Don't chew
gum anywhere on the premises or leave the damned stuff about.
Don't touch the piano unless you can play it. Don't open my
papers until I have seen them. Don't come to my door before
four in the afternoon or after seven in the evening. Don't ask
to borrow my books. Don't use my Christian name until I invite
it. Don't talk about yourself for hours on end . . . let me at least
say yes or no. Shut the door of the toilet when you use it. Keep
out of . . . ' " But the shouts of laughter from Felix drown him
out.

One morning he sees Tarl draw her little ones tenderly to
her, her cheek against theirs, explaining softly, persuasively,

"There's only two things you can't do here, darlings: play the piano and eat apples where Daniel can hear." "But wait," he tells Angela later, "till the list goes up."

"Poor little things," from Tarl. "They love the piano. If only I had a home where I could keep a piano. I've been married *ten years* and . . ."

"Eleven now, isn't it?"

"Oh-h-h . . ." hand to cheek.

Yet she can return a book. Dan can't believe his eyes when she walks in with it, cared for too, he doesn't know how. He clasps this precious first edition dedicated to his wife as though I myself had returned from the deserts of eternity, but, "I didn't find the Auden poem," stubbornly. "I didn't have time." Didn't have *time*. "But I know it's there. I *know*."

He waits carefully until he can control his temper, then, "I appreciate the exercise in forbearance you afford me."

"But she's a fool, Dan," from Felix. "I thought you said you couldn't abide fools."

"It's I who's the bloody fool."

"I do try," from Angela, "to let her know, Daddy, when she's at my place, how you're not to be disturbed. I said, 'None of us ever disturbs him during the week. I wouldn't myself even though I'm his daughter.' "

"When was that?"

"Oh, about a fortnight ago."

"That accounts for the extra visits during the week recently."

"The more I see how she uses you . . ."

He lays his hand on the top of the head of beautiful Mary, who looks a lot like me. "She's bigger and better than I am. Once she's got through these frightful thirties she'll be able to prove it."

"No one's stopping her from proving it. Why trample over you in the process?" Flash of a tear. "Mother would never have allowed it." I'd neither have allowed it or disallowed it. It's Dan's own affair to be met and solved, if at all, in his own medium.

"I owe it to art, Ange."

"One more reason for putting up with it."

"Besides, Tarl can return a book. There's an extraordinary thing. Something truly worth succoring in man or animal."

Angela brushes her face. "Oh, it's hot in here."

Brucey swings open the door wide, "F'esh egg for Mummie."

"I didn't use that check after all. I'd return it if I could find it." Her slim fingers seek in the raincoat pocket. Surprised, "Here it is." He takes the thing, slightly crumpled and certainly cat-eared, and drops it discreetly in his workbox. It looks just like a Pracket.

He is mainly unaware of what's going on behind the scenes next door and he never burdens Tarl with questions, having a regard for the sensitivity of others to pressure—and questions can be force. Not that he wants to know, God forbid, for the hidden core of alarm in his touchy mind awakes and throbs again these days so that he begins to sense a tide of destructiveness lapping in his direction. Not from the Prackets themselves, he believes, they being the least destructive of people . . . but from his own inadequacy in face of it. At the never-ending demands of his work for equanimity, its unceasing whines as though from a sickbed for equilibrium of the mind in which to operate its spiderweb machinery, he tries not to know what's happening over the fence, tries to ignore any knowledge of it that filters through. Yet quite enough does get through to bring his secret fear of Tarl out in the open where he tries to take the measure of it. At least he knows he's afraid.

"Borg," he says to a fisherman from the island who has crossed the harbor in his little boat one rainy afternoon—a man who has rejected marriage in case it interrupted his fishing and his nonstop interest in himself, in case it disturbed his constant fascinated examination of the content of his own mind. Dan rests a moment on his spade . . . three households he keeps in vegetables now. He is digging in the lupin to enrich the soil for the lettuce patch in the spring. "Borg, I want you to do something for me."

"No one says that on the island. Life is passing me by."

"If you get over that fench there, Borg, life will no longer pass you by. Just walk up through that orchard, find the house behind the trees, a hovel I believe, find your way round to the veranda rooms at the front and walk right in on a woman you're bound to find there. Just that. But it's for me, myself, I'm asking it, rather than for you."

Borg answers nothing, puts down the rake with which he has been helping and the next thing he is over the fence. When he returns about two spade rows later there is beneath his arm a leatherbound volume. But neither man says a thing. Neither does Tarl say a thing the next time she comes over. Nor the next time, the next or the next.

A few weeks before the end of the winter term word goes round about spring but I don't think Tarl has heard it. "These long, unending years of dreadful sadness." Crouched on the doorstep gazing at what is within her rather than at the trees about her. She seldom really ever sees anything specific before her. "I don't know what's happening to me. I've been out of touch with culture for years. Out of touch with life. No friends at all. No one ever comes to see me except the Child Welfare officer. One long black nightmare life is . . . a tunnel. I'm always so heavily sad. I'm crying most of the time. The kiddies say, 'We're supposed to be being brought up in the only right way but you're always crying.' But it does make me feel better coming here. The culture. Looking at all these overseas papers with the paintings and the new techniques. And the music you play to me and the level of talk. It reminds me of the days I knew."

"Have you finished your wine? I'll make you some coffee. I think there's some of your favorite coffee sponge that Angela . . ."

"There's only one thing I'm certain about. I'll never recover until I can free myself from Gavin. He batters at my mind as though he means to break it. I think he does. He might even batter my body. He got me down on my back on the floor last night and held my arms down sideways and he threatened to thrash me in the morning if I held Bennie back from school. He shouted at me, 'It's true what the magistrate said, that you are a dangerous woman.' I rushed into the police station, with the children and asked them for protection and I made a statement to them. I must save myself. I must get away from that hovel. I must get away for at least six months, I don't know where."

"Gavin's one thought is to save you. To get Benjamin to school so that he won't be taken from you. To keep his family together."

"I'd rather the law took Bennie than that Gavin should have him." They are all sitting round in the music room before the large fire, simply, gloriously doing nothing. Dan also, their pattern already established in his home. "But what I *really* came for . . . could you let me have some money? I hope you won't think I'm awful but . . ."

"No."

"I'd pay it back at the end of the month with my Child Allowance."

"Isn't that meant for the children?"

"I could sell my sewing machine."

"It's not I, it's my accountant. He won't let me keep any in my local bank. He doesn't approve of the way I walk round the street giving it away in armfuls." Mistake, that.

"Oh all right then," no anger. Then proudly, "My poverty is my jewel."

"It's the begging-bowl technique," he tells old Jim when he goes over to the Bay for a breather. "For her it's noble to beg and live off other people. But honestly, I'd have nothing left if I gave her everything she asked for. God knows what I've got was never begged for."

Jim is sixty and another exponent of freedom but he manages to get away with it by kindness and unbelievable charity, in one who has nothing anyway. He's beyond any influence. Not like Angela, who mops up everything she runs into. He lives in a real hovel in sound of the ocean. "What you've done, Dan, you've spoiled her as you do everyone you meet. Anyone else would have thrown her out long ago." Over the sandhill on the beach booms the everlasting Pacific.

"That's just it, they all do."

"I'm not without the suspicion—" he drinks the whiskey that Dan has brought him— "that there's something right at the bottom of it. Thoreau and so on. But isn't it time there was something right at the top of it?"

"She couldn't stand being right . . . I mean people saying she was."

"Nothing she does will ever be right, not in this society. By Western thinking, she'll remain wrong or mad. And that's it, y'see. Her pattern of values, it . . . yes it does, it does have a definitely Eastern quality, flavor, I think. And in the light of that she's not wrong. She's not mad, selfish, lazy or cruel. Matter of fact, in the light of her values she's courageous, energetic and sane. What she's trying to do, she's trying to save Benjamin from Western patterns. Now look, Dan, can you . . . I mean, who *doesn't* want to escape, tell me, from the . . . from all this ghastly pressure and racket of living? But have we got the guts or the desperation to—to . . . ?"

"*You* have."

"Dan, the magistrate himself would like to run barefoot with Benjamin. He's plainly on the child's side. Otherwise they'd have been convicted long ago. He'd have been taken by now, the boy. But he keeps on with these adjournments. And there's much to admire in Tarl. How many of us would stand up and openly defy the law of the land in order to practice our credos?

It's like Cranmer putting his hand in the flame." He throws his butt miles. "You've got to support her whether you like it or not."

"I do not."

"Oh, you writer guys. You all understand more than is good for you." His eyes reflect the sand dune as he looks out upon it. "And you pay too dearly for it." The boom of the breakers rolls in. "As far as I know there's neither cruelty nor kindness in the East. I've never seen the word 'love' between any of their covers nor the word 'hatred' either. They mate with each other, kill each other and go cheerfully on. It argues the free mind is automatically good." He rises and stretches. "How's the book?"

"Don't."

When Dan relays to Angela on one of their long drives home on Saturdays what Jim thinks about Tarl and the East she says merely, "It sounds convenient to me. Let's all go Eastern."

"I'm too crippled with Christianity."

"Well, turn some East back on Tarl. See how she likes it on the receiving end."

"She'd love it and come back for more." He doesn't add to her, All this love thy neighbor, care of the afflicted, good Samaritans, strangers within thy gates and such . . . I'm disgustingly riddled with it. Angela is too impressionable.

"But I do understand, Daddy dear, and I was kind to her last time she came. And she was nice to me too and we had a serious talk. Well, it was a lecture, really, on childbirth. My word, Daddy, she's up in that. You know what? Gavin delivered her last baby. Homer. There wasn't a single solitary thing she didn't have an answer for. But . . . I don't know why . . . her children don't play with ours. Did I tell you how she tried to get me to join her in establishing some place, some hidden camp . . . community in the wilds where we'd all do nothing? And if anyone did want to do something like paint or read, the others would mind the children. And we'd all eat wild fresh food and —and there'd be no one in charge and . . . as if I'd ever leave Rod. As if *I* could live like that, but . . ."

"Say no, say no if you need to."

"How much?"

In a matter of minutes Dan has bought another picture, something else that wouldn't sell in the past, presumably, which is hauled in from under a tree by Benjamin. The same old crumpled check is handy. "But that won't be any good, will it? You said there was nothing in your local bank."

"That's right, by Jove. I'll ask Ric about it. Take it in the meantime." Back it goes in the raincoat pocket. But when he asks Ric whether he has paid for the two or only one Ric laughs and does not answer. But obviously here's another flight. It's hardly warm enough though, not by a long way.

A cold dark Sunday evening before the last week of the school term. Dan has forgotten to turn on the outside light and his door is shut. Is that a step on the veranda? A soft knock. He turns over the page before him. "Come in."

It is the father ibex. He looks through the door and whispers, "Where's my family?"

"I don't know."

"I thought she might have told you."

"No."

"She didn't tell you?"

"She told me she wanted to go away but she didn't say where."

"Didn't she?"

"Come in. Sit down, Mr. Pracket."

"Gavin."

"Gavin. Sit down."

He settles in the armchair with the greatest care as though each movement were under strict control. He has no coat this very cold evening. His dark hair is tousled and his dark eyes burn.

Dan says, "They'll be all right."

"Not according to Caesar."

"This is only another little holiday."

"This is Caesar with his sword."

"Just a little holiday. Give them a . . ."

"Give unto Caesar that which is Caesar's."

"Caesar . . ."

"Ben is Caesar's. Ben must be at school next week or Caesar will take him from us."

Pause. "Yes."

"Bennie must be got to school somehow. They've got to be found in time. Give unto Caesar that which is Caesar's. But she's got the car. I've got college all day and in the evening I prepare my work. You must have some idea where they are, Mr. Francis."

"Shangri-La presumably."

THREE

❖❖❖❖❖❖❖

*One should never put on one's best trousers
to go out to battle for freedom.*

—Ibsen

❧ THE BELL CALLS loudly on Monday morning, School or else, Benjamin Pracket!

But where is Benjamin Pracket? Since Gavin called last night Dan has had in mind a picture of Tarl running before the police, her back to the wall with Benjamin. As he takes a moment on his way to work in his chair on the veranda, looking through the trees and across the playground, the spring day shakes with premonition.

Yet, believe it or not, here comes the Pracket car along the road. Praise all heaven and earth. Now . . . only this short movement from car to gate and the crisis will be safely over. Regrettably over, says an inner voice. Which parent is with him, he wonders? Now, these very moments, the drama being played out at the school. Praise God it's over, says his manifest face. Damn it, it's over, whispers the other. He rises in the bland spring sunshine and returns to the house for coffee, the ghoul of all men in him cheated that the pain should be safely over.

But when the Head passes through at lunch time he hears it is far from over. Benjamin is not at school. Tarl did indeed creep out of her hiding place but to drop Ramona only.

"But they've still got the rest of the week, Ric?"

But Ric doesn't discuss the subject. Neither does Tarl get over the fence to talk the whole thing over.

"Where's my family?" in the evening.

"I don't know."

"I thought they might have come here."

"No."

"You don't know where they are?"

"No."

"I've been looking for them all day. I took a day off from college. I've got to get hold of that son of mine." He looks Dan fair in the eye, his own fever-bright, unwavering. "They haven't been here today?"

"No."

"They haven't?"

"No they haven't."

He comes in respectfully over the step, as though Dan were worth it, in a way his wife never did, and sinks into the armchair, knees apart, elbows on them, covering his eyes with a hand—humanity's despair personified. Nearing forty, thick wavy hair growing well back on his forehead. An outdoor build and face. Not as tall as Dan and much better-looking. A bit plump maybe, his clothes conscientiously neglected, and these gray strides New Zealanders wear have hardly had a press at all, just managing to meet over his stomach. One supposes his shirt has seen an iron but there's no evidence to prove it and his tie hangs "just anyhow" like anything else in the Pracket family. He makes Dan think of southern forests rather than of a college classroom. Yet he's a soul, Dan reflects with interest, in the front line of life and in danger of being outflanked. He's a man of no mean sensation value to one living alone.

"She deceived me," he hears.

"I don't believe it."

"She deceived me."

"No . . . Gavin."

"You don't know what I know."

"Tarl wouldn't deceive. She's an artist. I'd trust her always."

"She did," looking up. "When I found her last night she promised to bring Ben this morning but she didn't."

"I don't call that deception. We often promise to do a thing, then our mood changes and our mind with it."

"It was coldly premeditated."

"I still don't believe it. I know her very well."

"You don't know her as well as I do. I found them last night, after seeing you, in an expensive flat at the Bay. Ten pounds a week job."

"She said she had to get away from that hovel."

"Ten pounds a week. How can I save for a home?"

"It's that hovel over the fence there. It . . ."

"She calls anything a hovel in time. This expensive flat would be a hovel too if she stayed there long enough, longer than she wanted to." Pause. "She pretended last night to be cooperating to get Ben to school. She promised to bring him back here this morning for me to take him along. But it was only to stop my keeping an eye on him, to forestall any preventive action I might take. She had no intention of bringing him back here this morning. She did arrive but only because Ramona was crying to come to school. But no Ben." A sigh.

"I said, 'Where's Ben?' And she said 'He's at Auntie's. You can get him yourself.' So I took the car and went back into town to her aunt's place but he wasn't there. So I came back and asked Tarl again where he was. She was white with fury. 'Find him if you can.' So I went over to the school and called Ramona out of her classroom. She didn't want to answer at first so I knew she'd been geared to deceive me too, and I said to her, 'You know Mummie's wrong, don't you?' And she said, 'Yes.'

"And I said, 'Well, tell me where Ben is. You know, dear, that if we don't get Ben to school this week he will be taken from us.' And she said, 'Mummie left him at the playground in town.' So I drove back to the playground but he wasn't there. So I came back to ask Tarl again where he was but she had disappeared. I've been searching for them all day . . . all the places where she was likely to be, every beach within reach, every riverbank and bush, any people she knew in town and every motel in the borough. I went to the flat at the Bay but it was locked, and no sign of them. I thought she might be here. She certainly did deceive me. It was all definitely premeditated."

Dan is silent a moment, then produces his only known solution to crises. "I'll make you some decent coffee."

"I mustn't disturb you."

"That's all right."

Gavin follows him humbly, respectfully, the path of the trusting, weary and anxious, for most comers believe in Dan. Along the dark veranda where he switches on, too late, the outside light, into the dark, carpeted hall, through the brooding music room where Tarl's two paintings hang and into the light and colors of the kitchen with its shining nickel plating where people are usually merry and where they tell him their secrets. And he sits on the chair by the fridge where Tarl has sat so often in rage, despair or hope, carefully in control of himself, and speaks in his softest voice, "This is tragedy."

"It is."

He receives the coffee most gratefully when Dan passes it. "You take sugar?" Dan asks. "Two I suppose."

"Just one, please."

Dan stands with his back to the bench as he usually does when people confide in him. "I still can't accept her deception. She's even told me she'd let him attend. She said it was Benjamin who refused. I said to her once, 'Why don't you really let Benjamin go to school?' And she said, surprised as anything, '*I* don't stop him.' And I said, 'Why doesn't he go then?' And she said, 'I don't know.' And I said, 'Have you ever asked him?' And she said, 'When I asked him he just said "I don't know." ' She wouldn't tell me anything untrue."

"You don't realize, Daniel. You see only one side of Tarl. What you don't know about is the fear and hatred of school she has created in the child's mind. I grant you, she could now quite safely suggest to him that he go to school but she knows very well he couldn't. You haven't seen her at work on the kiddies, the vicious language . . . oh yes . . . she uses on teachers and schools to them. The absolute hatred . . ."

"Gavin, I've got to defend her. Tarl must have someone whom she believes to be on her side, of whom she can be sure. From what I see and hear, everyone is against her. I've got to try and see the whole thing as she sees it, and to some extent I do. I *do* support her basic concept, freedom of the mind and the right to be different. It's her operation of it, only, I question. I've got to accompany her in mind. She's in darkness. She says so herself. Now I'd rather go into darkness with her and walk out with her, together, to the light. I . . . instead of standing comfortably in the light of reason and calling her from the darkness. It's a very hard thing to put into words."

"I appreciate that very much." He stares deeply into his cup, stirring the coffee as though somewhere in it he might find not only his family, not only the solutions to his problem, but a release from his soul's malady, and as Dan stands observing him a thought germinated way back in the winter takes firmer root and he talks with the foolish profundity of one in whom all answers are to be found—but are not—about obsessional artists needing to paint to avoid the obsession flowing out upon the family. Surprisingly, Gavin listens, examining with the trained eye of the scholar each one of Dan's words, standing them on trial; then he sums up with economy, "She must paint?" Pause. "She hasn't her materials." Reflects further, "But I've fixed her easel. It's in the car." A longer lap of thought to himself, then,

"She's a very fine artist, you know." Stirs his second coffee, "The trouble is I've been too busy. Three sixth forms I've got. Physics. I've forgotten it and I don't remember enough of the chemistry to teach it without preparing until eleven each evening, to keep one jump ahead. Zoology is my subject. Man himself for me. And Saturdays I go laboring. It's hard on Tarl and the kiddies.

"But somebody's got to keep the family. I've got to save somehow to get them a home. In the last year or two we've lived in four places—five now with that flat. But although she continually reproaches me for not providing a home, she's never let me get one. She keeps us on the move all round the world . . . America, Britain, the Continent, back to New Zealand, whatever appeals to her at the moment, off we go. She never has consulted me on anything—Tarl. She announces a thing, or doesn't, and does it. With no reference whatever to reason or to me. There's never been any other right way but Tarl's. If you disagree you're lost. Faced with any kind of authority at all she either fights or runs away. She knows no such things as submission or compromise. But I'm used to these flights of hers, these overheated pipe dreams.

"I remember a time in London . . . I wanted the holiday pay to catch up on bills and expenses in order to start the following term in the clear for once, but when I was at school she received a large payment from sales of her pictures and she put this together with the advance holiday pay and slipped off and bought a secondhand car and announced we were going for a holiday. No chance for me to look over this car. So we all set off but we hadn't even got out of town when the thing blew up. All was lost then.

"That's what it has been like all our married life, and so far I've always given Tarl her head in order to keep the family together, but now, for the first time, I've had to defy her. I've got to rule in this or we stand to lose Ben. I've got to crush my family to save them. This is just one time when she must not run away with Ben but . . ." fingers through hair . . . "she has. The sword of Caesar knows no compromise." He beats the fridge softly, "But can Tarl see this? That I'm trying, not to take Ben from her, but to save him for her. Poor girl, poor little girl, if only she could see reality."

He thinks to himself for a while with that look on his face of men recalling a dear lost love. "We were so happy at first, roaming like gypsies all over the world. It was not till Ben was born that disharmony appeared. His was the only planned pregnancy, the only time when she fulfilled herself. He is her favored child. She won't let him leave her for any reason. She has this irresistible hold on him. She has this boy in thrall. I beg her, 'If only you'd release the mind of this child.' " Silence, then. "She hates me, she *hates* me."

Follows a clear hour's worth of solid and meticulous analysis of his wife: her deprived, traumatic childhood, her agonized schooling, her subsequent rebelliousness, irrationalities and contradictions accompanied closely by her incomparable handling of children; all in fastidious scientific divination, cold in words though hot in feeling, with an overall flush of obsession as clearly discernible as any in his wife, until he closes softly with, "What shall I do?"

"What shall you do? Are you asking *me?*"

"I am."

"There's at least one thing no Pracket will get from me. Advice. And another thing. You'll never catch me—wittingly that is—taking sides in anyone's marriage. All that quarreling married people are short of is a third person to blame. To interfere in other people's lives is generally to assume an unwarrantable risk. Besides . . . what makes you think any advice from me would be any good? God Almighty, as if you'd follow it. Either of you. No, man, no. I mean to remain on both sides. To the finish. And I don't think that's going to be easy. Each of you so convinces me that I'm on both your sides. Simultaneously. Well . . . I'm on the side of the one who was here last."

Gavin laughs outright, revealing a silver filling way back in his teeth, and Dan feels round for his smokes. Thank God, he thinks, as the Head drops in on his way home from school at nine.

"I'm desperate, Ric," softly. "Here is Caesar with his sword. I've got to beat Tarl to save Ben. I've got to crush my family to save them. For the first time in our marriage I must defeat my wife."

"You must . . . beg your pardon?"

"I must defeat my . . ."

"Oh I see. You must defeat your wife. I see." But the Head likes practicalities. "What is her greatest need?"

"A soul mate."

Silence all round. The clatter of cups and the rumbling of the water pick up thoughts and toss them about like balls out in the playground until Gavin adds the obvious, "She wants Benjamin for her soul mate. He *is* that. But she'd never admit to it."

Milk running into the cups. "You in this round, Gavin?" And the Head gets on with the tangible trying to establish some sort of order in the Pracket chaos. It's a relief to have Ric about; he has the kind of presence that deflates crises, even his own, and this is his crisis, too, professionally. "When's the next court case, Gavin?" So far Dan has never spoken so indelicate a term as "court case." So . . . well, "indecent" is the word, rather.

"If he's not at school by Friday the first case is the following Wednesday. There will be two."

"And what," rationally, "will happen if you lose the first case?"

"Have a scone," from Dan. "One of Angela's."

A smile, "I've already stayed too long."

Dan does not dispute this.

"They can only fine me, Ric. But they'll hand the whole affair over to the Child Welfare department who will make a charge of neglect. Failure to send a child to school by seven, without substantial reason, constitutes neglect in the letter of the law. They'll give Ben another chance and if he still resists . . . if they can prove neglect . . . they'll take Ben. Or think they will." Adds sugar to his tea. "But no one will get my son from me. I'll produce him tomorrow morning. I spent some time this evening nailing up the windows of the 'hovel' from the outside. He eluded me that way last week. I'm going to spend tonight with them at the Bay to keep an eye on Ben. I'll get another day off from college tomorrow. I've got a sympathetic Head." Feverishly, "The whole fate of our family, our unity, depends on this: getting Ben to school this week."

The Head, turning it over, "Getting Ben to school this week. Ah. I can see Benjamin walking along that road tomorrow morning with his head up. He's . . ."

"That's what he would do," soft fist on fridge, "if she'd only release his mind. She's only got to say one word . . . but she refuses to say it."

"She's only got—what did you say?"

"Just one word but she . . ."

"I see. She's only got to say one word," thinking it over, turning it over, "but she refuses to say it. Yes I see. Well, you've got four days left, Gavin. You tell me that Benjamin has an exceptionally high I.Q. He'll be able to see for himself that his attendance will save him from . . . save his family from . . ."

"But Ric. What if I do get him to school? I'll lose Tarl. She'll never forgive me for defeating her. I lose either way. I can't win."

"You can't win," pondering on it. "But surely it would be true to say that Benjamin has enough mind of his own to . . ."

69

"His mind," thump, "has never been his own since the moment of conception. Tarl needs psychiatry to remove this mental block, this vicious hatred of any authority she's carried in her heart since early childhood, of anything to do with schooling, of 'Anyone In Charge' at all . . ." and so on until the cups are empty. "I need time, Ric. The magistrate Johnny has been lenient, he's been adjourning cases for eighteen months for us to agree between each other but it's not enough, you can't organize, legalize human frailties. I need time . . . more *time*." Thump.

"You need time, more time. Well all you've got to do, Gavin, is . . ."

" 'Time and I against any other two.' "

". . . is put him inside the school gate, never mind the building, just once, so that I'll be in a position to report to the Child Welfare that he has been present. I've already enrolled him, that first morning way back in February. Even if he goes home immediately. Once I can say the child has attended . . ." hands outspread . . . "then you've got all the time you want. You and time against any other two."

But this brings on all Gavin's fevered doubt about the damage such force might do to his son's mind, the shock, to which the Head counters in experienced exposition the delicacies and techniques of integrating a child, adding, "I have carefully prepared his teacher, a lovely young Maori girl. He needs only attend, later on, till morning interval and then go home, until he's achieved adjustment. A child who . . ."

But all roads lead back to Tarl. "She's teaching the kiddies to hate me, Ric. That's more than I can bear," until Dan loses the threads of marathon analysis in which he has learned more about Tarl than she's ever told him herself, more possibly than she knows about herself. Is the Head on the floor now? ". . . not my function to influence a parent beyond the gates of a school. It's no good asking me to influence your wife. When your son attends that will be my area of influence. As for fearing there might be any mishandling—everything will be done to integrate the boy. On the other hand if . . ."

"I'll need to be kept informed. At the first indication of any . . ."

"You may rest assured, Gavin, that I myself will do everything humanly and professionally possible to preserve the unity of your family and to understand the little chap."

Gavin is one of their parents now and, for that matter, one of God's creatures, whatever, if anything, that may be worth to a scientist, and Dan should as host stay on to the finish but he all but crawls off on hands and knees to bed in the middle of someone's sentence. . . .

A family dividing all over him, the sound of rending, of convulsions. Consciously as he opens the window for the night behind him, perceiving the high moon, he recalls this family as he saw it a year ago on the beach below his land. They were at the cottage when he and Angela arrived and drove in, Angela thinking the two lots of children would play together, as well as from a habitual neighborliness.

Tarl runs out in a pair of those silly little pants women wear secretly beneath their skirts but which Tarl has no secrecy about. This unself-consciousness about her body is the same as that about her mind; exposing both easily. When however the Prackets follow them down to the beach later with some simply marvelous tea, she's covered up again in the same old matadors, the apotheosis of allurement, but there's nothing tied round her head today and her hair turns out to be silky and sultry. Slight and lithe she lies on the sand beside her husband tenderly stroking his hair.

Seen all together for the first time and at close quarters the Pracket family strikes him with its gentle unity, closely and touchingly knit. Ramona is a lovely little girl, about nine at that time, with the body of a fairy and long black hair down her back. A faded dress, a little soiled, reaching to her knees and her feet slim and bare. The disputed elder boy, Benjamin, seven at the time, coos over Angela's baby like a bird, holding his fingers and examining his toes. A nice-looking boy, slight like the others with his hair longer than most, a deep black fringe on his forehead. The profile's good, a particularly nice line from nose to chin and his voice has something unusual in it. Is it authority in the throat of a child, or the confidence of deep-bred serenity? True, the four children cluster to their parents as though closing the ranks against unproved strangers so that Dan gets the impression from the car of a flock of animals of some exotic origin, faintly alarmed and bewildered to be divided from the herd, but the poignancy of a family remains, within the herd or without, the offspring radiating from and eddying back to their vital parental source . . . the meaning of symbiosis. Each child is so indivisibly a part of the family unit as to be barely distinguishable. The baby, Homer, constantly climbing over his parents claiming their attention.

"All this emphasis on clothes," Tarl is saying to Angela, poised on a tussock nearby. Ruefully, "Ramona wants me to

71

wear a dress. That's what comes of going to school, picking up this regrettable regard for what others think. I find myself entertaining her friends and the next thing I hear is, 'Mummie, why don't you wear a dress? All the other girls' mothers wear dresses.' But I simply haven't got a dress. No one has given me a dress for years."

"Why not," from Angela sparking, "try making a dress or even *buying* one?"

But Tarl doesn't hear on principle and continues, "See that? She wants to go home and change into a cleaner dress because you are here. School ideas again ... oh-h-h ..."

The moonlight is upon Dan's face and he draws the curtain a little. That was in the summer last year and that was the family together, the only time he saw it thus, but even then the seed of discord was germinating as everything alive germinates in the youth of life.

The bell calls Benjamin on Tuesday morning, again with urgency and hope. Benjamin Pracket, come to school! Do-or-die week, school or else! Ring a-ling, school or else!

Through the trees the clanging softens to a peal with a cadence of persuasion. Come and learn, Benjamin Pracket. Come and receive the knowledge passed down from former generations, that your civilization will endure. In order that the country you love so well may not disappear like the cities of the past in the Middle East, vanishing beneath the sands of the centuries and the corrosion of neglect. Do come and learn, little Bennie. ...

Dan sits longer in his chair this morning orientating himself for work, looking through the trees to the children. Will Gavin get Benjamin to school? What happened at the Bay last night where he went to keep an eye on his son? Who won over there? Is it spying to be sitting here watching? On the other hand is it his fault that the Prackets choose to play out their morning drama across his accustomed line of vision, and this is his legitimate line of vision on his way to work in the morning. Why admit to himself his craving for sensation given gratis to all by this family? Why not cover it over with masses and masses of sympathy and a pose of sacrificial nobility?

In any case he can't work anyway. Who could? How can a man settle down to virgin paper, with an image in mind of Tarl baled up by the police? He is not stainless steel. Wonderful, sensational and bloody image ...

Every tree, plant, bird, teacher and child is answering the call of the bell, excepting him and Benjamin; going about their business of growing and learning and seemingly happy about it. Just try killing out individuality in these voracious years of a child within a school or without; in the hands of the very worst teachers freedom still fills his lungs, let alone in the hands of a good one. Discipline frees the wings of the wildest spirit in a way that whim cannot.

Excepting Benjamin Pracket. By Tarl's reckoning he needs the world entirely to himself, entirely *for* himself, including the civilization in it obligingly supplied and worked for by a whole society . . . to preserve his soul's identity. To do what he wants in the way he wants, which often appears to be nothing. Which no doubt can be excellent for a boy in the context of nature but how good is it for his father in the text of the law facing Caesar from the dock?

By God there's the car. Is it going to school? It is . . . it stops. Do you see that, calling bell? You've done it. Congratulations, bell.

He tries to work till eleven then gives up the whole idea and plods to the kitchen for coffee. He's got that left-out feeling; drama happening elsewhere and he not the shining center of it.

Enter the female animal. Strides through the house, scattering drama right and left, collapses on chair, legs widely spread-eagled. Hands to cheeks, eyes closed in the best stage manner . . . a "soft shuddering moan."

"Congratulations, Tarl. Hurray. Benjamin's at . . ."

"He's not at school." Gasp.

"What?"

Utter outrage in every angle as though arranged by an artist for a sitting. She whispers, "Monster . . . brute."

Brandy, sugar, lemon juice . . . "Where is Benjamin now?"

"Hiding in the grass over there. Oh-h-h . . ."

"Where are Dessida and Homer?"

She does not see the glass he holds toward her. "The monster."

"Where are the younger two?" Still the out-held glass. Angela will laugh at this when she hears . . . this outstretched glass unseen.

"Over there with him." Eyes still closed. "I must get back. The monster," shudder, "the brute."

"Drink this. It will stop you shaking." Women love to be told they are shaking. The slow eyes open, a hand reaches forward

73

trembling authentically for the glass. *"Thank* you," the extreme of humility.

He starts on the noisy brewing of coffee, spoiling the whole scene. He'd do anything, he's so relieved that the drama is not over, that Benjamin didn't go. Good boy, Benjamin, holding out. Atta boy. The truly terrible disappointment he felt when he believed the boy was there . . . it is over. On with the triumphant coffee. Good coffee will bring anyone with their woes and their firsthand living. "Is he a monster, Tarl?" Turn on the sympathy, Dan. I know you.

"Thank you." A sip, then suddenly, "Yes he is. You don't know him as I know him. Would a humane father nail the outside of the windows and take the lock off the bathroom door to stop his son from escaping? That's what he did. Poor little Bennie was hiding in there. He dragged him out by the wrists and held him up like this." Demonstration. "He hauled him down the lane. He lifted him from the ground and carried the little thing by the wrists. Bennie was screaming and kicking. The two little ones ran madly after them, throwing stones and mud at their father. Oh it was dreadful . . . *dreadful!* Bennie started vomiting near the gate all over Gavin and he had to put him down. He was practically unconscious. Sobbing . . . a jerky sort of moaning." Demonstration. "He crawled away like a wounded animal on his hands and knees into the long grass. He's still lying there now. His little wrists are raw. The inhumanity of it. What d'you think of a man like that?"

Dan is so grateful for all this that in moving about getting the coffee and the cups ready he is making far too much excited clatter. The scene is suffering from it. An audience should be quiet. "Drink that and you'll feel better."

A grim sip from her glass, then up valiantly on her feet again, eyes a black blaze. "He betrayed us, the monster, the brute." Her raincoat swishes on the fridge as she strides from the kitchen to the music room. "It was he," from the other room, "who taught me all this about permissiveness and the freedom of the mind. He began teaching me from the moment I met him. And look at him now . . . nailing up windows. He betrayed us, the monster, the . . ." another sip . . . "brute." Dan takes an eager sip also.

"Only let the mind be free, he said," bitterly from the other room. "And everything else will follow. Thwart a child in nothing." Back on stage in the kitchen, eyes rolling dangerously. "Love and serve a child and he in turn will love and serve and strive to thwart others in nothing. But look at his thwarting this

74

morning. Meet all possible demands, he said, even to toast at two in the morning. Let him run round with his food if he wants to. Let him stand on the table with his bread in his hands, or in his feet, if that's the way he likes it. Eat his food with his fingers . . . always supposing there is some food . . . the animals seem to manage. Let him jump on the furniture when there is some furniture if the desire strikes him . . . there shouldn't be any in the first place. Children should only go to bed when they want to. A baby should fall asleep in his mother's arms just like the Maoris. Obey every whim whatever it is so that the mind may grow without the slightest pressure into its normal shape. Man is essentially good, he taught me, and will grow in goodness if the mind is free. Freedom . . ." the dark eyes roll to the window framing the fig tree outside. "Living from moment to moment, from whim to whim in the Everlasting Now. The magnificent unfolding of the Now." Radiance in her white face a moment before the collapse on the chair by the fridge again, hands over eyes. "But look at him now. Backing down before the law. Descending to the level of force." Very, very softly, "He betrayed us, the monster," fading away. "He betrayed us this morning, the brute."

He allows a good long pause for effect, it's only fair, then risks, "What I can never fathom, Tarl . . . why return to this country knowing well the laws? Why not some island in the Mediterranean or even the Arabian desert? I could name any number of places in Asia where you could all do nothing forever. Places like Isfahan, Zahidan, and there's a little place called Oomsbahn on a little island called Bahrein. The diseases I suppose. And of course there'd be no Child Allowance there."

But she never does answer this question. Dan privately likes to think that she read his books overseas and came back to be near him but it wouldn't do to say this openly to anyone. It would hardly contribute to his pose of professional modesty. All Tarl answers is, "There'd be no disease if the mind were free," and her gaze retreats to the fig tree through the kitchen window.

He examines the fig tree too with the new leaves barely budding. "I'm not saying I wouldn't follow anyone into court to defend the right to be different." Rash, that . . . the brandy. It's the kind of thing that could bring embarrassing results. He beaches in another place. "The spectacle of a child hiding, kicking, screaming and vomiting in order to avoid being taken to Mr. Richmond has to be seen to be believed. That's what children usually do when they are kept from him."

75

"Bennie's not ready to leave me," whispered Tarl being a master of evading the point when it suits her.

"Children love Mr. Richmond."

"Bennie has not yet said, 'I suppose I'll go to school.' "

"Let's take this coffee in the sun."

Dan is not a man to diddle round with trays but he's in my role this morning. He's even chosen a special cup for Tarl, the sort of thing I used to do, daffodil yellow, and a saucer the new green of shoots. How pathetic can men be when they try to play the role of a woman? And for once chance is on his side; there happens to be a piece of the coffee sponge she likes . . . he can do this sort of thing with no children about. On the veranda it is very beautiful, the uncared-for spring garden before them, very still except for the birds and an occasional sneaking cat . . . a relaxing forgiving place. He takes to his canvas chair while Tarl predictably ignores the other to squat on the brooding doorstep, clasping her legs, her cup beside her. And as her eyes charge fiercely ahead she whispers, "They'll never get Bennie from me." He heard Gavin say that too. "I'll beat them. I'll beat them all."

He looks at the black head with its tails of long hair and the yellow thing around it. The spring sun delineates the dark hairs on her legs, ponders on the worn flat shoes and sports tentatively in the yellow of the stiff rubber raincoat with its angular folds. Sometimes in the months ahead the weather will remove this permanent coat to reveal the slim thighs again. In the meantime there are always the riches of her eyes and the pathos of her slight hands and feet. The voices of the infants in their classes just round the totara tree which Benjamin nursing his wounds in the grass next door must surely hear too . . . carol, carouse and call in a glory of praise to life in the spring. But on Tarl's face is the groan of a soul in subterranean caverns.

On occasion vanity in Dan does step back a pace for a moment, then compassion awakes, a quite authentic compassion. Born of that infirmity of writers in which they enter the mind and being of another and become that other. In which case I would say it were not so much compassion at all as simply this infirmity. In any case he finds himself getting up, a little clumsily, steps over her huddling on his step, avoiding her cup there, takes some wine for support, settles down in the dimness of the music room at the keyboard and enlists the help of Stockhausen, whose music—or what he calls his music, but which most people claim to be invalid, meaningless and misleading—is more in character with the Pracket temperament than more regular composers. He explores these surprising ruminations on the keyboard, unable to watch as usual an original of wild torn trees above the piano not unlike the original on his door-step . . . on account of the unlikely score. And it comes to him in jagged flashes just what it is that offends him in this marathon marital conflict: the indecent exposure of souls, their own and each other's. Even when souls are comely it is to him reluctant ground off paper, much more so when they are not. Only lovers can get away with it, musicians, writers, trees and women in labor.

In time she comes creeping in, settles fearfully on the edge of the couch, or humbly maybe, and actually appears to be listening so that his vanity returns. "This," as he plays, "is the 'never-mind' music. I think he knew all about it." And he smiles at the wit in the manuscript. But he does not want anyone to see his own soul which, along with the composer's, is badly exposed in the music, so he rises from the whole thing restlessly, impatiently, and tries something else. Grandly, "I'll pick you all up in the car and take you to the land. For you all to get over this morning." Rash again . . . the wine. He escapes to the easier veranda.

Out here again she seems to be even sadder. What would my wife have done now? he thinks. She would have picked up that potted tulip and stood it before her, the bloom beneath her face. Or would have picked those few stray freesias from the for-gotten garden and said, "Smell this. I challenge you to feel any-thing but benign thoughts in the context of this scent." But Dan has forgotten the years behind us since I died. I did do that sort of thing when in love and young but had I lived and matured I would not have. In any case he can't possibly do it and feels he has failed again. But I myself know that Tarl registers his general intention with that pathological sensitivity of hers, the antennae of her spirit picking up the intangible with ease. Which is her great gift when she chooses to use it.

But she may be feeling better for she begins talking about something else: the expensive flat at the Bay, the peace and the freedom of it, the children on the beach in the early mornings. "I feel so different there. I haven't cried for days." There is even joy in her white face as she looks up, but is there anything harder to witness than joy on a face overlaying the darkness behind it? He regrets he has managed to cheer her.

"Have you been able to paint out there?" His only question ever.

"Not quite yet but I could."

77

"Gavin said last night you were a very fine artist."

"He's never said so to me."

"How like a husband."

"He argues that art is only consolation, that a true and free intercourse between people should supply all human needs."

"That's like his slogans too." Careful, don't take sides. "But of course he's right." But he says no more. To converse with Tarl at all is such an exercise in delicacy, such a lesson in withholding, an engagement with such high requirements that he is seldom in gear to do it. But even so he has been too clumsy. Irritable movement from Tarl, a sigh, "I must get back to Bennie."

"There's a friend of mine at the Bay. He's sixty. He lives on his own. He's frankly of the company of vagabonds but an extremely successful one. Gracious. I celebrate there when I get a book away. Number two-four-nine, the Waterfront. Jim Prenderghast."

No answer but she must have heard. Then Dessida and Homer come over the fence scuttling under the trees and spring excitedly upon their mother like puppies. At which he at once realizes they have been alone and that now they no longer are. The strain is lifted considerably. She receives them gratefully as though part of herself were restored and indeed she does look more herself with her young upon her. Soon, however, they are both well under way with the fruits of civilization until he says, "What about Benjamin over there in the grass? Isn't he ill? Doesn't he need attention?" For that matter, what about his own work in the room behind him? He knows that is ill and in need of attention.

"He's all right." Finishes her wine. "He likes being on his own." It is nearing lunch time by the sound of the reception class let loose, and the Head will soon pass this way. She knows it too and gets up, her shoulders curved, and goes down the steps calling the children. "Don't go, Mummie," they say.

"We've got to get back to Bennie, darlings." She swings Homer heavily on her hip and lifts these wonderful eyes to Dan from the bottom of the steps, like sleeping pools in the forest reflecting the wistful haunting darkness about it. "Well, are you going to take us all down to the land? We could pick up Ramona."

"I've had too much hooch."

"Ramona could do with the afternoon off."

"Too much alcohol I've had to take the car on the road." Only a quarter true.

The schoolchildren run out, eddying, whirling, calling and spreading under the school trees for lunch. She turns away with her heavy Homer, her sadness even heavier and her enslavement to whim heavier still. "Come on, Dessy. We've got to be there when Ramona gets home for lunch." She doesn't add, "But what I really came for . . ." or "I feel a little better now," so presumably he has failed. Brandy, coffee, sponge, wine, talk, music and all, not to mention the scent-and-color treatment implicit in the morning.

"Has that boy been here?"
"No."
"He hasn't?"
"He's over there hiding in the grass."
"Ay? Beg your pardon?"
"He's over there hiding in the grass."
"The grass." Thought, "You've done no work, I suppose."
" 'Nature knows no pause in . . .' what's it again now?"
"You haven't?"
"Haven't what?"
"Done any work?'
"Oh, that. Goethe said something about nature knowing no pause in progress and development. Ah, here it is. She 'attaches her curse on all inaction.' "

⚜ AFTER THE HEAD has gone, Dan takes another look at nature from the veranda, all that she offers a boy. He's been a great truant himself in the past. The blue line of the mountains in the distance, the blue sky spilling its blue down into the ravines, and he thinks of the blue harbor water. He remembers eeling in forbidden creeks beyond secret hills, padding forest pathways, roaming the hair-blown beach, ah . . . he even truanted from teaching all over Asia one time before he got me to marry him. He's on the side of truants at heart, for the moment anyway.

Felix said to him one morning before Dan forbade him to come in the morning, "Work's a terrible thing. And I mean it, Dan. A weak disgusting unnatural habit that too many people fall into. The thing's contagious too. Here you are, a man with

79

means, and you still won't come and play. What about happiness? Haven't we a right to happiness?"

"Happiness," Dan snarled. "Did I hear you say *happiness?* Happiness is only a precipitant. You don't go looking for it. The only time you find happiness is when you're staring the other way. Absorbed in some arduous work, something with continuity. Then it may fly off in sparks. Joy, Fee, is an astoundingly unplannable thing. Joy is a woman, I've found . . . shy, fickle, elusive, as unreliable as a cigarette lighter. Not to be lured, not to be caught except when she's unexpected. She'll hover then, suddenly show her face, smile at you and kiss you on the back of the neck. Woman . . . I've known her. Happiness. I've known her."

"I repeat that work's a terrible thing. It's ungainly, it's improper, it's . . . it doesn't grace the human creature. I still just can't understand how an otherwise quite decent chap like you can't call his time his own."

"I'll send a . . . someone I know along to you one day. You're going to get on."

What is it now? One o'clock. She has two more hours to put in over there till three o'clock when she collects Ramona and takes her back to the Bay. She wouldn't have had to endure these bad days next door had it not been for Ramona's tears to come to this debated school. They could all have been on the beach at the Bay, the children delightedly gathering pipis and shells while Tarl, hands in raincoat pockets, wandered far out to the water's edge to breathe in chokingly the horizon and drink in passionately the freedom. She certainly means her philosophy, to love and serve children.

Over that fence waits one of their parents counting terrible minutes. Were he a woman he'd go over, he thinks. What would his wife have done? In the music room hangs this portrait of me and he prowls humbly about it. Many months have gone by since I last appeared to him on the veranda in the evening, pleading to him from the shadows. A man in his early forties and a girl of nineteen with the abyss of the grave between us—our only tangible link . . . a portrait. To perpetuate the endless mystery of the face the artist must have exercised herself indeed. My eyes look directly ahead yet they follow the viewer wherever he moves . . . to the initiated a routine phenomenon but to Dan an outright miracle.

Yet it is not wholly on my account that he finally decides to make his first visit to the notorious "hovel." Nor the habit of the Christian ethic, nor even plain humanity. Nor is it wholly the urge to find out for himself exactly what this disputed boy is like in the privacy of his own habitat . . . he never fools himself where he can avoid it, which he claims to be his one valid virtue. He knows that he wants to be close to the source of sensation, in the front row of the stalls where he always sits, to see for himself for a change *what happened,* independently of the Pracket double version. Moreover, the role of the fine benefactor, understanding and healing all wounds, is one of his favorite roles. Also and not least, with a bit of plonk under his belt he finds he can take quite a bit of appealing eyes, especially wonderful eyes, lifted in pathos to him—in all of which he is not ashamed to be Man Everlasting.

Another injection of brandy to help him live up to himself, to leave the sickbed in the library where his work cries aloud for attention, to silence its groans before he dresses up "nicely" in his good strides and white sweater and gets hold of something for the youngsters as teachers have a way of doing; a bag of peanuts, conceivably, for the boys; and he goes into our bedroom, my dead bedroom, for something for the girls; a small bottle of scent he bought in Arabia to give me on his return to New Zealand, all of which he stows in a Teal flying bag of Angela's with the long strap over the shoulder.

Over the fence they are always climbing with the barbed wire on top and the blackberry. As he plows up through the long grass of the orchard he's astounded at his first view of the "hovel." Through the citrus trees it turns out to be one of these large white pretentious Christmas-cake dwellings with decorative icing dripping from the verandas, built in the century when New Zealanders were able to own such places, when taxes didn't smack them from the hand or death duties eliminate them and when the size of families justified them. Probably the homestead of a wide farming area, a station, cut up in pieces now. Pointed white turrets, jutting windows and verandas broad enough to accommodate several families on their own. And at each possible and impossible point all this elaborate wooden lacework they so loved early in the century before the price of labor forbade it. One of these grand eloquent stiff-silk buildings professing all manner of happiness within but which more often breed high tragedy—as it does at this very moment. A magnificent façade of well-being for many whereas two could be happy in a cave. In my brief walk on the earth I knew rapture in a cave myself and ecstasy in a hut of sods.

He comes upon her unawares. In his right mind he would

revolt at so invading the privacy of another without warning, but the brandy allays all that. He finds her crouched on the ground as usual, chin to knees, arms clasped around them, still in the permanent raincoat, stiff and as part of her as the bark of a tree or as the skin of an all-weather animal. Her eyes like magnolia petals stare ahead, seeing what? he wonders. She does not, he is surprised to note, jump at his sudden appearance as his own two women would have, but merely shows faint pleasure. Softly, "Oh, I was thinking about you." Not moving an inch, "I was thinking about that tulip in the pot. You wanted to put it under my face. You must have thought I was indifferent."

"It's good for bad moods, I believe."

No sign of the Benjamin he's come to see but Dessida and Homer are in the fowl yard playing hilariously with the hens, dozens of big white gentle hens dashing about like disconnected ideas. Dessida has a large bamboo stalk, scattering them to see them cluster and squawk. Yet their clucking is a soothing sound like subdued conversation. He says after a moment, "There's something to be said for the Hallibuts letting the children play with the hens."

"They don't let them play with the hens. They're all away at work or at school from eight till five."

He remains standing and she sitting as they watch the children and hens until she calls to Dessida, "It would be better without the stick, dear," at which she at once puts it down. Then two-year-old Homer—no, three—runs from the fowl house fondling a great white egg. "What a lovely egg, Homer, yes, but you'd better put it back." Soft and careful persuasion. And the egg goes back all right. None of this wrangling between mother and child tearing love to pieces; the discipline in this undisciplined family is like clear running water when there's no one In Charge about, and has to be seen to be believed. Tarl could appreciate Ric and his gentleness quite well possibly were he not the One In Charge. Presumably Benjamin still hides in the deep grass shedding the morning's agony, like cats that withdraw when they're sick. And he's left alone with his instinct.

The children pick up a fat hen each and caress and fondle them like babies. "Look at those lovely children," she croons, "so full of love for birds and animals. Little animals themselves. That's what I'd like to be ... an animal."

The air has the blue heat of the spring sky, voluptuously blue, and the trees shiver greenness about them. The hens are white ... white. Like his own sweater.

He merges with her thought, "Whitman has some lines, 'I'd like to go and live with animals . . .'" Pause, trying to recall them. "About none of them being respectable or unhappy over the whole earth." Pause again, remembering, "'They don't whine, they don't kneel to another who died two thousand years ago.' I've got the words wrong."

"Walt Whitman?" Her brooding eyes lift with a feeling in them just like trust.

"A great big something."

"What do you mean?"

"They couldn't quite classify him . . . poet, proser or singer. They only knew he was great and big. So they called him a 'something.'" But as usual she doesn't follow this up to develop his line of thinking. She so seldom crosses to another mind and accompanies it as an artist must . . . as one does in practiced conversation, artist or not. It's only within herself that she sees. Maybe her thoughts have already swung to something else like flying leaves changing course in the wind. Or maybe his talking about someone great and big oppresses her. In any case she begins getting up, perhaps realizing at last that a first visit from him, at least physically great and big, calls for some sort of action, he doesn't know. He never does. So he swings the conversation, if you can call it that, back from something great and big outside of herself to something weak and small and as within herself as her blood . . . Benjamin. He sits down on the grass, at which she does too. "I think Benjamin is afraid of me."

"Do you?"

"He may be."

"He hasn't said so."

"Hasn't he?"

"He never talks about anything like that."

"I came down on him once for eating apples near me. I've got an abrupt manner. It used to take my teachers at least a term to get used to me."

"He always wants to go over there when we go and doesn't want to come away."

"If he were not afraid of me there would be less for him to be afraid of."

"He's not afraid . . . Bennie."

"Well, why doesn't he go to school?"

"I don't know."

Not too much of this questioning. It's pressure . . . it's force.

"He still says if you ask him, 'I don't know.'"

"All right, we'll put it this way." Like the lawyer in court or

83

the Child Welfare officer. This and no more, then he'll stop. "Were it not for his fear of me there would be less to hide from." He's talking too normally, too logically.

"He's not *hiding*. He's just protecting himself as any animal would. You should see him at the Bay. The sea, the beach . . . the children are out early in the morning. It's no more than the unreasoning protective impulse of the wounded."

"That's his voice in the house, isn't it?"

Pause. "Yes . . . but he likes being by himself. 'No man,' " she quotes, " 'can be a lover of the true and the good unless he abhors the multitude.' The strongest man is he who stands alone."

The "multitude" puts the bag down beside him and calls to Dessida, whom he always approaches first being warm like her father and of the age of Angela's Mary. "Dessida, will you tell Benjamin I've got something in my bag for him?" What does Tarl's covered smile mean . . . amusement? Or compassion for him? Don't lovers of the true and the good, standing strongly alone, like "something in a bag"? Angela's babies are mad for it. He retreats into his spreading brandy and stretches prone on the grass to deny his unacceptable size and murmurs, "My age is a comfortable one. I like to sleep a little in the afternoon." He flashes a glance at her, "But I don't."

Closing his eyes he murmurs to himself, "Obsession. I'm never freed from it. Only in exhaustion or in my cups. Those two only . . . exhaustion . . . inebriation—the only two states I know that can discipline obsession. Discipline again. Can freedom from obsession, or freedom itself, never exist without discipline of some kind, without rows of iron bars . . ."

She leans sharply nearer, "What's that?" But he can't repeat it. She lowers herself on an elbow murmuring secret things so that he thinks it is the real inner Tarl speaking rather than the character she creates for others or for herself, her native esoteric self. What is she saying? "I do not find nature vulgar"? "I don't discredit discipline"? Ah, he heard that. ". . . discipline the mind itself to make my mind its own master. I try to cultivate an insight into its real nature. My fundamental object . . ." pause . . . "it is to get into the nature of my own mind and soul. I discipline my inner eye in order to look into the very reason of existence. I believe in my own inner purity and goodness. Whatever is superadded or violently torn away . . . it injures the wholeness of the spirit. I don't meditate. Meditation is something artificially put on. It doesn't belong to the native activity of my mind. Those fowls over there . . . what do they meditate on? They squawk and feed and breed—isn't that enough? Why should I fix my mind on something to . . . to—to *think,* only to be arrested in my life-activity? Nature is a bottomless abyss; no God to be fathomed."

But if he was near sleep in the first place he is even nearer now and he forgets at once what she says the moment she says it. As for releasing deliberately this revelation of herself at a time and in a circumstance when he certainly cannot assimilate it . . . well, that's Tarl. All that gets through to him is that she too is now prone on the grass beside him. Whatever her intention in that.

With the warmth of the sun inebriating his body quite as much as the plonk within it, he drowses uneasily. The trembling moment of communion, the knife-stab of realization of all she could be to him, begins registering on him physically, in exquisite danger until he hears Benjamin's voice. It comes from the fowl run now where he has joined the other two, conversing comfortably with the hens. Not that he takes obvious notice, but the electric rapport between them is at once destroyed, as so many other moments have been destroyed in the past by the presence of her children, their eternal priority in her dark heart, and as they always would be destroyed. The focus is safely shifted. He has come, after all, to see Benjamin, her favored son, her soul mate, and he sits up practically, responsibly. "I can't sleep on Hallibut's grass." But what he means, rather, is, I can't make love on Hallibut's grass.

"Neither can I." She sits up too.

It's no good calling Benjamin of course. He might as well try to lure an untamed horse or win the confidence of a wind-swept deer. It's like hiding a bridle behind him, creeping forward step by step coaxing, crooning, making horse or deer noises, with the animal watching warily. A touch on his neck and up would go his head and the next thing he'd have thundered off. You get children like that in school at times.

Tarl, dreaming upon Benjamin among the fowls, offers softly, "Bennie has a wonderful way with animals. He can walk up to any of them. He can catch things the others can't. They say to me, 'Mummie, why can't we catch them too? Why do they let only Bennie touch them?' " Dan has seen him catch the butterflies and, which is something for a boy, let them go unharmed. But he doesn't speak this even in agreement. From learning not to argue with her, then not to criticize, not even advise, let alone question, he is learning to not even agree; never to touch her untouchability or put the slightest pressure on her. To utter

85

nothing at all on the subject of herself; will the next lesson be to not even listen? No . . . she is one wild animal he'd never try to catch, always supposing he wanted to. Neither of them, her or Benjamin. Let them come to him, if at all, on their own elusive terms, which happen to be his own terms also with any woman or child, and a test of whether he's worth it.

So he turns his back on what she is telling him and looks the other way in case thoughts also are weighty upon her and says no more than "It's time you made me some tea, Tarl." At which she gets up gladly and goes in a way that makes him think she wants to do something for him if only they could agree on what it is. And agree long enough.

After a while he follows Tarl and as he walks below the verandas of this "hovel" historied now with her tears he notes there has been a lovely garden. Much of it still survives, flowers and scents still exult and a circle of unweeded freesias remains that could well supply a market. But who is he to point out the obvious? He'd hear all about "When my domestic situation is just right for me," and about the Halliburts and Gavin immobilizing her soul's action or more likely about the disgrace of labor anyway, the futility of the future and the importance of the Everlasting Now, all of which by now he could write down blindfold with one hand tied behind his back in anything up to twenty languages.

Their corner of the "hovel" consists of two front rooms, the tallest, best lit, most spacious and best; the impressive reception room and the best bedroom both with expensively high ceilings and many generous windows opening upon the veranda and a beautiful view of the estuary. Gracious full-grown trees just down the steps on the lawn. Rooms like these he's known before when courting me; carpeted, armchaired and with paintings on the walls; treasures brought back from overseas, terrific silver and china, all sorts of cakes and five-tiered sandwiches and I by the wide log fire. A white blouse I wore, I recall, that day when it first came to him he loved me.

Still the carpet left on this floor but nothing else. There's a bench of some kind on a wall, a low bed on each of two other walls but nothing else whatever. Didn't she mention one chair? But Tarl prefers the floor. He doesn't register precisely what's on the bench other than that there's a lot of it, and a thought fleets by of how Angela would sail in and make it clean and wholesome. In place of the squalor he sees Tarl in bloom making the best of her bargain; getting on with the landlady, finding something in her to praise, coming to terms with the others in the house and turning a creative eye upon the emptiness so that these two grand rooms become a magnetic center for any in search of sympathy. But Tarl is not Angela. If you set Angela down in a bare paddock or on the side of a cliff you'd get a mecca for those in need.

It's not the place but the personality in it, and Tarl is herself, that's all. Beside the flame that is Angela, Tarl is frost, excepting where children are concerned. But comparisons belong to mortals and if I ever found myself in the afterlife, looking back from the advantage of eternity, still blaming a person for what she is, I'd put down my phantom pen and pick up a phantom shovel.

The cold fact remains, however, that cleanliness and order do take time, also sacrifice and things like that, as well as a certain kind of personality with an eye for reality, whereas these are hardly part of Tarl's no-mind and the magnificent Do-Nothing. I can't see, myself, how graciousness and order can ever find a place in a home of Tarl's although plainly she likes these things. I can't see it anywhere even though on this side of the grave one sees everywhere. There's no future or past in my state, no horizons at all. According to Gavin any habitat of Tarl's inevitably takes the calling of a "hovel" so that the graces she craves must be sought elsewhere, preferably in the homes of the civilized. Which never fails to confound Dan, this taste for what she denounces. Yet even were she given Dan's home over the fence the bleakness of her spirit would bleaken it anyway before it ever sank to . . . or rose to . . . hoveldom. Already she's restless to be gone from this place. "No one ever comes to see me," she often cries. Conceivably so.

He hints at none of this but she reads much. As he comes in she looks up at him, steadily examining his face, in defiance, supplication and doubt. "You told me once," ruefully, "how you followed that friend of yours into his kitchen to make tea. Jim Prenderghast. That man who rejected materialism. The look on your face when you said, 'His kitchen.' Then you laughed out loud. Now you follow me into mine."

Carelessly, "But he's happy."

"I'm not unhappy," a flare. Implication can be force too, apparently, something further to toss the head about and gallop away from. "I'm the only one," tensely, "who *is* happy. It's all the others who are not."

"Of course. I'm corrected." Will he never learn not to trespass in these marathon interchanges and that to her any manner of pressure is murder? Indeed I covertly agree. What a clumsy thing a tongue can be. Dare he try again? "It's roomy and light in here, isn't it?" This pedestrianism does not qualify for an answer. But there *is* something wonderful in here, a kettle on a gas ring, and by God does he need a drink. Pathological compassion dehydrates a man. "Look at that marvelous kettle."

"I wonder where that cup is. We did have a cup. It must be outside somewhere." The yellow raincoat goes out, its stiff shoulders rounded, and he hears it calling the children to have a look for it. But he doesn't take the opportunity to stare inquisitively about Tarl's lair; at the wallpaper stained and torn from the freedom of young children, the despised carpet, deteriorated, despised for being a carpet in the first place and abused by the precipitants of living upon it, and at the bench with its account of chaotic eating; at this desolate analogy of Tarl's soul bared. He habitually recoils at the soul's exposure. Souls, he claims, should be seen only in a woman's face during labor, on a man's countenance on his deathbed or in the eyes of lovers at dawn; all of which he has known in his time and from which he gathers his values.

In time she returns with an authentic cup and then she shows him the bedroom and bathroom. Why? What on earth makes her think he wants to see them? Or does that not occur to her —it being she who wants him to see them? Oh this compulsive exposure of herself by proxy, this willfulness to uncover the secret contours of the unfulfilled heart. A woman fulfilled need show nothing of herself at all. She sits serene and smiles as I do from the portrait. In the serene woman any material disorder becomes an ornament. One does not measure a woman by her home, but the home by the personality in it. Some women get away with it. This bleakness in Tarl's home could be worn with grace had she grace herself.

But there's far too much being unsaid here between them. He doesn't hang round any longer waiting for the tea but walks outside to nature herself, ridiculous in his fine white sweater and his moneyed playboy shoes, at least eight guineas' worth of style, enough to house his ibex in a motel for a weekend. With assumed nonchalance only, he makes his way to the gate of the fowl run where he sees Benjamin playing and hesitates a moment there. What price the understanding of a disputed child? Can he do this thing? Will the brandy see him through to the finish or let him down too soon? A man should carry the stuff. Crises are unpredictable. He enters and settles down on one knee, his very best strides in the dirt among the scraps from the Hallibut kitchen, indeed that of the Prackets also; spines of fish, crayfish skins, cores of fruit, animal bones, potato peels and the white feathers of fowls. "Give me a hen too, Dessida."

Always Dessida first, which says much for her father's nature. Her black hair is long and curling down her back, tied behind her head, her face is round and joyful, she's four and is the one who's always laughing and never far from her mother's legs. She's the baby of the wandering days when laws had nothing to do with how they reared their children. A more sturdily built child than the others. Smiling like her father she carries to him a large white trusting wondering hen who sees no reason to protest, if she sees reason at all, and who lies in his arms with rather accomplished coquetry. Hasn't he always said he's fascinating and irresistible to the tender sex? Her whiteness is at one with his sweater. He appreciates it. Moreover he feels she's a bird of no mean passion, and since it is three or four years now since a woman last came to his arms, however clandestinely since Angela came to live so near—three or four deprived years since a tangible, real, breathing woman lay in his arms like this —his fondling is largely authentic. A discharge of what might have been on the grass a while ago. "What is your name?" he asks her.

" 'Isadore,' " he replies for her sultrily.

"And have you laid your egg today?" Not too frank for an Isadore.

" 'I don't lay eggs these days. I laid only two in my life but when they hatched my chickens were killed. They were killed in a car on a bridge.' "

"Give me a younger hen." He puts her down. Dessida produces another. "And what is your name?" he asks her.

" 'Alice in Wonderland,' " quaintly. He notices Benjamin listening.

But her body is shy against his and innocent of the movements that interest men. In some shame he inquires, "Do you lay eggs?"

" 'Only when I'm forced to,' " a high-pitched voice at which the children are breathless. " 'I did lay one this morning. It was a beautiful egg and Homer showed his mother. I think he liked it, that little boy. He didn't break my egg.' "

"No, he never breaks anything. He never touches my gramophone needle."

Here is the wild uncatchable one skirting ever nearer, to Dan and to Alice in his arms, Dessida and squatting Homer. But he doesn't look at Benjamin. Dan was good at catching horses when a boy and in his manhood too. At least as good as at catching women. He puts down little Alice, "I'll see you later, sweetheart. When you've grown up a little." With embarrassing excitement, "When you've learned your ABC."

Benjamin himself puts a hen in Dan's arms and he tries to hide his interest. "All these white hens . . . haven't you got a black one? Or one with reddish hair?" But he is not comfortable on one knee and down goes the other knee, his strides in the fowl-run filth. "And what is your name, Madame?"

Mysteriously, " 'Mona Lisa.' "

"And who is that boy who gave you to me?"

" 'That boy is Benjamin Pracket. I don't let men touch me as a rule but I don't mind Benjamin.' "

"You feel he understands you?"

" 'I'd get down out of my frame in the Louvre for a man like Benjamin Pracket. I would follow him. I'd follow him along the flower-headed roads and up the blue-heart mountains, I'd bathe in the streams with him. I'd follow him to the ninety-mile beach and gather pipis with him. I'd give my exclusive historic heart to a man like Benjamin Pracket.' "

"Would you lay an egg for me?" reverently from Benjamin.

" 'I don't talk of things like that.' "

Tarl has returned with the tea. She is back again over there on the grass where she has lain a moment beside him. "I'll have it here," he calls. And now here is Tarl in her vivid yellow, joined the company in the dirt and stink of the fowl run, standing so humbly beside him. "Oh how wonderful . . . wonderful . . ."

"It's not I but my wife."

"What did you say?"

"I was just thinking of someone else. I . . . was remembering a woman I knew."

He releases the secretive Mona Lisa and takes his tea, kneeling. It's in a white cup without a saucer. He takes a first sip. "This is smashing tea, Tarl." She herself has a plastic tumbler. And while he tastes it again, baby Homer digs a hole in the dirt.

Homer is a diamond child. In the first place delivered from his mother by no less than his father, with access to his mother's breast any time of night or day till the last drop dried, falling asleep in her arms every single night of his life to lie till morning beside her, and during the day too, thwarted in absolutely nothing since he first drew breath . . . he's the glowing proof of their theory, the perfect product of symbiosis. Added to which he is one of these rare children with the best of both parents in him, his father's I.Q. and his mother's art; his father's build, his mother's eyes, and the astounding humility of both. Oh yes, Dan's heard him cry, yelling tremendously at a fall backward down his steps, and Dan has seen Tarl cart him heavily all the way home on her hip because he demanded his own toilet. And he's seen him on her slim angled body in the crowds in town on a tired Friday night when she staggered to his car. "Push-chairs are cruel," she said that time in answer to his unspoken remark. "He looks like a poor little rich boy," he added laughing, "so expensively dressed, shoes, socks and all." "He asked for shoes and socks." "And all the time I know him to be a savage." She glowed with pride at the word.

He's a passionately happy boy, an incredibly good boy, his monument the open gramophone in Daniel's home. How nature loves the sensation of slinging a priceless gem into the stench of a fowl run. But not even this can stain the reflecting facets, the diamond-flashing of him.

He hides in his hole a scrap of crayfish. "Guess what's in here," he crows.

"A feather," Dan says.

"No."

"A stick."

"No."

Dessida, "A leaf?"

"No."

"A fishbone?" the rich voice of Benjamin.

"No."

Dan, "A little piece of crayfish?"

A shower of laughter. "Yes." He uncovers it and shows it proudly.

"Well I was the one who guessed it. It's my turn. Everyone shut your eyes." They all do, faithfully, no furtive peeping whatever. He gives Tarl his cup and finds himself digging a hole in the dirt and dung of Hallibut's fowl run with hands that have just left paper. Reams of pure white virgin paper that receives his intimate imagery. Yet these discredited Hallibuts . . . who remembers it was they who allowed the returning wanderers refuge in their orchard for six months of the summer, who called them onto their verandas on the days and nights of rain? Whom Gavin thought well enough of to ask the elder son to look after his elder son in the playground, should he go to school? Trusting Benjamin to a Hallibut boy in the great crisis of his life? Who put up with the Prackets anyway, which no one else seems able to do. We all have excretions of living but we are permitted to hide them. Did the Hallibuts require the

Prackets to choose their sport in their fowl run? Did they ask Dan, for that matter?

In his hole he hides the spine of a schnapper thrown out with the scraps from the kitchen . . . "Wonderful, oh-h-h . . ." from Tarl . . . and covers it again. "Open your eyes. Who can guess what's in this hole? Something beginning with F."

Benjamin at least knows F for it's he in time who guesses, F for Force, presumably . . . and he takes over the organization of this enthralling game, authoritatively and efficiently. Dan sees he's no fool at all. He finds in him qualities of natural leadership that would delight any teacher, and an economic tongue. He's rather magnificent in his lair. Slight and straight of build, brown-and-pink complexion, alert brown eyes, a fine profile from nose to chin and a head of storm-black hair cut low upon his forehead. He finds him sensitive, finely quick on the uptake, a lover of fun, a boy with a vocabulary and easy delivery and vastly charitable for a child. Moreover he has a patience with the two younger ones that is all but adult. Yet are these qualities remarkable in a child, or would most children be like this given the same nurturing of nature, the yoke of inhibitions removed from their necks? But the brandy tide is receding and the tide of obsession on the turn. This is not quite the occupation of his choice. He's found out what he came to find out and the astonishing party is over. He gets up stiffly as he does after having sat overlong at his table and brushes his strides, as if that made any difference. And takes his cup again from Tarl, the steam gone from it now. In any case who could drink fowl-run tea—Dan? "Well I must get back to work." A remark that is received with blank incredulity in the silence of amazement that anyone in his senses could not only mention the word "work" but plan to get back to it.

He retreats through the fowl-run gate, the company dolefully following, in fact compassionately following. "The attention span of that baby," he tells Tarl, "is overlong for his age. He's been playing the same game all this time with not one break in concentration." He knows better than to mention Benjamin.

Back on the grass where his bag is, they all sit down together. "There's something in that bag for you children," weakly. "Dessida," he adds. Lovely smile and in go her hands and out comes the rare scent from Arabia called "My Sin" bought in the depths of one night in some dark, deep, underground dive there, between dusk and dawn. "Some for you and some for Mummie and . . ."

"And some for Ramona too?"

"And leave some for Mary too, will you?" Pause . . . "She loves that stuff."

"And some for you?"

"Some for me. Here, you put some on my hands. This one too. Good. Thanks. And some on Mummie. Some on your hands, Homer? Some on Benjamin's too. And on your own little hands . . . last." She's made of love, this small girl, like her father. With the stench of the fowl run still on his clothes he's devoutly glad of this scent. Fortunate accident.

"These are nuts. Monkey nuts. Only monkeys can have them. Are you a monkey, Homer? Can you climb trees?"

"Yes," all flash and sparkle.

"Can you climb trees, Benjamin?" Careful. The first time Dan's addressed him in the year he has known him. The toss of the head and the gallop? Has he mistimed it? Couldn't he have chosen a less feeble question? So much hangs on something so small, as is the way with the world.

"Yes," a smile but the eyes slip away.

"You are both monkeys then?"

Sincere assent from both.

"In that case, you have the nuts." Then the plonk lets him down completely, utterly and suddenly, as the traitor drink will, or maybe it's not all drink. The relaxation possibly from too-concentrated, too-prolonged effort, the carelessness of success. He goes too far, shows the bridle. "I say, Ben, do put these cigarettes in this case for me." That's all right, it's the next. "Light one for me first, this one. Just like a gentleman." A *gentleman* in the context of the Prackets. Ghastly word . . .

And sure enough this is where the horse tosses his head. He giggles, looks foolish and doesn't do it. Fool, great fool. "I must get back to work," to that patient on the sickbed calling him. He unfolds himself and moves off quickly in failure, in overwhelming shame down through the jeering orchard leaving Tarl alone to her brooding.

Well down through the trees, however, he hears voices behind him and sees the horses galloping not away from him but after him, at which he plays a hilarious undignified game of chasing round and under the trees. But none of them touches him, nor he them; they do not carry catching to its usual conclusion as other children do, grabbing the "caught" with both hands. And he's glad of it too for some reason. Maybe they still glimpse the hidden bridle of authority, of Someone In Charge. He hopes it's not that. He'd rather think it was the overall untouchability of the entire family working in reverse. Besides he's far from touchable himself, a factor in his fastidiousness when choosing a mistress, spacing them so long apart. Within himself, probably, known only to the creatures of his imagination waiting in the library, he's the animal of them all.

"I wish I were a thief. I'd take an orange." He plucks one and stows it in his bag. "Don't tell the magistrate, will you?"

Understanding from Benjamin, "No."

Pride from Homer, "Mummie takes them."

"It's not that I mind odor *as* odor," he tells the portrait of me when he returns. "It's merely that I prefer my own."

I look at him through my painted eyes.

"Don't," he says, "ever ask me to do anything so hard again."

⚜ COME TO SCHOOL, calls the bell on Wednesday morning; come to school, Benjamin Pracket! We'll look after you, Benjamin. There's a young Maori teacher who smiles all day. And you don't have to start at the bottom, you can start in Standard Two with other children the same age as you. All sorts of interesting books to read full of amazing stories about birds, animals and water . . . a change, surely, from Police Court news and warning letters to your parents. And there's paint here too, Benjamin; vivid colors and brushes and paper and easels. Can't you hear us singing each morning from your lookout in the tree, and see us running together? Come to school at nine o'clock. Ring, ring, ring a ling. Come, Benjamin, do.

Dan can't take any more of these nine o'clocks with the bell calling Benjamin. He turns right round in the sun on the veranda, gets out the long new car and drives the twenty-five miles to get Angela and Co., "to be a buffer between me and the drama, Ange. If she runs away, Gavin says, it'll mean contempt of court and might even mean prison. That's if the law takes them both alive."

"That's not too good, y'know."

They are cruising through the incomparable spring countryside that is the domain of Benjamin. Benjamin's white daisies, Benjamin's blue chickweed and all his golden buttercups. Benjamin's cheeky birds and the white sheep on the hills and the serenely grazing horses. Even the shadows of the poplars and gums are his, fingering across the black bitumen like parallel iron bars. Which is the strange thing about freedom—ever associated with bars of some kind.

Later over lunch under the umbrella tree with both baby boys asleep and Mary at school, "If only the Prackets would leave me out of their drama. Oh get me off this subject."

"Does it ever cross her mind what she's doing to your life?"

"The only thing I've ever seen cross her mind is the idea of freedom."

"*Her* freedom. What about yours?"

"That's just it."

"What about it?"

"I dunno."

"You said last Saturday something about . . . what was it? 'restricting the claims of others on your inner emotions.' I remembered it."

"That's what I *say* but what do I *do?* I load myself with chains, then whine and rush down and get you to try to get me out of them. It's no good blaming Tarl. I know I'm a six-faced cataclysm but I *have* got one clear virtue: I know what I am. For instance I secretly rather like all this. I like the sensation. I'm angry with myself but I still like it. Yesterday going over there, y'know . . . this pouncing readiness in myself to take advantage of youth and grief and an open wound . . . that did anger me later. At least Tarl is herself. At every stage of her career you bump up against this refusal of hers to be anything but herself. She doesn't conform to convention because she can't. It's a hallmark of the great. And it makes me envious of her, as the false are always envious of the sincere. She leads the life I'd secretly like to live, as we'd all like to, including Blondie, Ric and the magistrate. She belongs to that class of people regarding whom it is impossible to postulate any social system of which they could be active members. Even that freedom community she proposed to you. She'd abandon it in no time. They are called crusaders but they're actually saboteurs of life."

"You mightn't think so, Daddy, but I understand. I know I'm not cultivated or anything like that but I . . . what I'm trying to say . . . I mean . . . Well I'm still on your side but I . . . yes I do understand Tarl."

"There's a strange new influence abroad. Whether it's from her as a woman or—or whether it comes from the forces she embodies, I . . . well so far I can't say. It's lapping around the neckline of Benjamin like a high tide, and around the feet of

Gavin who is taller in years. And around Ric a little I think, and . . . don't be alarmed . . . I think it's . . ."

"Coming your way?"

"Only the magistrate and Blondie seem to . . ."

"Who is Blondie?"

"Y'know, the Child Welfare officer. Decent chap. Only he and the magistrate seem to be able to keep clear. I wouldn't like to say it was a tide of destruction. I'm very bad at jumping to wrong conclusions. And by God I was weak enough to tell her where dear old Jim hangs out. Poor innocent defenseless Jim." But they both can't help smiling.

"I notice we're still on this subject."

"Most of us are. People, anyone caught up in this, are taking a second look at this thing called freedom and wondering what it means."

On the green table between them is the green tray with the colored cups, the silver teapot and her scones. The morning is so blue and green and flowered and birded and butterflied and filled with children's voices you'd never dream of what it conceals, what it secretes beneath its robes like a woman with a whetted knife. The morning is like the smile of a woman with hatred at heart. No woman is beautiful with hatred at heart. When the heart feeds on hatred and contempt the human being is facing the wrong way. Yet here reposes Angela in her productive youth, babies both outside and inside her, her very morning-blue eyes reflective and all this fair hair of hers cresting and surging down her back; impressionable and far too receptive, too innocently vulnerable to the knives of strife. Thought spreads, feeling is contagious. Ric with his talk of the power of the mind teaches all and sundry both inside the class and the home and outside them that only good thought and feeling should be sown at all. "I shouldn't be talking like this, Ange. It'll qualify your attitude to Tarl."

"I know my attitude to Tarl without you qualifying it, dear. And I can tell you right now it is not too favorable. When I see you constantly upset like this and your work blasted to pieces . . . why even we don't come up during the week in case we disturb you. Yet she claims the right to just sail in any time, in the morning too. What I can't understand is . . . well she's supposed to be an artist, isn't she? Doesn't she know about interruption? Even Rod and I do and we're not artists. We know how necessary peace of mind is to your work and—and how necessary your work is to you. And all the care Mr. Richmond takes to protect your work and—and yet she . . . talk about freedom . . ."

"You are critical. That's my doing."

"I've got eyes, Daddy."

"That's what I thought."

She laughs like anything and touches him.

"I'm not saying that their coming to me is not enrichment really. They're all so convincing. But God damn it, everyone's too convincing in this drama, from the magistrate through Blondie and Ric right down to Benjamin himself. They're *all* not only able in their subjects but their passions are contagious. I agree with each one utterly till the next comes along. A writer is on everyone's side. His response is a multiple response. It's life itself that's upsetting me—not they. Reality. Every time they arrive life breaks new records in reality. I'm simply not geared to reality. Reality makes me sick. I belong to unreality, to the estates of the imagination." Reaches for his smokes and leans back, "Yes, I'm on all sides. I get the strain of the whole damned show—every-damned-body's."

Her eyes blow up and her hands too. This gift of Angela's —so absent in Tarl—of catching alight from another's feeling, of anger as well as joy, which makes her tumbledown old farm homestead with its winter mud all but blocking off its accessibility—makes it a mecca for the gay and the sad. "Look, if she'd walk in now I'd . . . I'd . . . I'd give her a thrashing if I wasn't pregnant. Oh Daddy, you're so helplessly hopelessly kind."

"Why don't you be frank and say 'soft'?"

"*Soft*."

"Ay?"

"*Soft*. Gosh, I feel better."

They laugh for some time. Then, "Come on, my little Daddy, have some more tea."

"All right, any left?"

"I'll get some hot water." She begins to ease her weighted body to its feet.

"No I'll get it."

"It's my leg."

"Where?"

"Up here." Fingers a groin.

"What's the matter with it?"

"Oh, the doctor said it's pressure on a nerve or something. He said there's nothing to be done about it. Except have the baby."

"I'll get the water."

"You're not going to wait on me."

"I will wait on you. It's a change from waiting on . . ."

"Here, give me that jug."

"*I'm* going to get the water. You sit here. You get enough of that at home. I'll get anything for you, hot water included, as long as you have babies."

"I'll say I'm having babies." Again roars of laughter. Finally he lets her get up and she limps off slowly across the lawn but when she returns swaying like a ship at sea she says, "She said some wonderful things about having babies. She said the father or the lover should deliver the babies. She said it's the great biological occasions that are the unifiers. Isn't that beautiful? It makes me cry." She does, with several blue tears. "She said that women are always falling in love with their doctors over childbirth. It should be their own male they're feeling united to, feeling passionate about. And another thing. Not quite so beautiful." Fingers away the tears, one eye then the other. "She said that hospitals were divisive places. Dividing the child from the mother, the husband from the mother and the baby from the father and the . . . have I got them all in? She said a woman should go behind a bush and squat and have her baby outside. Like that. I . . ." a real blush . . . "I don't know so much about that."

Dan laughs loudly.

"What are you laughing for?"

"It's not what you're telling me, dear, it's just you, the way you say it. That belligerent look."

Later still he says, "It's the cleaning up after them. It gets me in my weakest point: my vanity. My dignity. How can I be a famous writer when I'm picking up nutshells from the red-room floor and carrying in dishes from the lawn and bringing in push-chairs and dolls' prams and . . . ?"

"I thought we were going to drop this subject. You only get worked up."

"What would my fans think of me if they . . . ?"

"Now please drink your tea. Put it out of your mind. You teach me how to put troublesome things out of my mind, so you should be able to."

"All the characters in this action are so fearfully clever."

"Me too?"

He surveys her appraisingly from under his lids, clears his throat doubtfully and says nothing, at which she laughs out loud and holds her frontage. Then they talk about Rodney and the farm and all the new calves and lambs arriving, the puppies and kittens and the baby rabbits Rod brought back home to Brucey and how he feeds them with a pipette until the other thing, working stubbornly underground, comes to the surface once more. From Dan again. " 'Freedom to be different,' " he quotes. " 'Freedom to be excellent.' And that's exactly what those children over there yesterday in the fowl run were. Different and excellent. Especially the disputed boy. Oh well, Ange, we'll have to do something constructive about it. I don't know what. Ric would be horrified to hear us speaking critically. Trouble is I'm not martyr material." Pause and thought, "I'm afraid I've influenced you unfavorably."

"You have influenced me but not unfavorably. Not in the way you think. As a matter of fact I understand. I've got an idea what to do. One of these days I'm going to offer to mind her children so she can get some painting done. When they're asleep I suppose. They'd never leave her awake." She begins putting the dishes together, one plate upon the other, one cup within another, and he notices that her sweet soft hands are beginning to show signs of wear; the skin is cracked a little around the thumb tip. "Well I'd better be making tracks. I must be home when Mary comes home from school. Just once I wasn't home——one single solitary time—and she said, 'Mummie, why are you *never* home when I come home from school?' Gosh . . . I can't get up. Fancy not being able to get up this early in the piece. It's my leg. It won't go."

"Carrying another man."

"This is a girl, or better be. Mary insists on a girl. I'm going to call her after Mother. Macushla."

He does not answer.

"I wish I could find a nursing home near me where they'd leave the baby with me in the room and not take her away to the nursery all the time to cry all night." She levers herself to her feet. "Daddy, do you think I'm big? Oh, my leg. You'd better carry the tray. It's after sitting down, y'see, and then getting up. I dunno, some girls have their babies with such decorum."

Dan can't answer. It's just as well that in eternity we are spared feeling. Eternity would not be worth it were we not spared that. Feeling would be beyond any endurance . . . and that is what hell is; looking back on life with this superknowledge and superperspective and superwisdom, with accompanying superfeeling, and not being able to do anything about what you see. One does have reflection, thought and memory, however. The state I see most is . . . I keep seeing the two-woman team of mother and daughter wandering in and out of shops to-gether. The married daughter slightly pregnant and the mother with her, usually wheeling the pram with the other baby in it. Thinking the same things, with the same purpose, the mother guiding the girl, advising, helping, cheering. Who in life, walking the earth inconsequently, sees the beauty of this particular sight? A sight so usual, so ordinary. The look on the grand-mother's face. I'm always glimpsing two pairs of shoulders entering a shop, two pairs of eyes looking in windows, two pairs of hands reaching to the two-year-old when he toddles the wrong way. The human mortal spectacle can be beautiful without a man. Yet Angela has none of this. Were I under this tree with her today there'd have been an exhaustive examination of the pain in the groin. Much about what the doctor said. Yet Dan sits here either silent or joking. It is a merciful eternal condition that one knows no regret. That's what hell would be . . . regret.

"There's Brucey awake."

"It's Reuben, isn't it?"

What has this long relaxed loving intimate conversation between them beneath the green of the tree and draped in the blue of the morning . . . what has it been about, anyway? About Angela and her need and her condition and her sore groin and her lame leg? A lovely long shapely leg to be lame. Only incidentally and briefly. It's all about Dan, the man, and his condition and his sore mind and his lame life. Not a lovely and shapely life to be lame. To think that my Angela over whom I lost my life is left to the mercy of men . . . *men*.

"Not, it's not Reuben, it's Brucey. I'll have to wake up Reuben. Oh Daddy, he's such a darling. He simply smiles all the time. He doesn't try to do anything, sit up or anything like that. He just lies and smiles."

"My impression of Reuben is that he was so delighted to be born at all that he's spent the first six months of his life rejoicing."

"Oh Daddy," tears, a hand on his arm, "what a lovely thing to say." In the middle of the tears she laughs and tosses her hair in that particular character of pride in a child only seen in a breeding mother. At the cot she picks up Reuben and his delighted smiles and lays his head on her breast and her hand upon his hand. The head on the breast. The beginning of security and universal love, without which a man never rests till he lays his head on the breast of the earth. Dead. Fortunate baby, Reuben. No wonder he smiles his short life through. Yet Angela herself never knew this . . . her head on her mother's breast. The lack is the source of her impassioned desire to breed many babies in the unconscious blind powerful hope that in the nursing of all these heads on her breast will she replace her own loss. Not that girls realize these things. They "just *know*," and "just *do*." They're so close to death and birth and love and danger, month after month, year after year, they cannot other than "just *know*." They have no need of reason. How often you hear young mothers say with apparent unreason, "But I *know*. I just *know*."

But all Dan says is, "On the way I'll put my fowl-run clothes into the dry cleaner's. As I said to the portrait of your mother yesterday when I got home, It's not that I dislike odor as such but . . ."

"When I think of that fowl-run scene . . ." On Dan's affairs again.

And still on them when driving Angela home. "I'm glad you feel kindly toward her, dear. You're a good girl. As for helping her to get back to her painting . . . I think there's no lack of talent but she might be too indolent and disorderly to work. That remains to be seen. If she had only talent she would follow the beaten track, but if she has more than talent she could be expected to be unpredictable and to blaze a trail of her own. Men of more than talent go their own way, and since Tarl does actually and persistently go her own way, geographically as well as intellectually, one can be excused for allowing that she may have more than talent."

When Dan turns the car way out in the country at Rod's place to come home, Angela and the babies stand on the wild tussocky bank of the roadside to wave him goodbye. And here's this universal tableau that he sees every week . . . another of these very ordinary sights of fundamental beauty and that artists have painted from one age to the next. The young mother in slight disarray with hair lifting in the wind, her body big with fruiting, the baby in her arms, the toddler at her knees and the girl, Mary, out a little from her. All but the baby waving. Does Dan see this as I do?

"Daddy," says Angela as he puts in the clutch. "Thank you so much for the day. I loved it. And I heard two very beautiful things lately."

"What?"

"You said, 'Reuben was so delighted to be born at all that he's spent the first six months of his life rejoicing.' I'll think and laugh about that forever."

"What was the other?" The car begins to creep, the tires crackling on the unpaved metal.

"She said it is the great biological occasions that are the unifiers."

"Oh . . . that." Turning the far corner, when he looks back he sees the little group still standing there. Angela lifts the baby's hand to wave.

The rest of the day passes precariously and he sees nothing of the "saboteur" of life. But someone says that Ramona came to school per bus from town so Tarl cannot be next door. But how did Ramona get from the Bay to town to catch the bus there? Another bus, the ferry, or did Tarl bring her as far as town? What action took place at the Bay this morning? In any case how could Tarl put in another day of anguish on her own next door waiting for Ramona, as she did yesterday? Only Dan knows about that. He is both glad to be spared from, yet frustrated to be apart from, the center of sensation.

He takes the precaution of going out in the evening, a thing he very seldom does. He goes inland up Fort Road to where Felix and his wife hang out. Felix is a man of almost insufferable rectitude on whom religion has a suffocating hold, giving him a permanently offended attitude to life, and although he has a voice so rich that it could "give an air of verse to a recipe for stewed hare" he delights in insipidities and remains unshakably ordinary. Yet he belongs to the strange unclassified company who make their way to Dan's door asking no invitation and expecting no return visit. Dan himself holds the private view that this company is extravagantly rewarded from the richness of his own mind and feels magnanimous about them. They are valuable to him. They do him the favor of interrupting him, needing and admiring him. He invariably assembles his best prose, however flabby and subpoetic, for such as Felix with his admirable audience potential. "I think," he tells Felix over coffee, "she's one of these in whom the poet's outlook is not just a timorous cultural attitude, not a thing apart, but an inherent ingredient of life itself . . ." he likes to sling the heavy word "life" about when wishing to impress . . . "for which no apologies are due. I'm not, but I wish I were, attracted by her freedom of spirit. If only her inexhaustible unreason amused me."

"She's mad," from Felix flatly. "Clean off her head."

Dan likes to appear noble where possible, when he can get away with it. "She has many fine qualities."

But driving home through the romantic city, round the colored-lit harbor and through the nylon brilliance of the evening streets he is recalling something else. The way trifles stick in the memory while the more important events escape. He sees the primeval group of Angela and her children, as they were when he looked back from the corner this afternoon, standing on the high bank in the wind, touched by the lowering sun and silhouetted against the mountains. And hears again the timbre of her voice as she said, "It's the great biological occasions that are the unifiers."

❧ BENJAMIN, calls the bell on Thursday with anxiety in its ring, aren't you coming to school? Do-or-die week, school or else . . . can't you hear me, Benjamin? Four days now I've called you and there's only one more day. Your teacher is waiting for you. Don't let her down, please, Benjamin. Just come for today, at least. There's holidays tomorrow. A whole fortnight to live your life "as you should in accordance with your original nature." Hell is in yourself, Benjamin. When you completely ignore other people, that is hell, Benjamin. The hell of mortals, Benjamin.

Of this boy-versus-law week Dan, in spite of his appreciation, has nearly had enough. It's too much of a dose of persistent reality. He does mail instead of work and gives that up by eleven. He feels that he holds in the palm of his hand, the palm of his heart, the travail of all concerned which, as he often proclaims, is one of the more minor infirmities of a writer. He tries to memorize the Whitman on animals, dead years gone, with which to impress Tarl.

Later in the afternoon he hears that Tarl, awaiting Ramona next door, made one of these characteristic moves that provoke him to ponder on her motives. Leaving Benjamin behind next door, of course, she takes the two younger ones and walks into the teeth of the school she denounces to attend a minor class concert—Ramona's class, where she couldn't miss creating sensation of a kind. As for Dan, he firmly tries to believe—tries to prefer to believe—that she attends simply for Ramona's sake, although that hasn't the same story value. Besides it's easier at times to be on her side.

But he's insulted that she didn't come over.

"I'm desperate, Ric."

The Head and Dan are attending the college opera tonight and it is the Head who opens the door. "Come in, Gavin."

He follows the Head down the hall and pauses framed in the music-room door. The spring evening is mercilessly cold, but he wears no more than a worn gray jersey and summer-weight strides. In one hand he holds a bundle of plastic material which could be a coat.

You'd think Desperation would walk in with sunken eyes and white haggard face as Tarl's does, but it walks in just as well with a smile and pink cheeks shaped for fun. And his mouth, like Dessida's, always was so easy to smile with, showing a silver tooth. But one glance at his eyes and the rest fails. Also out of place in the cheerful face is the impression of taut control far more electric than exploding rage, while his bodily movements are the extremely careful steps of one negotiating blindfold a series of precipices which, in effect, he is. His courtesy is seriously overdrawn and the voice he uses these days has more in it of profound respect for man than Dan has ever occasioned. At once, right or wrong, Dan is on his side.

"Where's my family?" Softly.

"I don't know." Wood on the fire. "Sit down. Have some coffee? You're just in time."

"I'd love that." Forced normality. "I saw the outside light on. It's always such an invitation." From the edge of his chair, "She continues to deceive me, Ric."

The Head turns over a key in his pocket and another in his mind, examining this while Dan passes him coffee.

"She still pretends to be cooperating and I still trust. I spent Tuesday night at the Bay with them and she promised again to help get Ben to school in the morning. I rose early to watch him but he'd already flown. She'd got him up before dawn and hid him on the slopes of the Mount. Tarl claims she had nothing to do with it but you can't tell me a little chap of eight, even Ben, could wake himself in the early hours and go out alone in the darkness.

"I went back again last night by ferry and this time I set an alarm clock for four A.M. When I got up this morning he was still in bed. I hung round where I could watch him until about seven, then went in to wake him. But instead of Ben it was a bundle of clothes arranged exactly in the form of a boy's body." A smile of admiration. "It had the stamp of an artist. Ben had gone long before. But she still said she knew nothing about it." He continues in appreciation rather than recrimination, "She promised to pick me up in the car after college this afternoon to take me back to the Bay with them so that I could watch Ben for the night again but she didn't come. Tomorrow's the last day, Ric. I've missed the ferry but I still must get to the Bay tonight. Ben must be at school in the morning, otherwise we'll land this charge of neglect next Wednesday from the Child Welfare department. And we might lose the child." Yet he conveys the impression that it is the battle that counts rather than the defeat or victory. He stares into his coffee. "I'm hoping that she'll be there."

Thirteen miles round the city to the Bay, but no time in Ric's new car. As they drive through the fairyland lights of this tourist resort of the century and around the nylon harbor Gavin doesn't stop talking about his wife. And it occurs to Dan as they stab the frosty night that there is little reason why Tarl should "be there." Not this last night. In which case she has won this round. A fantail could see it. But what a waste of breath to say so. No good standing in the way of these floods of fever surging between man and wife, though he's strongly on Gavin's side for the moment.

"I do appreciate that, Ric. Just drop me within walking distance, will you? They might take flight if they see a car."

They set him down near the wharf, and it turns out that this plastic bundle he holds is actually a coat and he dons it as though he believed it. "I'll see you and your son in the morning," says the Head, who sincerely believes what he says. And away strides this father of four children looking just like any other father walking home to his family where he will be received with food, warmth, tempestuous interchange. Only Dan knows differently. He watches Gavin as he walks off in the frosty dark, his head high in the right place and a determinedly hopeful step, just like a procession of one. Then Ric wheels the car.

At half-time with the lights up, Ric is told that Mr. Pracket is outside and wants a ride home after the show, "if you please." Outside they find Gavin with his teeth chattering in the frost and once more he holds the plastic bundle in his hand. "They've gone, Ric."

"Ay? Beg your pardon? They've . . . ?"

"Gone. They've gone."

"Oh I see. Gone. They're gone. That what you said?"

"I got in a window to make sure." Hammering at the door of the flat for his family. Is there anyone there? he calls out but only echoes answer. "That's where I tore this coat. But all was darkness and empty. She meant to go, Ric. She knew this morning. She asked me to put the rubbish bin out in the street and I said, 'But the rubbish man doesn't call on Thursday. He calls Friday.' And she said, 'Oh put it out anyway since it's ready.' And I didn't guess even then. She's been deceiving me all this week and I've been trusting her. That's how she defeated me. I can't find them at this time of night and she's got the car. And I've got nothing in my pocket. I gave it all to a taxi chappie who brought me halfway here. I walked the rest. I haven't got two razoos to rub together."

Ric offers to drive him home right now but, "I'll go back to my classroom and do preparation. Catch up on my work. I've missed so much this week." His teeth are knocking ludicrously. "I'll meet you after the show," and so on.

All the way home he talks swiftly of his wife, back into her childhood again as if they had never heard it. Minutely analyzing Tarl; proving with the finest scientific formula how fatally wrong she is, as if intellectual analysis, dogmatic tenet or any symbolic formula could gain access to Tarl's system of thinking founded on anything but routine logic. And what, anyway, if he should prove it chaotic? This apocalyptic encounter of the human passions with the spiritual search for wholeness and light . . . does the chaos from such a collision need proving? When did this bloody conflict not arise between the passions and the spirit in the lives of professional sensitives? And in the fighting of it out who is more irrational than the determined rationalist that Gavin claims to be? For that matter where does his own frenzy fit into the framework of his rationalism? Never have I seen a more wayward passion outside a strait jacket, let alone inside reason. None is more irrational than the dedicated rationalist hurled forward on the crests of feeling. But when Dan tries to protest this, Gavin slings him aside with the kind of slogan he slings at poor Tarl presumably. "A highly arguable technicality," sort of thing leaving Dan utterly if temporarily on the side of the wife.

"But," Gavin streams on softly, "although sentiment has guided me over the years with her, anger has guided me lately. I've never shown anger to them before but I had to try everything conceivable. I thought anger might work where indulgence failed but anger provokes worse reactions in her than I had ever dreamed of." Pause for breath. "I threatened to spank her one night if she opposed Ben's going to school in the morning. I told her I'd put her over my knee." Pause again. "But she went to the police after that, asked for protection and made a statement. She could use that sometime. I took a false step there . . . No, anger has failed worse than indulgence. I must now let reason guide me."

Ric has the courage to change the subject. "Do you teachers mean to strike?"

"That is not yet resolved. The conference is in Auckland next week. I'm the delegate from here, or was. But I can't go since Tarl has the car. And now that they've left Hallibut's it's up to me to clean up after them before I leave myself. Buy new wallpaper, repaper both rooms for a start. There's a lot of burning and burying of rubbish, accumulated tins and such. Shampoo that big carpet and scrub our end of the verandas. On my own it'll take several days. Also there's the court case next week. I've got to perpare my case and brief the lawyer. I had my address prepared for the conference but I've had to ask another chappie to take my place. I did want to go. This is the center of protest. I led that rebellion. I'd give my back teeth to be there."

But all roads lead back to Tarl. "What the poor girl can't realize is that although we are still at one on the bringing up of the children, this is the sword of Caesar. That we must give unto Caesar that which is Caesar's; that in obeying the law I'm not destroying but saving the unity of the family. If only she could see reality. If only she'd release the mind of the child."

Ric's feet remain on the ground. "She might see reality if you showed her the inside of a court. Took her there. Have you ever tried that?"

"Only once. But we had to stop her talking. Her rebellious attitude only lost us ground. The magistrate johnny called her a 'dangerous woman.' "

Now, as they sit in the car at his gate they have a lengthy analysis of the case itself, its pros and cons, but the Head's endurance is marvelous. "Come on with us and have some supper." It's very cold sitting there.

"No thanks, Ric, I must get some sleep. I've got a big day tomorrow. There's still a chance of finding them in time to put one of Ben's feet inside the school gate. I'll take another day off. The rector will give it to me. He's a chappie of much humanity and has been taking my classes this week while I've been tracking my family. I'll have to withhold that car when I see it again. That's one thing I'll . . ."

Even Ric hides a yawn, it's well after eleven now, nearer twelve. "Well, remember, Gavin . . . just one foot inside the gate. Do you want some money?"

"No, thanks, Ric. I'll draw some from the bank tomorrow."

"Where is Gavin?"

The rector and his first assistant turn up in the very middle of the night looking for him, to make sure he is all right. "We've been knocking at his door but he doesn't answer. We couldn't get away straight after the show, supper, speeches, but the minute it was over . . . Is he over there?"

"He was exhausted, couldn't have heard. Come in," shivering in pajamas, "and get warm. Which is more than I said to the prowler last week." The talk is of Gavin but like everything else ends up with Tarl. "It's hard," Dan finds himself summing up, "impossible for any one of us to understand any other fully but . . . yes it's safe enough to say that her values are different from ours. They've an Eastern quality, an Eastern source which is . . . unintelligible in terms of our wooden Western philosophies. It's not to our credit, and I include myself, gentlemen, I do . . . that when we encounter someone unintelligible we at once use the word 'mad.' Even to say she is ill is an oversimplification. To use her own words, Gavin himself taught her all this permissiveness and now, faced with the law, he's backing down. She feels he's betrayed them all."

"She feels he's betrayed them all," from the rector, in this way teachers have of repeating a thought, carefully weighing what is said.

"God damn it, I've *no idea* whose side I'm on. Unless I am on everyone's."

⚜ FRIDAY . . .

The bell calls Benjamin. It calls him urgently now and with a little fear. You must come, Benjamin Pracket! Whether you like school or not you must come to save yourself. You cannot want to be taken, Benjamin, away from your brother and sisters. And who will love you as your mother does? And as your father does? You think he doesn't love you but everyone knows he does. Just put your feet . . . one foot . . . one *toe!* . . . inside the school gate, then off to the wilds again. Come on, Benjamin, save yourself.

Benjamin . . . you must never confuse freedom with naturalism or with libertinism, which means following your own inclination without questioning its origin and value. There's a great difference between human action and that of animals—

animals lack moral intuition and any religious consciousness. They know nothing of exerting themselves in order to improve their condition or of how to progress to higher virtues. It's a wonderful thing to be a little boy, Benjamin, with all the capacity of humanity latent in you. Come to school today and exercise your boydom.

But when a girl brings up Dan's mail he hears there's still no Benjamin. And no Ramona either. Tarl has won this round. He trusts she's at least happy about it. Where is she, he wonders, at this moment? No longer, he is sure, sitting knee to chin, her legs locked in her arms, her inner eye on a reality beyond reality as he found her over there on Tuesday. No, she'll be striding, breathing deeply toward the blue horizon. At least it is legal holidays again. She and the children can lawfully relax for a fortnight to get over doing nothing . . . a whole term of nothing . . . while Gavin cleans up after it. Of which he has quite a bit to do, both at the "hovel" and at court. "I'm proud of my messes," Tarl once said. "I'm not one of these dried-up dirt-cleaners secretly hating household drudgery, obeying experts rather than instincts, thieving children's freedom. These Child Welfare officers and public health nurses spreading their high-standards propaganda worse than germs. They're the sirens who delude mothers into domestic mediocrity. I'm not lazy. Out in the wilderness in my houseless home I can work tirelessly gathering wood with a baby on my back and find it utter soul-rest. I can pound away energetically for hours washing clothes in a forest stream or rock pool. But that dreadful house routine sits on my head like an iron oven. Living rooms are dying rooms . . . just great big subdivided coffins. I'll choose the earth and dig my toes in."

With Tarl well gone Dan too has a spot of cleaning up to do after the family, but in mind rather than in substance. Taking the place of his created people is the company of Pracket imagery dominating the mindscape: jumping out windows, nailing up windows, taking off locks, wrist-wrenching, mud-throwing, kitchen collapses, vanishing of a boy in the dawns, alarm clock, form in the bed, where is my family, dash by night to the Bay, "not here" at the flat, to the finale of the cloak-and-dagger scene in the middle of the night . . . not to mention the family of children itself tossed and bewildered between one parent and the other, catching the hot breath of each. Alarmed, affrighted, young, defenseless. The whole parade punctuated by the nine-o'clock bell and set between the covers of a book called *Strife*.

True, his fragile creatures, his enchanted phantoms still roam the land of no horizons, the bizarre livid sky of the imagination, but they have less light and life. Their bodies are stiffening and they dress in shrouds. Now he's laboriously composing. They no longer propel themselves, no longer live lives of their own. Instead of little more than recording what he sees and hears, he finds himself formally "writing," which is just like work and easily as flat. How else can art be with vision in brutish slumber?

As for me . . . I never appear to him now on the veranda when the evening is still and the moon high. Too many others now come from the night.

⚜ DID THEY THINK Tarl had gone?

As soon as Gavin has fought his way through the current court case—the first in the pair—lost it, and seen the file handed over to the Child Welfare department to make its charge of neglect, as soon as the strike conference he craved is over and that lost too without him, and as soon as he has completed scrubbing, shampooing, repapering on his own, burning and burying away all trace of his family in the celebrated "hovel" . . . the moment the two rooms are spruce, new and quite civilized again, the moment she is no longer desperately needed by him as a helpmeet . . . Tarl reappears next door. A few days earlier would have been another thing but this neat timing has all sorts of value. What is victory without viewing the vanquished? Besides, think of the sensation part. Tarl has a by no means coarse talent for timing.

Naive dream . . . that the disturbance next door is over and that Dan can treat his ailing imagery. For a while he is audience to a tale of flights and returns more in character with a wildcat creeping back to a dump of food scraps and dashing off when it senses danger than with a calm disciple of the Everlasting Now. A story into which he vainly tries to fit her doctrine of liberation of the mind from self-deception. But the stubborn reasoning of the Western mind, ever trying to reduce all to the banal familiar, founders dolefully in this mystic area. All he can see clearly is that her behavior seems cheerfully, even deliberately divorced from reason . . . if human behavior ever wed reason . . . which would be wholly fascinating but for the pathos. Yet when he thinks compassionately enough upon it and allows the ruthless spotlight of truth to burn down upon the stage, then this chaos in Tarl's life, however enigmatical its manifestations, falls into place as a step forward in the personal progress of one striving to throw off rationalism as a preliminary advance toward wholeness.

"But what a lesson, Jim," as they expand under the tree with whiskey, "for any confined wives in this country dying to plunge out through a little back gate never to retrace their steps, but too startled at the sudden fury in themselves, too loving to hurt those left. But Tarl's not afraid of her fury, not impeded by sacrificial kindness. Tarl *does* plunge out the gate. Picks up her young, counting no cost, and the next thing here she is madly at liberty on some resounding beach, striding over the tidal flats with her offspring frolicking about her; over the shellfish, through the pools to the beckoning water line, breathing vast volumes of nature; her hands not in a sink but in her raincoat pockets, and her view, not a tight-lipped fence but the enormous laughter of the ocean. It's magnificent to watch, Jim . . . if you can forget those hurt in the process and if you can avoid the question of who is the richer: the runner or the run from, the taker or the giver . . . the hurter or the fearfully hurt.

"And *what* a way to keep a husband at heel. Contempt holds a man as well as love, even better so on occasion. I do admire her 'not here' technique. And God, it's good to see her wake up suburbia, flouting its laws written and unwritten in our alarmed faces. For it's not so much the fact that one defies as how one goes about it. You can get away with anything if you do it with an air. And Tarl's a master of defiance . . . a master of how to go about it, how to get away with it. Especially when it pays in sensation. She's aware of her uniqueness and says she's proud of it."

"No wonder society hates her. Poor little thing."

"Not so much the 'poor little thing' either. Society is secretly if unwittingly on her side. I wouldn't mind betting that the old boy on the bench wouldn't mind ducking off in the way that she does, to dip his white stiff toes in the brine. *I'm* on her side, for one, a little more frankly than others. Irresistibly so." Blows out smoke reflectively, "For the moment, that is."

But in the evening in slippered mood by the fire with a good meal inside him, here is his flexible allegiance swinging to the magistrate when he comes upon his plaintive headlines: "Failure to Send Child to School." "This matter," he argues in print, "has been before me for over a year and I have tried every possible means of getting the child to school. He is being deprived of his right to education." Someone In Charge indeed. Yet it's a jolly shame about this magistrate. He's all for this magistrate. Anyway the headlines will gratify Tarl, whatever she thinks of his legal clichés. From that point of view, the humiliation of the English language, Tarl may not see this as quite such an excellent reading lesson for Benjamin. But better than nothing. How could Benjamin avoid understanding the words that follow, big though they are: "Defendant described efforts, including the use of force, to get his son to school." An ibex could work them out, or a fantail, given the same motive.

Closing the paper, however, soon he is back on Tarl's side, accommodatingly enough and thinking her mystic thoughts with her. Before returning to work at seven he recalls the vision in her eyes and the vibration of her voice, "I must be untouched by lust or suffering, profit and loss, by all this rising and falling; by concern for others, enjoyment, fear; nor must I cling to any creature." Will she herself ever be able to translate these abstractions into the coarse realities of her own living? Will her exercised mind ever achieve that entire revolution where "I will be no more troubled by anger and hatred, bitten by envy and ambition, stung by sorrow and chagrin, overwhelmed by melancholy and despair"? Will she ever know the bliss she seeks?

How could Tarl stand up in court and explain to the bench that a Western school is hardly the place for Benjamin to come in touch with the inner workings of his own being without resorting to the external and superadded, that any semblance of authority is to be firmly rejected, that whatever authority there is comes from within and that absolute faith is placed in his own inner being; that even the reasoning faculty is not final or absolute but, on the contrary, hinders the mind from coming into direct communication with itself? What would our earnest magistrate make of it were Tarl to tell him that what she wants Benjamin to grasp is not the racket of "education" but the central fact of life, and that in the most direct and vital manner, so that when he understands it he will attain absolute peace of mind and live as he ought to live? All of which she would, without doubt, tell him too, were she given the chance, spitting out the wood of his Western argument.

It is seven and time for work and as he lays down the local paper one more thought crystallizes from the fluidity within him: it may not be wholly the going-to-school issue that enrages Tarl, but the defeat of Gavin himself, not as an erring father, a too-ardent lover or even a person, but as reason embodied. After all, we are all entitled to fight for survival, which in Tarl's terms means wholeness. But who, from the legal eyries of the law, through the orthodox desks of educational authority to the conforming community, could be expected to understand this? Who . . . other than Dan . . . perceives in Tarl not "the laziest and most selfish person I have ever met," "off her head," and a "dangerous woman" but a rare adventurous spirit enduring the travail of a demoniacal birth, beset with unknown terrors and dangers, menaced by deluding mirages, labyrinthine mazes and the worst of all fates threatening the venturer . . . the silent abysmal loneliness in the time she calls her own?

And who—with the possible exception of Angela—has compassion for Tarl in her prolonged fixed battle with the inconvenience of human passions in this arduous striving for wholeness and who sees her antisocial behavior as the emergence of something good, and Tarl as better than they'll ever be? No one who lives by the Christian ethic, however devout, compassionate. Tarl's public travails provide us with admirable entertainment but her private ones are unintelligible. Fighting her lone battle against private temperament as well as public prejudice, her situation suggests not tragedy, but only low comedy, in the district.

By the time he has lumbered up the hall, turned on the outside light and is crossing the evening veranda it comes to him that by a whim of that arch-whimmer, fate, it may be he who is chosen to see further into what appears to be, and to allow a certain legitimacy, a kind of grand overall justification of her intransigence, in short, to return to her in kind the permissiveness she believes in . . . to "stand by" in some vague way. But, stirred by the immediacy of the action in the storm center itself, caught in the stretching tensions and reeling from the onslaughts of the frenzied cast on the stage, not to mention his own anguish over his work, he never seems to achieve the equilibrium in which to work it out; to ascertain exactly what it is that life wants of him. He gets no further than the intuition that Tarl is not what she appears to be. She may be something more. Her behavior, her erratic appearances and disappearances, is not unlike that of the creatures of his imagination. And it is this hardly thought out, hardly arrived at conclusion, this hardly admitted benign overtone to his thinking that injects him with sufficient endurance to try all over again and to play the uncomfortable uncharacteristic role of audience anonymity.

"Daniel!"

"Hullo. It's Tarl. How are you?"

"Where have you been? It was terrible to look over here and see no movement. No lights at night. *Dreadful.*"

"Oh?"

"No outside light."

Pause. "I thought you'd all have been at the beach on a lovely day like this. Holidays and such."

"We would have been," ruefully, "but Gavin said we had to clean up after ourselves before we could have the car. So I refused to go. All this fuss because the place happens to be clean again. But where have you *been?*" Only Tarl is allowed to leave the auditorium.

He composes an impressive sentence that he might use for the press one day. "I've been to Auckland." Thinking it out ahead . . . "I had to go and try again to have a more authentic photo taken of myself for the press." Now it's ready. "I claim a certain native ugliness in my own right but the question remains whether I have, so far, achieved the hyperbole of hideousness with which . . ." think—think . . . "the press of the world accredits me." Angela would have screamed with laughter and held her frontage but Tarl covers her mouth with a hand in case a smile gets through. Which is just as well. Smiles don't suit her face at all. Laughs make her ugly. But the effort is wasted. He decides to tell it to Angela on Saturday. "Anyway how's everything over there? It's nice to have you back again."

"Oh, I feel this heavy pall of organized security falling about me again." Restlessly, "I need movement. I have a special need for repeated changes of scene." The mere listing of Tarl's addresses is already dizzying.

"I understand."

"Even away at the Bay. I thought I would have left the boredom behind me but it dogged me there too." The last *cri de coeur* of the imprisoned. "How long I'll see this out over there I don't know. I'm determined to save Bennie from living death."

"Living death?"

Superbly, "The living death of suburban domesticity."

"I wonder if Benjamin sees it that way."

"He's my companion in spiritual adventure."

Another day during the holidays they come upon him in the garden mowing, in a mowing temper. "He brings the entire weight of his scientific artillery to bear on proving me wrong."

Wipes his face with a dirty handkerchief and blows his nose. "He always speaks well of you here."

Ominous silence.

"I'm fond of Gavin actually."

"The *time-server*."

"So are others. The rector told me the other night . . . the other middle of the night . . . that Gavin is very much liked by the boys at college. He said he was the only one who could handle the really bad boys and get them to work. He said, 'He's valuable on the staff.' "

"The time-server. He's renounced the valiant purposes of his youth and has become a time-server. He'll learn in time that a brilliant career is only dust and ashes."

"I am still fond of him. I think he talks very well. Last week he . . ."

"Oh he can talk all right. He's good at convincing people. He can be most charming, *I* know. But you don't hear the kind of talking he goes in for at home. Hours he spends on proving me wrong. Everything I say and do is *wrong*."

"I might take him on about that." He remembers tardily his recent resolution. "This firing of scientific slogans at an artist . . . it's wasted in the area of sentiment. Besides you're not *all* wrong. You . . ."

"Last Sunday I was cleaning out the ashes." What about the "We have no fires these frosty nights," last time? "So that he'd give us the car. Homer kept getting in the fireplace, rolling in the ashes, then rolling about on the carpet he'd just shampooed. And all I said to Ramona was—*all I said!*—was 'It's not Homer's fault, Ramona. This is what comes of having carpets at all, of getting too far away from nature. There'd have been none of this dirty housework had we stayed with nature.'

"He'd been sitting at the bench marking exercise books and all of a sudden he got up—he *got up!* He started on all about my not seeing reality. He strode up and down reviewing the wretched past, dragging up all that happened, pinning down the reasons why we'd failed, pointing out all my mistakes. The children and I just *cowered*. Then he went over all the court cases. 'The history of our interminable court cases,' he roared, 'reads like a catalogue.' He beat and beat at my mind for hours trying to corner me and prove me *wrong*. Questions so fast I couldn't keep up. No time to work out answers. And when I did manage to reply he pointed at me," demonstration, "and said, 'Ah, *got* you. You said *that* before and now you say this.'

"Then he started on the children." They're having a wonderful time at the moment with Dan's civilization, Dessida wheeling Homer about in the push-chair, Ramona reading a book on the step and Benjamin stalking a butterfly. "Blaming me for everything. All of which he taught me in the first place." Nostrils quivering successfully. " 'Why haven't you taught them manners? Why haven't you taught them how to eat? Look at that food on the floor. Look at that sandal in the butter. Why aren't there any utensils? That boy can't use a knife and fork. Look at them all, they eat like bushwhackers. How can they meet society?' And he slapped Ramona for eating in bed.

"And poor little Bennie. He picked up Bennie by the wrists and swung him up high and shook him like a rat. 'Look at him, look at him, the cripple. Look what you've done to my son. Doesn't know how to eat, can't use a fork, can't read or write, hides when he sees people. Spends the best part of his childhood up trees. A miserable social failure . . . a useless cringing cripple.' *Three whole hours* of it. I suffered a physiological and psychological upheaval. I trembled, my heart pounded, I shrank into long shuddering moans. I felt so faint I cried for two hours and was tired for three days.

"Then he wanted to know where the money had gone. His big salaries. I said, 'I don't know.' " Her voice has the hoarseness of one who takes a gloomy pleasure in a sad avowal. "I said, I said, 'Don't you interfere with my poverty. I have little left to me now but my poverty and I insist that this at least shall be respected.'

"And look at him in court last week. Look at him. From the start he promised to educate the children himself and stand up to the law when he ran into it. He even had begun a thesis on School Phobias when we returned to New Zealand in support of his case. He said he'd fight the law, he said he'd change it but he's had one chance after another in court for a year and he still backs down every time. He backs down, the coward. Instead of proving our theory he argues there's something wrong with *me*. There's far more wrong with him, the brute. It's he who needs psychiatry." Her face is drained quite white with fury and her eyes spit dark stars. "I've got to get away from Gavin, from the impact of his mind on mine. For a week at least, a month, six months . . . a year."

When the snowball tree is in bloom he can't resist ringing her up for the first time and asking her to come over and see it. A fact he carefully keeps from Angela and the Head. He supposes she sees it when she looks at it . . . he doesn't know.

At least the four children rave. But Tarl's eyes as ever only see inward upon the bitterness, or anything else there. "He's full of remorse, Daniel" with mixed rue and relish, huddled knees to chin on the step. "He's been telling everyone everything. He's told the whole staff at college about him and me, and everyone else he meets."

A Maori friend of Dan's said he picked up Gavin Pracket once on the way home from town, walking; he said he began talking of his trouble, and arriving at his corner, remained sitting there talking until the other had to excuse himself as it was getting dark. The second Ancient Mariner.

Rueful gratification, "He's quite remorseful, Daniel. Poor old Gavin. At times I feel quite warm towards him." She is looking for once at the shirt Dan wears, exquisitely ironed by Mrs. Richmond. "Poor old Gavin. He's only got two shirts he irons himself. I wonder if *I* could do them like that." Calming, cooling, "It's not true about Bennie. He uses a fork most gracefully. But what I really came for . . ."

"Don't go, Mummie. Stay here."

Takes Homer from the push-chair, swings him up on hip. "We can't stay, dear. Mr. Francis has things to do."

"Don't blame me to the child, God damn it."

She apologizes with tremendous emphasis. But she glows to have aroused in him an emotional response. Or is it respect for emotion released, whatever it is? She allows anyone his rages . . . except Gavin. "Come on, children. *I* want you. *I* haven't got things to do. *I'm* not busy. Dessy? Are you there, Ramona? Come on, Bennie." And off they flock beneath the trees as though Dan had treated them cruelly. As though he had driven them inhumanely away from their only water hole.

"Daniel!"

Five pairs of upturned eyes. The children are learning the begging-bowl technique very well indeed, if nothing else. They are learning to actually *seek* humiliation. "I know I shouldn't disturb you again but I simply *had* to come. I *had* to. I waited till I stopped crying. D'you mind if I spend a minute in the garden? Just one minute, then we'll go. I always feel so much better after coming here. I feel I can hang on longer." Pause in the door of the library. How astoundingly lovely the group looks in the doorway. But he still turns over his work and fingers his hairline where a sudden sweat is pressing through. "How are you? It's always so pleasant to see you."

Later beneath the tree, "I always seem to talk too much

when I come. When I get home I just writhe to recall it. I'm determined not to talk today. After I've said just one thing. I *must*. D'you mind if I say just *one thing?*" The beautiful eyes illumined with supplication.

"Whatever you say is interesting. By God I'll have to cut back this blasted tree. An umbrella tree is one thing but a closed umbrella is another."

"What I really came for . . . I want advice. I don't know what to do. Will you tell me what to do?"

"I'm too much of a bloody—sorry. I'm too much of a fool."

Bright appreciation of his temper. "All right then," softly. "Never mind."

He suddenly stands, "You Prackets," he shouts to the spring so that every tree from here to the mountains rattles and every bird holds its ears, "you Prackets remain insoluble."

The adoration in her face, a permissiveness, "You don't *mind* us coming, do you?"

Reaches for his smokes, "I'm not likely to refuse a refresher course in human behavior; not when it's laid on my doorstep."

The thing about holidays, however . . . legal holidays I mean . . . is that they come to an end in time, excepting Pracket holidays. The reopening of school to Tarl is no more than a cue to take off and school is bound to reopen. At the first whiff of the expected she's obsessed by the opposite, at the first smell of authority she gathers her brood about her, clucking, and dashes off grandly to freedom, preferably the actual hour when the bells are calling. What has the case next week got to do with freedom? Nothing that Tarl can see. She doesn't even mention it on Friday. "Look, this is urgent. Desperate. I want you to do something for me." Gasps, holds head, center stage. "I want you to drive me and the kiddies down to Angela's. Right now. And not say anything to Gavin. This is a Desperate Situation."

"I'll not deceive Gavin."

"Deceive? *Deceive* . . . did you say?"

"I allow no manner of deception in my house." Ric's house. She is absolutely staggered.

"Wouldn't you *think* . . ." from Angela on Saturday. "Oh Daddy. Fancy coming to you of all people. The former head-master and a friend of the headmaster—coming to *you*. Let alone expecting you to hide them at *your daughter's* place. Honestly, Daddy, she's . . ."

"Hold it, hold it. You and I don't use that word. On the contrary she's astonishingly clever. Me . . . the very last person to ask such a thing. Therefore she comes to me, *therefore*. It shocked you, didn't it? That's just what Tarl wants: emotional reaction. She eats it as we eat bread."

"You're never without an excuse for her, are you?"

"At least I'm unique in that."

"Anyway, how did she think we were going to put them all up? Their five on top of our six . . . don't forget our man . . . six and a half, don't forget the baby on the way. In our little house?"

"Oh, they've got sleeping bags and that. Not all of them get undressed or go in for sheets, I believe, that sort of thing. I think Ramona does. I'm not saying they don't like nice beds but someone else's. But Ange. Can you see me carting the Prackets to and from Shangri-La? God Almighty."

"But Daddy, we couldn't afford it, not another family on top of ours. Gavin's got a terrific salary. Where does the money *go?*" Then the voice softens and she kisses the baby. "I would have put them up of course." Then a flare-up again. "D'you know what she . . . oh I told you about that. About that community she wants me to help her establish. Where we'd all mind each other's children and be free and that. As *if . . .*"

On the following Sunday evening before school reopens after the spring holidays Ric puts his head in Dan's door on his way home from church. He doesn't usually appear at the weekend. He looks gentle and elegant and proper in his dark tailored suit but there is shame on his face, even pain. "Really, this family of mine, I don't know . . ."

"Prackets."

"I was just driving in the gate and Gavin appeared from the darkness in a terrible state. He had a torch. He said his family had got away. She . . ."

"*Hoo*-ray."

". . . managed to get the car. He's borrowed Mrs. Suldoon's and gone to look for them. At this time of night. He said he'd had his eye on them all day in case this happened. I don't know, I'm sure."

"Hoo . . ."

"Now don't raise your hopes. We've . . ."

". . . *ray.*"

". . . heard all this before."

❧ BENJAMIN, calls the bell sadly in the morning, will you never have done with holidays? And Ramona—astonished—where the devil have you got to? Don't tell me you've dropped us too. We thought you loved your lessons. Your work was so good the teacher put it on the wall. We all thought you were fearfully clever. Are you . . . have you succumbed to the Do-Nothing too? Ramona . . . Ramona . . .

"Where's my family?"
Nine o'clock in the morning.
"You're inclined to overdo that question: 'Where's my family?' "
"They've gone. They got away."
"Come in, Gavin. Sit down."
"She deceived me, she deceived me, she deceived me. All this week she's been pretending to cooperate. On Sunday, yesterday, we seemed almost happy. We spent the morning doing the washing together, talking quietly and normally to each other about school in the morning but she was secretly packing the car. She even got Ramona's clothes ready for school and prepared her lunch for the morning, deceiving Ramona too. Then just before dark she said, 'Come on, kiddies. I'm going to return the Education Act to Mr. Richmond. He told me to put it in his mailbox. All hop in the car.' And that's the last I saw of them. Mrs. Suldoon round the corner rang me and told me they'd asked her to take them in for the night. Tarl told her I'd been sharpening the carving knife to cut all their throats. And that after our harmonious day together. But Mrs. Suldoon told her that her house was already full of visitors and off they went into the night. I borrowed the Suldoons' car, spent the whole night searching for them. The bookseller rang me from town this morning telling me that the book *The Lonely Traveler* was no longer in print. There never was a book called that and I had never ordered it. It was her way of sending a message to me."
"God damn it, it's a straight-out game of cops-and-robbers."
"You should see how they've left my lovely clean rooms."
"Cops-and-robbers. Courts-and-Tarls."
"D'you know where they are, Dan?"
"Who—me?" Have they gone to Jim's? he wonders. "No. If

I did know I'd say I knew, but I wouldn't tell you where. As you know, your wife trusts me."

"I appreciate that. I appreciate all you do for her. She always comes back from here so much calmer. Better."

"I suppose you've had no breakfast. Come and I'll make you some coffee." Through the quiet long morning house, the way of the weary and defied, the one behind the other down the dim hall through the music room where Tarl's pictures no longer hang—he has stowed them away out of sight in a cupboard—to the colorful shining nickel kitchen with its windows upon the fig tree. The light filters mysteriously through the fig tree to enter the kitchen. The buds are showing. "Do you love her?"

Fist on fridge, "I want her, I want her, I want her."

"D'you ever let her know it these days or do you concentrate on proving her wrong?"

Fingers stray on the nickel surface of the fridge.

"D'you ever pass her a cup of tea? D'you buy her the food she likes? Even Angela brings the coffee sponge she likes."

He is thinking and so is Dan. He is thinking of his wife and Dan of his. "D'you ever call her by some pet name only the two of you know? D'you ever kiss her," pause, "in the wrong places at the wrong times? D'you . . ." He looks at the new pale green buds on the bare body of the fig tree and stops. Do you kiss long long kisses over doing the dishes, undress each other and pull down the blinds? Do you dance together in the kitchen solemnly, bowing, pirouetting? Do you drive deep exciting trips together alone into the heart of the country or way up north in the wastelands where the roads are dry sand or crushed white shell, where the ocean in the bays is thundering and the sides of your tent billowing? Do you lie together in the night to the billowing and thundering, mouth on mouth? . . .

Gavin's eyes lit with memory lift a moment to the fig tree too, then cast down again. "We were very happy for years when we first went away. We'd love to get out on the open road singing, heading for nowhere." Then is silent again. And Dan waits, inviting Gavin's thought to find its own way through the years behind in privacy and at his own pace. Two men in a kitchen on a soft spring morning recalling women's kisses, with the difference that Gavin's are recoverable. From the senior classes across the road a reminiscent draft of air carries the voices of the children in a pulsing Maori chant welcoming some visitor or other but I don't think Gavin hears it. Neither does he appear to apprehend Dan's accompanying reverie but, obsessed

121

with his own, pursues his own low chant, inner groans in a cavity of mourning. "We were kissing each other at the beginning of this year in that cottage below your land, on the beach but . . . then as the legal duress closed in upon us, as Ben reared higher between us we . . . his permanent place between us we . . . since then there's been nothing. I do go in to her at night now sometimes and cuddle her and talk softly to her but . . . there's . . . but no response whatever. She's cold . . . cold in my arms."

She's dead . . . dead in my arms.

The chant from the children swells at the will of the wanton wind, as the memory of me swells too at the will of wanton circumstances releasing within Dan his homage to me jailed by the shortening years. "I can say this, Gavin: she loves you. Whether she knows it or not." He cuts Gavin some strong bread and butter and sniffs. "Last week you fell into the shirt test. The Shirt Test. If a woman truly loves a man she wants to do his shirts." A glance at the rag he wears. "She hasn't, of course, but she wanted to. You passed the mighty Shirt Test."

Is there anything more searing than a lover's laughter above the agony in his heart? Tragedy holds to itself this capacity of throwing up a cover of effervescence to obscure its subterranean working, highlighting itself by contrast. "And," Dan adds, refilling his mug, "she speaks tenderly of you at times, as recently as these holidays. More than once she has said to me, 'Poor old Gavin. I feel quite warm toward him.' You'll come together in time when all this . . . all these explosions are over. It's this dynamic reciprocal awareness between you that I'm banking on. From that awareness stem both love and hate. I know love in all its guises . . . you might not think so seeing the kind of life I lead now but . . . and I know that you two love each other. Gavin," passes him the sugar, "all will be well."

Fist, "She hates me, she hates me, she hates me."

"Love in reverse."

Hoarsely, "The part I cannot bear is her turning the kiddies against me. She's with them all the time. And she's teaching Ben to deceive; to escape, to hide, to run from anything he dislikes. That's not Ben. He's a real man of a boy. She's teaching him to hate me. I can't win."

"He'll work it out for himself when he's older."

". . . To hate me."

"He's got brains. He'll see for himself."

"I can't win."

"It does make very sad listening."

He pulls out a cigarette from a cheap packet examining it with distrust. "I don't believe in smoking, I don't smoke, but these days . . ." a hard breath . . . "I indulge myself, in this at least."

Later, rising and stretching, Dan says, "Some evening, Gavin, I'm going to take you on till six in the morning on 'How to handle an artist.'" At which Gavin looks up at him and his wide smile reaches its full quota of teeth right to the silver one at the back. Dan pockets his hands, "But it's hardly the time now for philosophy with Caesar's sword drawn, and Damocles' sword dangling."

The smile closes again. "Another day off. I'll lose my job in the end. Could *you* get Tarl to send Ben to school? Would *you* influence Tarl?"

"Me influence Tarl? Does the man draw breath who can influence Tarl? There's no such thing as 'influencing Tarl.' Do *I* have to tell you that? Or any other Pracket for that matter. You included. The two of you are always right . . . *dead* right. I'm not joking. I believe it. I believe you both. No, Gavin, life makes its own arrangements and adjustments without any reference to us. Life is just like Tarl, and Tarl like life. Take my hazy word for it. Nor does life make such a bad job of it either, at least as good as Tarl does. The more heavily the soul falls the sooner it reaches bedrock. A good place for a soul to be. The more travail in one's life with a woman . . ." but Gavin doesn't hear a word he's saying . . . "the more rapturous the . . ."

"I must make a man of my son."

"Y'know, Pracket, I don't enjoy this role of righteousness thrust upon me. The all-knowing, all-receiving, all-healing God. You miscast me. I'm not my books. I'm not. I'm a thoroughgoing hypocrite from any angle. And another thing, for your information . . ."

Doesn't hear a word. "Sometimes I think my cause was lost before I started."

"I'm a lost cause myself."

"But I must think my way carefully through all this and no longer let anger guide me."

"I see no solution to the problems of the Prackets."

He smiles and rises. He likes smiling, as Dessida and Homer do. He puts down his empty mug respectfully, not because Dan is anyone in particular—the Prackets are immune to incidentals like fame—but because for the moment Dan represents humanity in general. He'd treat Paddy Tu the same, which is the basis of his success with the bad boys at college. He treats them all with respect. Then he hitches his strides like girding for battle and looks back through the long mellow house to the sun on the trees and the smile of the flowers, a masterpiece framed in the doorway. "Now I must find my 'Lonely Traveler.'"

FOUR

I am more resolute because all have denied me, than I could ever have been had all accepted me . . .

—WHITMAN

❧ "OH, ISN'T Jim Prenderghast lovely? We did arrive very late at night. He put us in the little bach next door to him, oh-h-h . . . He gave us bedding and food and lent me books and even gave me a first edition. Dessida runs into him at all times and he comes over every evening to see us. Just over the sand dunes from the sea. We spend our days on the beach. And we met his friend the vagabond scholar and Bennie simply loves him. He's going to help Bennie with a collection of shells."

"Did you get some painting done?"

"N-no. I can't with the children. Besides, people crowd round. I dislike the touch of strangers . . . even the physical nearness of people. I detest to be overlooked when I'm working and I can't bear comment. It drives me frantic." A sip of her wine. "It subjugates my soul."

They are in the kitchen. "But what I really came for . . . I hope you won't think I'm awful. Could you let me have a saucepan? Just a little one. And a bowl? I want to make the little kiddies a pudding."

"I'm not strong on saucepans and bowls but aa . . ." He gives her these things. "Would you like a handful of forks? Do you people go in for knives?"

"Oh how wonderful . . . *thank* you. Tha-a-ank you. No, we've got no knives." Gavin's salary runs to four figures. "Could I have a few spoons too?"

127

"But where does the money *go*?" from Angela. "Gosh if we had that income."

"Ay? Oh, aa . . . I think the Prackets are above such trivialities as where money goes."

"Funny, isn't it?"

"My word she came down on my kitchen stuff."

"As a matter of fact, Daddy, I could have done with some of that kitchen gear myself if it was going begging."

"I didn't mind the pot going, actually. It had a wobbly base—you know? And the forks. Now these forks, they . . . I used them in a school orchestra once. You hit one on the other for a ringing sound. The children were—well they were not exactly delicate. I was young at the time. Well, these forks . . ."

Angela starts laughing and holds her frontage. "Don't make me laugh, Daddy."

"And the knives, they . . . old Auntie Jessie sent them to your mother. Part of old Auntie's trousseau seventy years before your mother's. They . . ."

Angela screams with laughter. "But," he adds, "I *was* sorry to see the bowl go. I kept the milk money in it. But I could see their need was greater than mine. All their begging scenes are short of a bowl. She . . ."

"Oh, you've got to hand it to her."

"Ay?"

"She's a master of the pitiful scene."

"Pitiful scene. Just imagine that arrival scene at Jim's in the middle of the night. The slight humble mother with child on hip looking up with poignant eyes. Madonna-and-Child effect. And all the other pairs of eyes at varying levels pleading from the darkness. A canvas titled 'The Lonely Traveler' by one Tarl Pracket."

Angela stands with effort and reaches to a cupboard above her for this stuff she takes for nausea. "If only I could have a baby with decorum."

I picture myself as a full-grown middle-age woman looking after Angela.

"Don't make me laugh again, Daddy."

"I can be very funny, y'know." He goes to the music room, then comes striding back into the kitchen holding his forehead and gasping. "Oh-h-h," flings upon chair legs astride, eyes closed, and moans. "I'll only stay one minute. Just *one minute*. But what I *really* came for . . . I hope you don't think I'm awful. Could you let me have a saucepan and a bowl?" Then pathetically, "I want to make the children a pudding, poor little things.

They never have any pudding. And some knives and forks and spoons?"

"Please stop, Daddy."

He *should* stop. I would never have allowed it.

"I don't suppose I could have your dinner service, could I? For poor little Bennie? And the grand piano? The poor—*poor!*—little children never have any music, I've been married for *ten years* and . . ."

Some time later beneath the tree he admits, "Ric wouldn't like this critical attitude in us."

"She's really terribly clever, I know."

"She's messianic rather than clever. All this carry-on of hers . . . it's just sparks flying from the central furnace. The blazing crusading for freedom in the minds of children. I never forget she can return a book. I never forget how Dessida returned the scent I lent her with some left for Mary. Nor how Homer leaves the needle of my gramophone alone. Ever since he was quite little."

"I wish I could say the same of Brucey. They're the first young family I've ever seen in my life that didn't quarrel or cry. I've heard them say to each other, 'You have it.' It's what she says . . . love and serve children and they in turn will love and serve. Once I've had this baby, Daddy, I'll mind her children. I could if I knew there was a sound purpose to it. To let her paint."

"There are many qualities in her I admire. Her contempt for secrecy is one. And the absence of pride, and of ambition. And I've never ever seen any jealousy. Her modesty is astounding. Feeling strong makes one modest. She seems to be quite indifferent to her reputation. She is free of the sense of supreme responsibility which is the sense of sin. She appears to be one of these rare characters who are capable of a . . . of setting an ideal aim above her own happiness. Such an unquestioning sacrifice seems to be even essential to her character. This sounds strong but I do get the feeling at times that she may belong to the elect company of those who mold the conscience of their race."

"I've had this ready to say to you for a long time." The raincoat in the kitchen has red eyelids on pale tragic cheeks, its head hangs down, its hands press its face. "Couldn't you harness your crises, Tarl? All that Mrs. Hallibut business. Instead of letting it immobilize you and drive you crazy, just go inside and draw her. A few minutes of line. Sketch Homer sticking that knife into all those Hallibut pumpkins gathered for the market. And her face when she sees it. Draw the taps running that Homer leaves on. Release the hells. Harness the bloody lot. Sorry, the whole lot. Lift a brush and make one stroke and you'll wake up in the morning different. A new world altogether. You'll suddenly be fond of everybody; even the law. A new technique to meet a new situation. Three-minute sketches lasting no longer than the time the baby's back is turned."

"Some things are too painful to harness."

"Y-yes, but maybe other times when . . ."

"I'm not in the state of mind." Closes her eyes and covers them.

Damn, he's been too clumsy. Advice again. "I should remember that."

Her head lifts like that of a horse sniffing the breeze and her voice changes; sniffing the air loaded with the sweet scents of distant lush pastures. "I'm going away for six months and I'm divorcing Gavin."

"Don't you do that. Sometimes I advise, by God. You must not remove the father from the children. The one other being who is natively interested in them. No one will fight for them as Gavin does. He'd lay down his life for any one of you. He's practically doing it now. You never know when you'll need him, you or one of the children." Heat in his words.

Amazement from Tarl. "As if being married to anybody had anything to do with gaining access to the whole personality, to the entire unconscious. On the contrary, marriage is an obstacle." Authoritatively, "I've got to make a settled home for the children, Daniel. I've got to get them away from Gavin. Bennie's like a little animal with the hounds after him. But Gavin says we've got to stay on at the Hallibuts' in that *hovel,* until he can save enough to buy a home. The children need one *now.* Especially Ramona." Her voice lowers again and she gazes wistfully beyond him to some far mystical distance which he cannot see. "I'm always searching for Shangri-La."

Her landfall is a long long way, the longest of all roads. It is one of the times when the whole of her face looks lovely, burning with the intensity of one who sees through illusion, when it dawns on one how contrary to life are all rational deductions when you come upon something alive. As her eyes blaze beyond him in his ugliness and beyond the tree in its beauty they reveal how passionately would she tear open those doors which others would gladly slink past.

130

He frowns in concentration, as he does when following closely the movement of the spirit in another, his mind leaving its own habitat to enter hers and accompany it side by side, an exercise engaging the whole of his energy. He examines his red wine which seems to hold the radiance from Tarl, glowing in her momentary wholeness. And he senses that in the working of her mind, secure amid the clashings of everyday living, is something calm, quiet, silent, undisturbable, which appears to be viewing eternity; that this inner quietude and silence is not mere idleness or inactivity, nor the silence of the desert shorn of all vegetation nor that of a corpse forever gone to sleep and decay, but the silence of the eternal abyss in which all contrasts and conditions are buried. It is the silence of nature in her oneness and allness.

It is some time before he collapses and has to desert her in her vision. He waits respectfully until she moves, looks upon the floor and finally sips her red wine in its crystal glass as though tasting in it on her tongue what her spirit has tasted in the crystal glass of vision. And when she at last speaks it is with a profound serenity even though she speaks of the seven years' service from which . . . with the anguish over, the arduous years of solitude, inaction, boredom, wandering, crises and self-denial . . . one finally harvests the fruit.

Another day this week, as she squats on his doorstep he says, "But you are creating. Your concepts are your brushes and the children your canvas and the painting that emerges is dazzling."

"Others see it as a daub."

"There's nothing more like a daub than a masterpiece."

Later still this same morning he goes on, "I believe Benjamin would be all right at school, this school, anyway, where the Maori staff laughs all day, but I simultaneously believe he should not go. I'm strongly on Gavin's side yet just as strongly on yours. I support the law of the land but think it should be defied. A writer cannot exorcise from himself the faculty of becoming each protagonist in turn, in person, even simultaneously. I'm hopelessly and helplessly on everyone's side." At which she covertly smiles but only behind a hand.

Neither of them mentions the Court looming up next week; why waste words on trivia? Side by side with the soul's travail, Caesar is inconsequentia, to be ignored as some minor irritation or acknowledged as no more than another reading lesson for Benjamin, or as a reason in a language comprehensible to the Philistine for taking off on another flight.

131

As the school children crow nearby in the playground and as she luxuriates in her melancholy on his step, he sits in his canvas chair holding the Whitman, the white pages a glare in the sun to eyes used to shade. The children have followed her over, not Benjamin, and he has let them go to Angela's children's brushes and paint. There must be some way of consoling Tarl if he could but put his finger on it. He begins reading to her:

> *"I think I could turn and live with animals, they are so placid*
> *and self-contain'd,*
> *I stand and look at them long and long . . ."*

to the end of the long verse, and its last line,

> *"Not one is respectable or unhappy over the whole earth."*

She listens wistfully, indulgently as though Homer were showing her something. He reads it again as any teacher would, then turns to the "Camerado" and reads that, but he still raises no more than patient silence. Piqued, he plunges in further and talks like a fool of social love circulating in a community, in particular between a home and a school. "But there's a breakdown in the cycle somewhere."

"Um." Only a forgiving pity for him in her soft eyes.

He goes into the library behind him and brings out his small leatherbound book of Rembrandt's unfinished line drawings and puts it in her hand. "Given to me by my art teacher at training college twenty years ago. He's dead now."

"*Tha-a-ank* you."

"It was old when someone gave it to him."

"Oh-h-h . . ." with reverence.

"And it comes from my 'Never-lend' shelf."

When they have gone and before he begins cleaning up he reads "Dear Camerado" again. Surely Tarl heard in it her own fierce thoughts.

> *". . . I know I am restless, and make others so;*
> *I know my words are weapons, full of danger, full of*
> *death . . .*
> *For I confront peace, security, and all the settled laws, to*
> *unsettle them;*
> *I am more resolute because all have denied me, than I could*
> *ever have been had all accepted me;*
> *I heed not, and have never heeded, either experience, cau-*
> *tions, majorities, nor ridicule . . ."*

Must his own work perish that hers might endure? Whose work is of the most value to others? Something instructs him that it is Tarl's. Even in the most Stygian darkness of mind with the light of vision extinguished he perceives that it is Tarl's. For him . . . no more than the selfish ecstasy of the creative orgasm, whereas her freedom of inquiry is the last hope of man. She may actually be one of the tiny minority that never fails to rouse the furious hatred of the majority. How else does she survive the arduous life a freed mind inspires and brave the obloquy to which she's exposed? The impulse must be overwhelming. Certainly she believes herself to be doing the greatest service parent can to child but it could be even more. There are times when he thinks this service may be the greatest man can do to man.

It is this indomitable quality of her mind at its best, popularly termed stubbornness, that gives him hope for her, allays his growing jealousy and resentment, and helps him to believe that in spite of the dangers she brings on herself she might yet grow whole; that she could, as other crusaders from other dark times, emerge with renewed vigor and with at least enough confidence to not only withstand the prevailing hostility but also overcome the black nightmares within herself which create her world of suffering and cause her astounding folly. For she does sense the road to a happy life, and if only the law would allow her to travel it . . . who knows? She might yet lead her tortured family to a land of light and joy.

⚜ "DANIEL!"

"Tarl. How are . . . ?"

"I've got a request, d'you mind? Can you tell me somewhere to go? The children and I are ill with the strain. I've been crying for three days. Poor little Bennie, he's in a pitiful state." Through the window he is holding a monarch butterfly. She strides back to the door, "Oh I must cry. . . ."

"Do." At which she fails and returns center stage.

He clears his throat. "Now let me see, somewhere to go." She used up Jim Prenderghast. "You could go to Felix Sand. Up Fort Road, a few miles inland from town. He's always calling out for interesting people."

"But would you tell Gavin?"

"I'd tell him I knew, but not where."

"Well I can't go there," with an air of refusing a favor.

"If you did go there I'd ring him first. He's a man with a regard for the proprieties. He trims a little black mustache."

"Ooo-ooh . . ." Horror.

"But he's quite a good-natured man, impulsive. Except that his temper is unreliable and his jokes are a little on the heavy side. He's a man who never fell into the mistake of undervaluing himself. He . . ."

"How long are these people going to stay?" Felix on the phone in the morning. "We can barely feed ourselves with my wife out of work. I want to make it quite plain to you, Daniel, that our bach is not available for casuals. We keep it for our friends."

"I see. I take it that Mrs. Pracket's Madonna-and-Child tableau has failed to work this time. I would have . . ."

"It definitely has not. They arrived by taxi with no warning whatever and dismissed it before they came in. It's all so utterly sordid. This proximity to a court case."

"She's a very interesting person, Fee. A well-known artist. I . . ."

Comes down an octave. "I picked something like that. Something different, a sensibility. They can stay a day or two longer. It happens that my wife is fascinated by the children. They're very nice children. Beautiful. They're as gentle as kittens and bunnies."

"I'd have rung you first had I known she was going. She said she wasn't."

"As long as it's quite plain to you that . . ."

"When you've had enough let me know. I'll let her husband know where she is."

"Where's my family?" Four o'clock. "Do you . . . ?"

"I've just made the tea. Have some?"

"D'you know where they are?"

"I do."

His eyes wait, unwavering.

"But don't ask me where, I'd have to tell you. Just take my word for it, the children are in clover. Have a scone?"

"Thanks." Awful control on the chair by the fridge.

"Mrs. Ric made these scones. I pass the Scone Test as well as the Shirt Test."

"If you don't tell me by Friday I'll have to engage the police to . . ."

"For God's sake leave the police out of it."

"I will ask you on Friday. I've got to have her over the weekend to work on her to get her to cooperate in court next week." A sip of the hot tea. "I tried to get the visiting psychiatrist to say that Ben is not school material but he's a washout. No understanding of a child whatever. Even so, Daniel, if I win the case I'll still lose Tarl. If I lose the case I'll lose Ben. I lose either way. I can't win."

"No one can win. Like a nuclear war."

"This is tragedy."

"Yes."

Silence.

"I must get back to Ramona. She preferred to stay with me and go to school. She's on her own over there. I've got at least one of the family." But he is still here when the Head passes through at five—to whom Gavin, all over again, minutely analyzes his whole plan of action for the court next week, bemoaning the inadequate lawyer whom Tarl had chosen. "He knows nothing of the complex make-up of a child or anything of the subtleties of human relationships. All he can say is, 'This letter was written so-and-so therefore at that time he meant so-and-so.'"

The next thing Dan hears is these two civilized compassionate men discussing from necessity the pros and cons of carrying Benjamin to school—a method loudly articulated by the entire district. "By God if I had him . . ." and so on. To place his two wild bare feet on the ground within the gate for no more than one split second, conscious, unconscious or vomiting; both equally concerned at any possible damage to the child's mind, examining the proposition from all sides: on the one hand, carried to school in his father's arms to be held there a moment, then returned to the heart of his family; on the other, carried in the law's cold arms away from his family to be held in some alien home for at least a year. Until they move on to the care of the child at school, which makes more heartening listening, the prepared teacher and, "Young Hallibut," from Gavin, "has agreed to keep an eye on my son in the playground. He'll be quite safe with Albie." Until Ric says, "Now Gavin, it's time to consider what you'll do after the case, should you lose it."

"They'll never get my son from me."

"That won't do, Gavin."

"I'll appeal."

"You must be geared for all eventualities."

"Daniel!"

The raincoat has gone at last with the warmer weather and the tight white things are back. The children whirl down the hall after her like a cluster of chaffinches on the fig tree in autumn. "This is a Desperate Situation. I want you to do something for me."

"Wine? How are you?"

"Oh life is dreadful . . . *dreadful*. I want you to come to court next week and give evidence."

"*Me?*"

"All you've got to do is say you know the children and that Bennie is not neglected." Stare. "You said you would?"

"Me? Did I?"

"You said you would."

"I did?"

Sharply, "Will you then, or not?"

A big change takes place in Dan at the disrespect. The carefully cultivated charity of a year and a half goes down before resentment. An almost ever-present resentment. "I . . . I can't think in an emergency. I'll have to wait and find out what I think."

"Oh no no," from Gavin at five. "That would defeat my purpose."

"Oh no," from the Head. "You'll certainly not go to court for any reason. It would disturb your work. I won't allow it."

Gavin, "I haven't had time to find them yet. I might have to ask you on Friday."

"Sordid," shrieks Felix on the phone. "Squalid."

"I take it she has overplayed the interesting people role."

"She's overplayed my endurance. She's got plenty of money. Far more than us. Why come and live on us when she can afford to cruise round in taxis?"

"I'll let her husband know where she . . ."

" 'Interesting'? I'll say she's interesting. The scene at our home last night when *he* found them and *she* refused to go home . . . 'Interesting.' She waited till this morning when *he* was safely at college and *we* were safely out, then she sneaked out by taxi without a word. The *sponge*. I want to make it quite clear, Daniel, that . . ." and so on. All very clear. The birds outside are calling for codeine. Well that's the end of Felix. A theoretical loss only. Indeed he is so pleased at the loss of Felix that he sweeps out the library for the first time this year and burns all the rubbish except his novel. Nice work, Tarl.

"Daniel . . ."

On the phone on Monday. So Gavin didn't catch her to work on her for the weekend.

"I'm back with Mr. Prenderghast. I feel more independence here. I felt too restricted at your other friend's."

"How are you?"

"Unnerved and quailing. And I'm worrying about Ramona. What does she do between school over and Gavin coming home, do you know, Daniel?"

"I think Mr. Richmond sends her home with another little girl to wait."

"Ramona told me on the phone how you called her and Gavin in from the playground on Saturday afternoon when he was giving her ball practice. You called them in to the fire. She said she just loved being there. She said, 'I just *love* Mr. Francis.' She is longing to come back to you. Did you have Gavin for a meal as you said you might?"

"I forgot."

"Now then, Daddy," from Angela on toll, "I know you. Don't you let me hear that you've taken Gavin and Ramona in to stay. Just give Tarl one leg in and . . ."

"The law," says Gavin by the fire in the evening where Dan has called the two of them in again from the frost-coming playground. Ramona is warming her hands crouching near the flames and her father has a bottle of beer beside him. "Just one bottle, thanks, no more." These spring evenings can be so biting. "The law places the whole onus on me to persuade my wife to see reason. It's a bad thing between us. She has asked her lawyer to prepare separation and divorce papers."

"I told her not to do that."

"Oh it's nothing. I've had that kind of behavior for years. She's been talking divorce since May. But she can't divorce me." Ramona listening, sadly. "She's got no evidence."

"I won't stay more than a minute," the following morning. "My lawyer wants to know right now," with authority, "if you'll give evidence in court tomorrow."

He turns off the Boulez. "I'm not allowed to."

Stupefied, "Not *allowed?*" She follows him round, staring at him. "Who won't allow you?"

"Ric. Gavin."

Astounded. "But all he wants you to say is . . ."

"I don't take direction from your lawyer."

Hands pressed to cheeks, poised on one foot, one heel forward, staring at the floor. "But all he wants . . . you said you would stand up in any court in this country to defend the right of the one to be different."

"I did. But I've never said I'd take sides between a man and his wife. There's a distinction."

"But all he wants . . ."

"I don't argue."

"I'll give him a ring. He's waiting." When she returns, "You could be subpoenaed."

"What's that mean?"

"Cookies, Mummie, cookies," from Homer. Dan passes him the tin. "Eat them outside, little boy."

"It means if you are summoned to court you've got to come."

"Oh? There's always the hazard I might not say what your lawyer has arranged."

The bell releases the school for lunch and Tarl makes off up the shadowy hall to the sunlight outside calling the children after her. She swings up Homer like the whole weight of her family on her hip, the entire bulk of humanity, "Come on, Bennie," and lurches off across the lawn. Dan hastens abjectly after her, "You know I can't do this thing. It's taking sides."

Temper, "What did Gavin say? What did he *say?*"

"He said it would be defeating his purpose of keeping the family united."

Contempt, even anger, in her voice, "I'll see you later." And staggers off to the fence leaving him standing there on his own lawn, the biggest fool on the stage.

From Ric a few moments later, "Have 'they' been here?"

Dan's teeth are hard together. "Familiarity I hate from high or low; intimacy I allow from my friends only. Which is my measure of a friend . . . the capacity to distinguish between these two."

He returns to the kitchen to treat himself this time, but instead of making himself the coffee or the tea or pouring the wine—all that he does to comfort others—he stands there with his fingers on the bench staring through the window at the fig tree. He can forgive just about anything from Tarl as long as she entertains him, makes him feel from her generous sensationalism. A man asks no more than to feel, whatever it is. But a man of Dan's seething vanity, even though he is partially aware of it, cannot take contempt, or its symbol, familiarity. His one cry to Angela throughout is that Tarl has approached him as an equal. "It means nothing to her at all, Ange . . . my position and my . . . my professional position and my, and my . . . I'm so much older than her. She's always uncovering me. She gets too close to me. She gets to know the inside of me. A privilege. She —she simply takes it. She's never earned it. What has she ever done for me? She's never even uttered the words 'How are you?' I hate it." After all I have done for her, he reflects to himself. She has never ever paid me the respect due to a man of position. Now she despises me. It's true what Angela has always said, that I spoil her. That I spoil everyone. I have spoiled her.

Standing immobilized, humiliated beyond endurance, with his fingers unmoving on the bench, staring unseeing at the new buds outside, he experiences a further change in himself. Something comes up from within him that has never seen daylight before. His covert but growing resentment and jealousy go further than overturning his authentic charity and his deliberate nobility of purpose to put Tarl's work before his own. Suddenly the impulse breaks through to the light that he would destroy her. A moment of hasty contempt from Tarl under overpowering stress, and Dan is revealed to himself for what man actually is. Much more sinner than saint. Such small actions it takes to determine large movements.

Dan has a formula for revenge proved successful in the past when he lived in society: make himself necessary to the enemy, even loved, in order to wound him more fatally—and he's not without his power over others. For all his sincere attempts at self-honesty the cards have usually been stacked in favor of himself. In all voluntary saviors there is a touch of the insincere. Self-criticism often obscures self-infatuation. True, Dan suspects he is a fraud and worries about betraying the truth and protests loftily to himself of his responsibility to humanity, but he is disposed to protest too much.

He is shocked to perceive this in himself . . . the desire to destroy Tarl. What about his genuine pity and compassion? But he is relieved. Great pressures are released below. He actually feels cleaner, purer. He relaxes, moves, and at last makes himself lunch. Recovers his normal face. The whole experience covers itself, he even forgets it and continues to be, manifestly at least, the same ambling, charming, charitable, permissive savior and server to those who come. But "The wish to kill cannot be killed."

"She certainly has a difficult husband," from dear old Jim on the phone. "Those rationalists are worse than Christians. You couldn't shift that fellow with a sledge hammer. But she . . . yes she certainly has an *idée fixe* about the children. Yes he did come here after them, he tracked them down, but he missed them. I'd sent them on to a friend of mine who claims to be enlightened. Arnold." He chuckles ruefully, "He hasn't been the same since."

"I only sent her to you because I wanted a breather."

"Oh, she'd disturb anyone."

And that's the end of Jim. Not to be celebrated.

From Dan's reading of the report in the paper everyone appears to have lost the case except the magistrate. The child is placed under the supervision of the Child Welfare department for one year, to "direct, if necessary, where he shall live." Although he hears from Gavin on the Saturday evening when he has called him and Ramona in to the fire again, from the playground, that Blondie, the Child Welfare officer, due to take Benjamin on Monday, intends to play the game with an even lighter hand. He offers them one more chance on Monday to get Benjamin to school, so that the whole affair is almost back where it started: School or else on Monday morning. "These do-or-die Mondays," he complains to the Head, "they're like a repeating decimal. I think I'll take off someplace for a while. I'll take flight myself."

"I'll not allow you to be driven from your own home." *His* own home, to be accurate.

"We've got to have the rooms up to standard now," Tarl wails on Sunday. "A Child Welfare woman supervises us. You never know when she's coming." So she's back again next door.

"I suppose you get a few laughs out of that."

"No, but I get some crying."

"That makes very sad telling."

He does not get up and tend her today although she is extra sad.

⚜ BENJAMIN, calls the bell on Monday morning, its voice dispirited, here's the Monday morning to end all Mondays. Can't you walk a few yards from one gate to another . . . you who conquer horizons? I don't think you'll suffer; suffering takes practice. After this morning, Benjamin, I warn you . . . I'll call you no more.

Dan sighs from his shoes to his brains at what's going on next door at this moment and sinks in his chair on the veranda. How can the sun remain benign like love? The birds themselves are holding their breath. The shadows of the towering gum tree reach their leaf patterns across the green veranda, lacy, still and two-dimensional, and yet he exists in tumult. Where is love over the fence—the old-fashioned sacrificial love? Where is marriage over the fence? Ah, if they only knew what it was to lose it. If only they had the insight, or rather the outsight, the capacity to see and feel people other than themselves . . . to read in him what his long weary womanless life has been . . . to see the sons he did not have.

A morning of extraordinary sensibility. Breathless. Not only the birds but the flowers too and the trees and the children in the playground. Breathlessness of waiting nature . . .

"Mum, Mum, come back."

It's Ramona from the "hovel." His heart hits about in his throat.

"Daniel . . . Daniel."

. . . From the fence. What is it . . . blood? Has a hand lifted and struck? Is there a prostrate body? All these are in her voice.

He kicks back his chair and belts down through the trees to the fence. Tarl is here, Homer on hip . . . these two, at least, alive.

"Look at that, look at that."

He looks at that, expecting nothing less than a monster striding down the lane with a child slung by a foot over its shoulder, his guts dripping from his mouth and a trail of blood. "Look at what?"

"At *that*."

But all he sees is Gavin ambling down the lane with Benjamin by the hand, not without purpose in his step but . . . not in a manner he'd call exactly pally but . . . at least moving in the same direction and at the same pace. No blood, no guts, no mud being thrown.

"Is that fair? He carried him from the bathroom by the wrists. The monster, the brute. What do you think of that?"

Something in this staging of father and son setting out together to meet the world . . . something of himself . . . That's me with my son. . . . He trembles and the tears break with funny gasps. Whispers, "He has to do it. He's trying to save him."

Tarl's back to him is silent, respectful at the emotion of another. A gratified back, to have wrenched from him the ultimate response at last. A surprised back, to have succeeded beyond her hopes while Homer on hip stares over her shoulder in respect also as he's been taught to do, but in amazement too at his face, at the strange man-noises. Dan returns up the garden between the grapes and the oranges, under the boughs of an old apple tree which quietly and respectfully breaks its buds, across the grass that is called a lawn and up on the veranda, to the privacy of the morning. And from here he sees Benjamin stalled. Against the background of singing from both sides of the road he is sitting in the hiding of the mailbox at his father's feet. Dan crosses the playground to the gate to help but Gavin waves him back. Later he rings the Head and hears that Benjamin is safely at school, settled happily with the others, talking and working with them.

From the kitchen with his hands on the grinder, soon after, he is aware of a form in the hall silhouetted against the garden. It is a man. It is Gavin. Slowly and heavily he walks down the hall with nothing to say, for once. "Hurray," Dan applauds, "you've done it." Gavin sits on the chair by the fridge and his eyes lift to Dan.

"You're a wonderful father," Dan gushes.

He sees the eyes upon him fill with economic tears in the first brief weeping he has witnessed in a Pracket. "He's very happy. I rang the Head," from Dan. "He's already forgotten it all. Tell me, how did you get him from the mailbox to the school?"

"I just talked him into it. Free of Tarl he could listen."

He senses another presence and this time it is Tarl. Looking back through the house he sees her sitting on the steps, her back to them. Up the hall, striding, "It's all over. Everything's wonderful. He's happy. What a courageous boy! Have some coffee, freshly brewed. Come and celebrate."

"No thanks."

"You must have some of this blackest coffee."

"No thanks. Ramona is in bed with the mumps." Her back to him.

Gavin follows up the hall carefully, guiltily, doubtfully and out in the dangerous sun on the veranda. Defeated by his own victory. The woman he's in love with stands at the bottom of the steps in her tight white matadors looking at him, her unsheathed eyes two knives of fury, her face as white as her pants. Bad enough her defeat indeed, but what about his usurping her own haven in her hour of crisis, ensconcing himself in the kitchen on her chair, receiving coffee and consolation by the wise old fridge?

Here they stand together, apart, the two of them, the parents of his flock of ibex, with lightning striking the morning. The only time he has seen them together since that balmy morning on the beach a year ago when she lay beside him and stroked his hair while he admired Angela's ankles. Ah how the loving part.

"May I have the car keys, please? I want to get fish for Ramona."

In silence, his eyes prophetically upon her, he draws the keys from his pocket and passes them to her. She turns and strides off beneath the trees, her small shoulders a huge reproach to the two men watching her. "This effort," Dan says, "to remain on both sides . . . it's been the most needle-fine exercise in discretion I've ever been privileged to do. My success is hardly notable."

"I've saved Ben but I've lost Tarl."

"Me too, I see."

In the evening as he shuffles along the veranda to work there's a large full moon peering through the lower branches of the gum tree, her face flushed red as though still inflamed from the fever of the morning. Existing, like them, in tumult. But late at night when he returns she has risen above the trees and has shrunk and paled somewhat. She has cooled considerably since he saw her hot though the boughs. Emerged from her tumult her face is white with the whiteness of a rebel cooled. She is white with the pallor of my own face peering from the darkness of eternity.

High in the black sky the moon reflects upon him, a mortal upon a veranda, as though nothing ever happened down there. Moon . . . how can you? How can you maintain a face so calm after watching humanity for eons? Blind and dead you are, as we would be, did we cease to vibrate to life. Blind and dead like you, moon.

FIVE

In those same fields tonight
frost will whiten the grass your feet trod
in pretended freedom. A hawk
will hang in the dusky sky, float
groundward, alight on a possum's dead guts.

—CHARLES DOYLE, *New Zealand*

❧ THE BELL also burst into tears to see Benjamin at school, but they could all have saved their tears. Not that he does not attend for a while. "It's a simply *wonderful* school," from no less than Tarl herself the very next Monday morning with the bell calling in triumph. "This is the only school for my children. Bennie was the hero the very first day. All the little children crowded round him to see his two rows of bottom teeth. 'Come and see Bennie's plenty teefs.'" She smiles behind a hand. "And the teachers, they're so kind. He's very fond of them. The whole atmosphere is so friendly and relaxed. And Mr. Richmond's patience, it's marvelous." You even hear that Benjamin returned to school after school on the first afternoon, until the buses went.

But as the days and weeks turn over into the beginning of summer, does Dan or does he not see Benjamin these days when Tarl climbs over the fence? Is that his shadow in a tree? His silhouette behind the grapevine? Does he hear a rustle in the grass behind the snowball tree? Yes, there are three of them again. What about school?

Yet, to be fair, could a boy like Benjamin go to school these days, these glorious days of inconsequent rain, the balm and the caressing of it, enlacing the soul of a boy? Do rabbits and ibex go to school, the beckoning birds in the sky? Yes, now that Dan focuses his mind upon it, here is Benjamin again cheerfully holidaying in the very home of the headmaster himself. Could he not have chosen somewhere else? "He's very contented at school," from Tarl, "but there's a little Maori boy there, Paddy Tu, he sits with Bennie. He annoys Bennie. He pushes his hand when he writes and . . . would you tell Mr. Richmond?"

"I'm not the liaison officer round here. You tell the Head yourself. As a matter of fact he comes down on bullies. That's the only time he lifts his hand. He hates persecution."

"Oh that Paddy Tu," from the senior mistress.

"I'll sit Paddy with someone else," from Benjamin's young teacher.

"Yes," from the father ibex, "if we could just have that little tiger moved away from Bennie." Proudly, "I'd like to be kept informed on the progress in this matter."

"Let him put up with it," from Angela, whose time is near. "Stand up for himself. Mary does. She doesn't know how lucky she is having Mr. Richmond for a Head."

"What they should do," from Tarl, "is pick out a group of the better children of the district and teach them on their own together, with Bennie. So he wouldn't be irritated."

"Irritated?" from Dan. "God damn it, surely I don't have to remind *you,* of all people, that life is one long irritation. You can't remove irritation from living and learning. Anyway, you go and suggest it to the Head—not me."

"What else could we expect?" from the Head. "But isn't that life all over, that he should be sitting with Paddy Tu? Well, well, we get all sorts."

Benjamin proceeds to take more regular holidays from the exhaustion of Doing Something. Getting on for nine now, this boy. Not that I don't understand. This requirement to put something into living as well as taking it out, and having to endure circumstances not designed exactly to his own particular liking must be incomprehensible to a fine young ibex. And he might have got away with it longer too, had he not chosen the headmaster's own residence to recuperate in. "Has that boy been here again?" Dan can hardly say no. The Head rings the father asking him to spare him the embarrassment before his staff of a truant doing his truanting in full view of the school, adding, "If he's well enough to spend hours at my home he's well enough to come to school. I'm letting you know I won't have it. You'll correct this situation, Gavin, or he'll be reported to the Child Welfare. Don't forget he is legally theirs."

"I'm astonished. I knew nothing about it, Ric. I've been led to believe he was attending regularly. I'll look into this at once."

With the result that, after a terrible row at home, for which Dan treats Tarl afterwards, Benjamin pays the school the honor of another day or two of his presence and the Head receives a remarkably sweet letter from his mother apologizing tremendously for embarrassing him and saying she had *no idea* she had been.

Until the whitebait begin running. Then Benjamin seriously feels the need of another holiday, a few more extra weeks, from the labor of putting back into living a fraction of what he takes out of it, but not at the schoolhouse this time. He stays home when Tarl comes over. Blondie, in a routine check, warns the parents, but Tarl, with years now of experience behind her in circumventing the law, of fighting it to the teeth in and out of cars and hideouts, in and out of court, is more than equal to a minor engagement like this.

"Bennie's not very well, Daniel. Every now and again he gets pains. Usually in the morning. When Gavin forces him to go to school he holds his stomach, poor little thing. No, it is his chest, I think. Yes, his chest. I had to call in the doctor, Daniel." Presses her cheeks. "He said Bennie would *have* to stay home for a while. He told me to let him know how Bennie was. But oh, it was lovely having a caller. Even a doctor. Simply no one comes to see me. By the way, Daniel, do you like whitebait?"

"He's always quite well," ponders Gavin, "when I come home at night. I'll examine the whole situation this weekend when I have a little time." The air of Supreme Commander of some D-Day landing.

Apparently he does. On the following Monday morning in Dan's kitchen, shudders, moans, head-holding. "We've had a dreadful weekend. We're *all ill*. You should have seen the children cowering. Ramona had an attack of asthma and I had a physiological and psychological collapse. I had to give Ramona steam in the middle of the night. And Bennie, he was too ill . . . he had such dreadful pains all over him . . . to go *anywhere* this morning." Dan sees him pink-cheeked out in the garden, smiling and swinging on a bough of the pepper tree, not in view of the school, of course.

"Has that boy been here again?"
Dan blows out smoke.
"I'll have another word with his father."
"God spare me another word with his father. It's I who collect in the end."
"It's your own work I'm trying to protect."

"Oh I'll get it done somehow."

"But," to Angela, "I dunno. I wonder what God's trying to prove?"

"I wonder," from the mother, "if you'd ask Mr. Richmond to keep Ramona inside during sports periods. She tries so hard to run and keep up with the others it brings on her asthma." Concentrated thought. "They could give her something artistic to do in school."

"I wonder," from the father, "if you'd ask Ric to see that Ramona is given extra coaching with sport. She's not as efficient at ball handling as the others."

"He," from Tarl, "doesn't see Ramona gasping at night. *He* doesn't have to nurse her at night. *He* sleeps in the other room. And make no mistake about that, Daniel: I don't see Gavin Pracket between the time I go to bed and the time I get up." Fire for a moment, then, "Poor little Ramona. She says, 'Mummie, why do I have to be sick and not the others?' I explain to her that she was our first baby, how we were desperately trying to do the right thing and were led astray by dreadful 'infant care.' I tell her all about that soul-soiling experience of feeding a baby by the clock and putting the little thing down to cry. She still cries, Ramona. She cries when she can't go to school." Puzzled, "She says she loves school."

"Ramona," from Gavin, "is beset with the desire to succeed. She never had the training in inner serenity the other three had. They are free of such spiritual distortion. Ramona knows about Ben's higher I.Q., realizes he is the favored child and feels she must establish herself, at least scholastically, well ahead of Benjamin. It would never do for Ben to catch up to her. Should that threaten to occur we would have to remove Ramona."

"They never," Dan tells Angela, "either of them, give any credit to the school for Ramona's happiness there."

"Oh . . . *them.* They'll learn."

Dan often beholds this lovely fairylike creature through the trees bobbing down the lane to school. Tarl has her beautifully turned out in school uniform, excellently sewn, meticulously laundered and shorter than the usual. You see these pretty slim legs so pathetic to him as a man, swinging from the hips. And her long black hair is brushed to the very last strand, neatly tied behind with ribbon—so refreshing from the "cut-it-off" fashion. Articulate and with charming manners. A credit indeed to the two of them. "Tarl," says Angela with open admiration, "can do anything when she likes. Well. She's terribly clever."

"Ric adores Ramona. She's all that he looks for in a child. She's got that sense of order that he has. She's everything. Reliable, respectful, charming, pretty, clever . . . he's proud of her as one of his pupils."

When Benjamin has finished having a "sort of pain" somewhere, a stroke of luck befalls him. He manages to contract the mumps. "He'd never have caught them," avers his mother, "had his mind been right. It's all this stress making the child ill." As for the mumps germ itself, it misses no opportunity to prove the contrary so that all the children get them. Even Gavin can't deny it. "The little chap," he confides to the Head, "really can't come to school. Tarl's right for once. But I'll send him along straight after." I believe Benjamin does visit the school straight after. Dan himself sees him there. He sees him sitting on the grass one afternoon of outside sport, when another school is visiting. Naturally he'd choose such an afternoon. He seems perfectly happy, too, but plays entirely to himself with the grass stalks and a few insects he lures as though he were the only one present. Indeed he has considerably more affinity with these insects who lead thoroughly successful lives without a trace of reason than with the boys about him. Their instincts coincide with Benjamin's. Tarl attends too, sitting on the grass among the other parents but with knees drawn up and her white face in a book, reading with concentration. Offended for the Head's sake, Dan does not speak to her. Bloody little so-and-so, why come at all?

"But he can't come next week," Tarl warns. "The Welfare man himself said I've got to take Bennie to the dentist. He doesn't like the look of all those rows of teeth on his bottom jaw."

"But don't milk teeth know how to drop out on their own? Or do teeth also have to be directed by the Welfare State what to do these days?"

"It's because of a trauma he experienced at a dentist once overseas. When he got out he fainted on the pavement. Now his teeth refuse to drop out and keep on growing more rows all the time."

"How many rows has he got now?"

Rueful pride, "Three."

"Good score."

There are times when Dan admires this boy. Honestly, to quote Angela, you've got to hand it to him. When he and the others have exhausted the mumps, not the mumps exhausted them, he succeeds in attracting the measles. True, the measles are throughout the school but what has that got to do with Benjamin's catching them? The measles germ could be shivering down in the antarctic from the point of view of contact, but Benjamin would still manage to catch them. *In extremis,* if it meant his freedom. They come as a gift to him direct from the hand of fate. No school, no Welfare, not even the law can make a ruling on fate. Fate herself could be a devotee of the Ever-lasting Now in her partiality for whim. "The children," from Tarl, "have never had illnesses before. It's the strain making them ill. They wouldn't have caught them had their minds been right, had they been closer to nature. Nature overlooks these weaknesses of bourgeoisdom with the sea rippling at your feet."

Did they think they'd got Benjamin to school?

❧ AND DID Dan think he had lost Tarl?

With Benjamin on the roll at school, reasons for getting over the fence prolificate like bacteria in favorable conditions. "Daniel . . . I wonder if I could borrow those marmot brushes of yours. I must get a portrait done. I always get this terrible sort of nervous urgent feeling to paint a picture when an exhibition looms up. Something seems to *make* me."

Dan frowns hard in concentration wondering where the brushes are. Finally he remembers, hauls them out from a drawer and hands them to her. After a week, however, she returns them. "I couldn't do it. You frowned when you gave me the brushes."

A few days later she comes tearing in, running, children tearing after. "I've had a wonderful idea. What about that old class-room? I could have that for a studio. Would you ask?

"That room is used for extra classes and films. And I think they house the four-and-a-half-year-olds there." So Tarl wants to go to school too now?

"Oh well . . . I just thought . . ."

"Daniel!"

Late one Sunday evening, head round door, "I wonder if . . . do you mind if I ask you something? Have you got any spare benzine? I'm due to paint Angela. Auntie is over there with the children but only till ten o'clock. I'm already late and the tank is empty."

"I don't keep spare benzine."

"I'm desperate. I've got to get there."

"Ric has my car at church. His is in dock."

"I'll have to ring the garage."

"Yes."

"D'you mind if I use your phone?"

"No."

"You wouldn't ring for me, would you?"

"No."

Exit. No ire. Door closed softly. She's gentle with a door as though closing a book, as though handling a young child.

Three pressed anxious sittings . . . "Daddy," sings Angela, "it was so lovely that when she showed it to me finished I wanted to run to the door and call out, Come and see, everybody." But Dan only sees it photographed in the local paper in an article on the exhibition: a eulogy which is at least a change, a variation in Benjamin's private reading material, his mother being praised for once. Neither does he have the chance to buy it with the "sold" ticket on it. He hears that some other man wants it. Somebody said it was Borg from the island who came over and booked it, penciled in his claim. But somebody else said it was Gavin. "She should have given it to you, Daddy. It's the only thing you've ever wanted from her, isn't it?"

"That comes of wanting at all."

Tarl, humbly, a little bewildered, "I do feel a little better. Sort of, y'know. I haven't cried since then."

"Mummie doesn't want this paper," says Ramona one evening. "She told me to bring it back. She wants some of that green school paper she saw here. She's making some pictures of the roadsides." Learning the art of the begging bowl.

"There's none of that left here, Ramona."

"She said could you go down to school and get some more."

"It's school paper, not mine." He sends over some more white paper. Ramona comes back through the darkness, "She doesn't like this. She said some of your own pale-green paper will do. She had her own paper but someone cut up a chocolate sponge on it. She's in a hurry because she has to go down to Angela's and get the children."

"Daniel . . . Daniel!"

Twilight on the seven-o'clock veranda. Where are they calling from? Running down the lane in the darkness to put the milk bottles out. He hears the children laughing and squealing.

"Daniel."

Like my voice from the darkness of eternity.

"Come over."

Who is he calling to come over? Not Tarl as she is but as he would wish. In the falsity of distance, at times she seems to be what he'd wish: soft-voiced, low-tongued, silent-footed, large-eyed, appealing in white tight matadors outlining her tender thighs. Here come their voices now and their need and themselves over the fence where the dahlias grow and the pulling thorned blackberry. Here on his veranda in the intimate twilight shot with fleeting moths. Here swarm his flock of ibex, clustering, whispering, eddying as he sits in his canvas chair. No man in his senses would turn on the light. Her face is pale in the shadows and her eyes are dark secrets with no stars in them. They lift to his, speaking the language of mystery, the language women use to make love. The desirous eye-talk foretelling only one thing, and that thing urgently soon. This is how love should be . . . spontaneous in the touching gloom with Tarl kneeling beside him, her thought and sensibility twining like seeking, hoping fingers. Seeking, thrilling fingers, so that he remembers that moment months ago when they lay side by side on the Hallibut grass. As lonely men do to the women of their desire, he reveals himself. His mind opens like a magnolia blossom, large and male, ejecting its scent to lure her. And he thinks she is listening to him, for once turned outward from herself. His vanity can believe nothing other.

Now she is speaking but it is some time before he knows what she's saying, her voice as soft as the moth on his beard. The Halliburts bathing for a wedding last Saturday. "All of them, Daniel. *All*. Steam billowing throughout the house and towels by the dozen on the line. All these bodies being washed for a wedding . . . *ugh*. Furtive whisperings, discussions on clothes, 'Where's the clothes brush?' Suggestive jokes in the hearing of the children." Up come the knees to her chin and her soft arms clasp them. "Twenty-four more days till the holidays. Gavin said if we could last twenty-four more days he'd see we all got away for good. I count every single day as it passes. I watch the clock and say, 'Soon it will be six and the day will be over. Only the night to get through somehow, then one more day has gone.' But Daniel . . ." change of voice. More businesslike, "What I really came for . . . could you tell us a place to go in the holidays? Somewhere just right for me, where there's No One In Charge at all?"

He gets up and turns on the outside light and resumes his chair again. Jim used up. Felix used up. "Remember Borg Hammerstein? Lives on a real island, sea all round, inner harbor on one side, ocean the other. 'And what did we see?'" he sings lightly, "'We saw the sea.'" Goodbye, Borg, my friend.

For some reason she doesn't answer. He picks up Tosti's "Goodbye," crooning to himself, "Goodbye forever. Goodbye forever." Homer runs in from the darkness repeating, "Goodbye forever," and smiles and laughs.

In time she uncoils herself lithely like an animal and drifts to the bottom of the steps. "I've often called you in the evening, when we go down for the milk but you haven't answered."

"I haven't heard you before."

He remains at the top of the steps, ponderous, overbig, with Tarl barefoot on the grass below. A familiar tableau. The outside light above him casts an unlikely halo upon his little flock of ibex revealing Tarl's upward-turned eyes. Is it pathos in them or is it supplication or is it frank longing? In mind he sees the setting of an island for six hot weeks with Tarl and Borg and the sea all round them and he hears the boom of the surf, rhythmic like pounding pulses. True, Tarl has a husband, but marital morality has little to do with pounding surf and pulses.

Tarl says, "I remember what you say sometimes and think about it."

"You shouldn't."

Pause, "N-no."

"Little, if any, of what I say is ever worth remembering."

"Isn't it?"

"I don't know that the role of mentor has been apportioned me by the Infinite."

"Oh, I see," in good faith.

They flock off over the night grass, dewed, making soft intimate animal noises under the night-sky trees, into the enshrouding darkness. But on the stage of his mind they remain brightly lit in the spotlight shed by feeling. Music when soft voices die vibrates in the memory but Tarl vibrates longer.

"Daniel?"

But there's no magic tonight. He looks up sourly from his table and doesn't turn over his work. Neither does he ask, "How are you?"

"I've just come to ask for something. We won't disturb you.

I wonder if I could borrow your gramophone and records. I want to give the little kiddies an evening of music." Four small faces about her.

"Oh."

"Poor little kiddies. They don't get much singing." They would at school, and Dessida is five. Tarl's jaws are moving quietly on chewing gum, which makes him murderous at any time.

"Don't they?"

"So you won't let us have them then?" Hovering like moths in his doorway, antennae quivering. Agog.

"There's plenty of that at school."

"All right then." No ire. "I just thought . . ." Casual chewing. "Never mind, come on, kiddies. We'll go down to Angela's and I'll paint Bennie." Other children would be in bed by now, not wandering wantonly in the night.

He hears first that Ramona, the darling of the Head's heart, is ill, measles on top of asthma. She is very much one of his children, this pink-and-white fairy, wings all but visible, among the hundreds of brown Maori children. For the first time, his jealousy and sense of vengeance out of sight under a gray sodden morning, he rings up Tarl and warns her he is coming over. "All right," dispirited, "how wonderful."

Running steps along the verandas, "Here he is."

"I hope you people have got the kettle on. I've got to be back at work at nine." To Tarl at the door, "How are they all?"

There's a place for pride in man, simply in being man. Gavin knows this. Even animals show pride of animal. But in Tarl's early-morning eyes, in her slept-in deshabille, he reads such a built-in cosmic anguish that he's overcome with his sense of protection. He wants to cover her exposure of herself, to deny it, by concealing what he feels. He tries like hell to be light-hearted but he is so darkened himself by the tomb of her eyes that all he can say is, "How are you?" as he enters.

But he gets an excellent cup of tea out of it. No saucer or anything like that, of course, but the cup is big and serviceable and actually has a handle.

"Mum, Mum," from Homer standing on the bench amid the food. "I'm hungry."

"I must get Homer his breakfast. He's hungry." Which turns out to be a plate of icing sugar which he eats with a spoon squatting on the "table" where he is. The other measled three are playing a civilized game, Snakes and Ladders, on the bed, led by Ramona. They don't look terribly ill. The bed must be Ramona's, it is pink and made and clean. Tarl's a lovely mother to Ramona, giving in to her on all civilized fronts when Ramona wishes it. And, by thunder! What's that?

"A masterpiece."

High on a barren wall, aloof and alone, an exquisite portrait of Angela.

"Are you going to buy it?" Collective excitement from the children. Even Homer pauses in his icing-sugar breakfast. Freedom . . . horizons are in their faces.

"It belongs to Borg, doesn't it?"

"Gavin."

"How much is it?"

"*He* won't pay me twenty guineas."

"Oh. It's Gavin's."

"You might as well take it. No one sees it here."

He recalls a remark of Gavin's on Angela, "She has such a genuine grasp on the world of relationships. And she knows reality when she sees it. She's a real girl . . . real." He says tentatively, "It might as well wait at my place till he does pay you." With radiance in him he reaches it down, the only manifestation of joy in the "hovel," beside the living children. "Tarl . . . you've got a future."

"Future? There's no such thing as the future. There's only the present. The Everlasting Now."

"That's right. I forgot."

"Gavin said he wished he could stroke Angela's flowing ankles."

"Daniel?"

He finds them on his veranda when he comes home from town after a session with the architect. "The man hasn't got a chance," he says. "I change the data each time I see him. He draws me a sketch and I turn up and supply a whole lot of different data, further ideas. I don't know how he can stand it. One of these days he'll . . ."

"Oh Daniel, we've had a dreadful time this morning. The Child Welfare man made me, forced me to take Bennie to the dentist again. As if four rows of bottom teeth had . . ."

"*Four?*"

" . . . anything to do with Bennie's access to his real nature. He . . ."

"Did you say *four?*"

Pride and alarm, "Four rows now."

157

"I *thought* his profile was changing."

"The dentist, oh Daniel, he was dreadful. He accused me of 'neglecting the boy's mouth' and all about how there were free dental nurses at the school. I tried to explain that they'd right themselves as soon as his mind was free but he groaned aloud. *Out loud!* And he said, 'So you're one of *those*.' Oh-h-h . . . we just slunk out."

"Oh dentists . . . they've got no vocabulary."

"Now I've got to go home and write a letter to him to explain how it came about."

"Don't dream of writing a letter. Don't think of putting the best of yourself on paper to any medical man. In fact never put anything on paper or say anything in the darkness that you wouldn't say to a person's face in the daylight. It only breeds embarrassment. Four rows of bottom teeth? The child doesn't need dentists; he needs congratulations."

She laughs like anything . . . for her. Silently. But it doesn't suit her. "Oh well, that's over. I feel much better."

⚜ THE SCHOOL is preparing for end-of-year break-up functions before the summer holidays. No one within hearing could mistake it. How Tarl explains away to herself, secretly, darkly and miserably this widespread outbreak of children's singing, music and dancing each morning from either side of the road, and each afternoon too, she does not reveal to him, much less inquire of anyone, "How's it going?" Even though sometimes when a teacher has released the singing groups of the "Hallelujah Chorus" from the classrooms nearby, bubbling in bright color and voice down the steps and over the grass like a summer wave breaking he'll find her on his veranda waiting to ask for something. And when a senior teacher has been taking the bulk chorus of one hundred and fifty with the wall doors wide open, he's noticed her underneath Old Man Totara near the house listening, the two little ones frisking and the star truant no doubt up a tree like an opossum watching from his eyrie his fellow creatures. Her reconciliation of all this with her concept of schooling must be at least arduous if she ever achieves it at all.

An afternoon for the junior school and an evening for the senior. Neither half attends the function of the other, an axiomatic, understood and respected rule based on numbers and levels of work. But although there is no Benjamin present as the juniors work on their program day by day, there is when the afternoon comes. For some reason his mother brings him herself, where he is entertained for two hours by the rest of the juniors, accepts with some cheerful right of his own a present from Father Christmas, manages to walk near enough to a teacher to collect a bag of lollies and is not too embarrassed, shy or wild to reach out a hand for an ice cream. Then, when the other children play outside with their new things, Benjamin joins the parents with his mother to stay himself further with tea and cakes. "Lucky Benjamin Pracket," a parent observes but well out of hearing of the Head. Not that they see the whole two hours, since Dessida cries at the sight of the clown and Tarl takes her home, followed with understanding by the others.

Comes the senior evening where juniors are not admitted. Excepting Benjamin of course. His mother walks right in with him. Indeed the entire Pracket flock is present from Gavin right down to Homer on his shoulders. For once apparently the two parents agree, not only to go to the same place together but to endure the ordeal of school, at all, right into the jaws of order and discipline, not to mention civilization, where they are entertained exuberantly for the evening and fed lavishly at supper. "Plainly," from another parent, "all these weeks of work are for the benefit of the Pracket family who make no contribution themselves. After all, I ask you, why not skim the cream from the school? Why not luxuriate in the efforts of the children? It costs them nothing. Why don't we all go Pracket? Wonderful philosophy."

"The take-take boy," someone whispers.

The Head turns belligerently, "I must remind you that you're criticizing one of my families. I resent your derogatory manner. I won't have it. We consider them an excellent family with a great potential. Adjustment takes time. They make their contribution by their appreciative presence."

"Daniel . . ."

He is flat on his back on his bed in the green room deep in the heart of the house, having talked clean through the night with the guest speaker of the night before until the birds tuned up in the morning. But they find him all right. In creeps Tarl with her young complete, and they cluster round his bed. Neither has the fantail any respect for a man's privacy. He twirls in too when he is moved to. So do flies come in during summer, and mosquitoes. He pulls the cover over him. "How are you?"

Tarl praises sincerely and lavishly the evening before until, "But what I really came for . . . I hope you don't mind my always asking you for something. That was the trouble with our landladies . . . the borrowing. I wonder if I could borrow three suitcases? We're going to the island in three days. Only three more days, oh-h-h . . ." Eyes closed, hands to cheeks. "Borg has a cottage for us. We leave by the ferry on Saturday morning. We're never coming back to Hallibut's."

Dan thinks with rapidity. "I've lent one suitcase to Angela to take to the nursing home to have the baby." True. "I lent her another for the clothes for the new baby." Also true, accidentally. "Another went to Mary when she goes to stay with a friend while her mother is away." Half true. "And the last is for Reuben when he comes to me." Not true but brilliant. "Bruce is staying with his father."

"Oh. Well, could I leave a couple of our own suitcases here? Stuff we don't want at the moment. Rubbish. People shouldn't have possessions."

He quotes, " 'No, he replied, with cool unruffled compulsion.' "

"All right then."

But she asks no permission to bring in from the veranda a parcel of paintings she has done over the past months with Angela supervising the children—"Mind, you, Daddy, I'd rather have had the baby first—" and puts them in the blue room where Dan finds them on the dressing table later.

"And another thing, Daddy, it's time I gave her a dress. I'm thoroughly sick of those pants. They're not a bit motherly. Every single solitary time she comes here she's got on those pants. My dresses are wasted anyway hanging there in the wardrobe between babies. I only wear decent dresses a few months a year. Gee I'm sick of smocks. This is the very very *last time* I'm going to have a baby."

"Six whole Pracketless weeks," Dan sighs to the Head getting over the year in the kitchen, like a writer getting over a book. "For God's sake let's get drunk."

The Head sinks on the chair by the fridge, covers his eyes with a hand and does not reply.

"They're not coming back to Hallibut's, y'know."

"Now don't you be too sure about that, my boy. Gavin remains here. He told me he's got two concurrent jobs in town for the holidays, one by day and one by night. He means to save up enough with the family away to put a deposit on a home. Amazing . . . the way he remains friendly. After all the clashes we've had over the children. I've never seen a flash of anger in him all this term. He doesn't cultivate quarrels. He goes on treating me as a friend."

"What home is he going to put a deposit on?"

"D'you want to know?"

"Yes."

"Shall I tell you?"

"Go on." This doesn't sound too good.

"That green house round the corner by the river. Mrs. Suldoon's."

"They're going to be here forever?"

"I prefer to wait and see."

"God . . . where's the plonk?"

Stretched out with his paper on the veranda on a paradise of a Saturday morning. At this very moment the ferry with his little flock of ibex on board is turning its nose to the water and Tarl is gasping in the seductive breeze, seeing sensuously the outline of the island ahead with its skyline of dark pine forests where waits all that is "just right" for her: children, surf, nature, lover, no husband, No One In Charge, nothing to do and her heart's desire . . . freedom. Already she's forgotten him in the breeze from Shangri-La.

SIX

. . . It is myself I seek,
and something permanent from the casual week.

— Louis Johnson

⚜ A MAN WANTS to respect the imagery in his mind, this luminous dynamic source of action, this embryo of vision which some call the soul. Imagery ignites emotion which in turn inspires action, and it is action that reaches others. And what else has life but this reaching to others? The man who nurtures his imagery is himself nurtured, and to the extent that he respects it is he respected.

In youth a man's imagery is hidden within the walls of his personality and his face does not reveal it. Few perceive what he really is until these walls are cleft; until some external blast or an internal passion thins them, no one meets his soul face to face and his imagery remains intact.

The imaginative power of some men however is so strong that passion combusts earlier and assaults the walls containing it. At which his recesses no longer have a reliable covering, a division between himself and others. Through the flimsy structure his imagery escapes; he merges more easily with others, his mind enters their minds living in liaison with them so that a man actually becomes other people. Before life has got far on its way these fusions are habit rather than accident, enriching sympathy. But to the extent that he lives another's identity is his own diluted, and his imagery is no longer his own. Lucky the man with imagery so dull that at least it remains his own.

That any inquisitive acquaintance can now see through these

thinning divisions between one man's mind and another's, can perceive what he intimately is, is but a minor payment for powerful imagery. The major cost is his absence of choice in the matter, his inability to save himself from living the pain of others. What chance has the man with little more than tissue paper between himself and others to remain himself?

Moreover, where is the artist who does not register his emotions physically? He records those of others also. Lucky the man with pale imagination, his emotions safely sealed, for he is himself only. Blessed is that man.

But Dan is not that man. He's not any particular man half the time. How can you be a particular man when you become everyone you meet? See with their eyes, hear with their ears and feel the things that they do? There's nothing to be done about it. But it is no fun, and the less you are others the better. But how can he explain this to the variety of everyones who come up the steps to his door? He exists in multiple tumult.

To Doctor Bob, "I'm pathologically compassionate, Bob. It's not a nice thing. It can't even be called a respectable obsession. It's this fatal inescapable identification of the artist with others. He becomes, he *is*, these people. All right. These others are in pain. Therefore he's in pain. And to alleviate his own pain he must first alleviate that of these others. You find a man like me living the lives of others . . . a great sponge mopping up everything near him. I live their lives not *as though* they were my own, but *because* they are my own. Very very nice for art, of course. But for me as a man . . . a man? Who, me? I'm not a man, Bob. I am nobody. I am everybody. I'm not I: I'm that fantail flirting out there. I'm Angela and Rod and the babies. I'm not I: I'm the Head, the staff and all the schoolchildren. I'm the Child Welfare officer. I'm the magistrate himself. I'm everyone I hear about and all who arrive at my door. Above all, at the moment, I'm every Pracket: Gavin, Tarl, Ramona, Benjamin, Dessida and Homer. Which is the reason I'm always on everyone's side, because each side is my own. It's why I die of conflict.

" 'A kind, most compassionate man,' you hear them say, that Daniel Francis.' Forget it. In my own right as a man I don't exist. With no choice in the matter I'm a multiple soul. Compassion? No, I have none. My own comfort is my concern."

Nevertheless, imagery can take quite a battering and come out alive. It survives any number of arrivals at his door. On the other hand, like anything else alive, imagery can take a certain amount and no more. At the moment he thinks his imagery

166

still breathes, if only just, and that what appears to be death is sleep. Care now and his creatures will wake again during the six weeks' peace from next door.

Yet he asks Gavin over to share the meal at the end of Christmas day. Angela and the new baby are staying here fresh from the nursing home. Gavin is obviously tired but does not once say so. He's a porter at the hospital by day and a cleaner in town by night. "You," says Dan, "a Master of Science. Why the devil couldn't you get something in your line?"

"I did apply to the lab but it was too late. But I'd rather be doing this. It doesn't hurt a man to work with his hands." And it doesn't hurt a man to work for his family. Humility is grandeur with this motive. Prackets just don't see humiliation as the rest of them do. Gavin is proud of the nature of his occupation, carting sick humanity about the wards by day and cleaning up after the well by night. Dan is beginning to pick up from them the synonymity of humility and the absence of humiliation; the absence of pride, jealousy and ambition to which the rest of them are enslaved. How much lesser a soul is his than theirs. At least he has learned this minor point. He renews his efforts to release himself from the chains of righteousness and to cut his way out from smugness. Not that he wants to be like them . . . but he'd like to be as free as they are from the limitations of society. Were it not for the disciplines of his work he feels he could shame the animals.

Ric brings over presents before departing with his family to the Lakes. "And how's the family, Gavin?"

"All very well and happy, Ric. Doing nothing. That's what they like. I went over on the ferry last Friday. From their cottage in the pines the inner harbor is only one minute and the ocean four minutes. Our kiddies play with island kiddies, eleven or twelve altogether." To Dan, "Both Borg and Tarl sent you their love and want you to come and see them."

"Thank you very much."

"There's nothing too complicated about the ferry."

"No. But the nature of my work requires me to forfeit social pleasures."

"They're living pretty cheaply over there. I've got a chance to earn enough in six weeks for a deposit on Suldoon's house round the corner. That's the house she wants, or says she wants. She likes the way it looks along the estuary to the sea." He doesn't add that it is also near the school and in reach of Dan. "She's been saying lately that she wants to settle down at last in one spot for the sake of the kiddies. They can't always find their things. They get left in suitcases all over the country in other people's houses." His eyes dwell on the silver on the table and the crystal. "It's just that I'm always so poor, whatever I earn."

"You're a very rich man, Gavin. You've got something to fight your guts out for, which is more than I have. The integration of your family, the love of your children and a woman you're madly in love with. Also you've got the means with which to fight: health, education and the right age when a man's powers are brightest and when achievement of desires is life or death. What more could Christmas day put on the plate of a man?"

"Now, now, your words run away with you, Dan."

Angela calls from the bedroom after dinner when they are in the music room over coffee, "How is Tarl, Gavin?"

"Tarl cut me to the quick, Angela. When I went over on Friday she said children don't need the presence of a father, that their only need is the female parent, as it is with animals."

Rod, who has brought Angela, retires to the library to read the book Dan gave him on Africa. Angela says, "I still say she loves you, Gavin."

"You wouldn't if you saw us on the island on Friday. She barely spoke to me at all."

"What about the children? How did they receive you?" Angela can say anything.

"They didn't seem to mind me there."

Neither asks after Benjamin and neither after Borg. As Gavin rises to go back over the fence for an hour's sleep before returning to his charring in town Dan says, "You are very tired."

"Work never hurt a man."

To Angela when he has gone, "So they'll be back again."

"Nothing surer. It's you she's still after. Before she went she hinted to me that she meant to stay near you forever."

"Bloody rot. Sorry."

Rod says, "We all have the right to self-preservation, Dan. Even that book on Africa is full of it. You've got to protect yourself from people like that. You've got to be ruthless, Dan. I am—now, I reject this sort of thing when it comes to me. Now you remember what I'm saying, Dan—be ruthless. That's my Christmas present."

"Pass me the baby, darling," from Angela.

Dan is alone again when soft steps come to his veranda, which turn out to be those of Borg. He brings the island with him. In his water-clear eyes you can all see the shells and fish-lets on the bottom, you smell the salt of the sea and the resin of the forest. He is all ocean gales and fishing nets. Dan is hit by the image of Tarl in mind, in white shorts on her back on the sand, those wonderful eyes of hers full of the sky. He thinks of bumping surf and pulses. . . .

Borg is not tall. He's in khaki shorts and his legs are good. His voice has the same extraordinary humility of the Prackets. You get this unwavering look. These children of nature are good with eyes, the whole lot of them, as though they had noth-ing to hide whatever and wouldn't conceal it if they had. Forty-odd.

"You take my chair at the table for a change. I'll take the armchair."

"I'd be proud to wear your mantle."

"Get it over. Not that I need to be told."

"Yes. It's Tarl."

There's many a distinction between men and animals. Attack an animal lair and the female will defend it. Attack a human home and the male will defend it . . . or should. After hours of the most amazing revelations from Borg that Dan has ever heard, read or written of . . . after several bottles of lager over his most unlikely moral outlook, Dan drives him down to the shore to pick up his little boat. And as he drives he falls back heavily on a teacher's ethic, to commit oneself on the side of children. And upon the solid old Christian ethic of preserving a home. Dan attacks the Pracket home, the only simple way he knows of saving it.

"But they have wonderful children," Borg replies. "As for Tarl—no woman could replace her."

This same evening on the phone, "I'm going up north to-morrow, Ange. I'm not waiting till Monday. A good thing I got the car greased this morning. Wonder what that camp stove is like. What I feel like is a run along the New Zealand roads. You know the close personal interest I've got in the roads of this country. My income tax has largely financed them. I feel quite proud in places. Especially of the expensive new bridges. I always stop at the bulldozers. Get out and chat with the men on the earth-moving machines. These . . ."

"Why tomorrow and not Monday? I know you. You're up-set."

"No I'm not."

"As long as you don't leave New Zealand."

"I'm not likely to leave a country when I've practically financed the place."

"Call in here on your way and I'll have some food prepared for you. I'll make you an apple shortcake."

In a fortnight he is back. He returns to work in the library and calls his creatures to him.

"I saw the outside light on."

"Oh, Gavin, it's you."

"It's always such an invitation."

"Come in."

"You're busy?"

"No. How are you?" He turns over his work and wipes sweat from his hairline.

"I shouldn't disturb you."

"Between jobs? I'll make you some coffee."

Later in the kitchen, "Borg has been good to my family. I ran into him on the jetty. I think he's trying to aid an adjustment between Tarl and me. One of the things he told me was that when Tarl returned a book he had lent her she said, 'There's hope for me yet.' But Tarl would be mad with fury if she knew we had discussed her."

"You two men and your paragraphs . . ."

When Gavin has gone Dan takes to his bed for another fortnight. He doesn't let Angela know, upsetting a girl with a baby at the breast. But Rod walks in one day. "I thought you said you were never going back up north again, Dan."

"I had to."

"You ought to get that beard off, Dan. You could sweep a cowbail with it."

"How's Angela?"

"Good, thanks. She cries a bit sometimes. She always cries with a new baby. Because her mother won't see it."

"That's silly. Her mother does see them. The mind doesn't die after death. It lives on in any heart that loved it. She's silly to talk like that . . . to cry. Oh well . . ." He takes the plate Rod gives him. "How's the hay?"

"We were still bailing at nine o'clock last night. Rain coming."

"When the hay lets up I want you to do something for me. I want you to get hold of a bulldozer and carve out the site for my house on the land. The plan is ready. Oh well, work again. The only solution to my . . . my difficulty."

"You shouldn't have gone up north, Dan. You should have gone south."

"Ay? Oh no."

"You got ill the last time you went up north."

"Oh . . ."

"Was her grave all right?" The way youth comes out with things.

"Yes. Now . . . back to work."

"That goes for me too."

"That land job . . . before the rain comes . . . ay?"

There's no other human reaction Dan knows of like that of an artist to interruption, the sudden transition from the unreal world to the real. Or, as it appears to him, from his real world to the unreal. Not only the awakening but the realization that for the time of writing at least he's had life inside out. He doubts if he ever recovers from each separate ordeal, if the mark it makes is ever fully erased from the susceptible mechanism.

Composition must ever remain a matter of seclusion and locked doors to a writer, and no inviting outside light. How else can he cultivate and maintain the conditions necessary to his creatures? The creating mind in its fluid state needs the oblivion of the womb and the temperature of it also; a molten state in which imagery is maneuverable. Interweaving, interflowing, intermerging, interchanging in the complex processes of fusion. And this is where the crisis is; this moment when he calls on all his angels and devils for exact equilibrium. Here is the crisis . . . this breathlessness in the mind before the idea flashed whole. . . .

"This outside light of yours, Dan, beckoning through the trees. You've no idea what it looks like from my side of the fence. A focus of comfort."

"Who's that?"

"I can see you're working."

"Who's that?"

"I can see I'm . . ."

"Is that Gavin?"

". . . disturbing you."

"Yes, it's Gavin. Come in. Oh yes, sit down. Aa . . . aa . . . how are you?"

"I've had a note from Tarl."

"Tarl . . . who's that? Oh yes, your wife. That's right."

"Tarl has begun divorce proceedings in town." He passes

Dan a small folded square of cheap paper. "I found this in the mailbox just now. Read it."

"No."

The hand with the note remains outstretched.

"I don't need to read it. I could write it out word for word."

"But I've just earned the deposit for Suldoon's house. The loans came through yesterday from the State Advances. The first time in our married life that I've been in the position to give her a home. That's what she said she wanted . . . a home." Withdraws the outstretched hand. "I can't take any more court. I can't face it."

"No."

"The foolish girl. The poor little foolish girl. She doesn't really mean this. I know these recurring outbursts with no reason guiding her whatever. She can't divorce me. She can't even get a separation."

"Why not?"

"Both have to sign a separation."

"She could get a divorce."

"No. A divorce is based on a charge. That charge must be proved. She has no charge against me."

"Didn't she make a statement to the police once?"

"I've never struck her."

Dan turns over his work. His hairline is wet and he wipes it. Then reaches for his smokes. And says nothing.

"All this coming up right now with college starting on Tuesday. Six A Physics. I can't face it. I can't believe it. It's another of her wild statements. The thing is . . . how to keep her out of court?"

"I'll make you some coffee. You're tired."

"I shouldn't disturb you."

"Coffee."

"It's the outside light."

Dan grasps the table and levers himself upon his feet and tries to get one foot to operate after the other, holding the table as he passes Gavin.

"What's the matter?" rising.

"Nothing. I often walk like this."

"You're ill."

"I'm not. I get stiff sitting. My feet hanging down fourteen hours at a stretch, they swell. An occupational disease."

"You are."

"I'm not. I'll loosen up in a minute."

The old worn track of the weary and desperate through the

house to the kitchen. While he is brewing, Gavin asks, "How did you enjoy your holiday?"

"Holiday? Oh." He lies, "I've been down on the land this last fortnight knocking it into shape. Before the bulldozer. I had a ring from my son-in-law, Rod. He was going to bring the bulldozer this week but he says now that we'd better wait till the rain has come. The ground's too hard to work with. It's like concrete. Hence all this stiffness. We sedentary jokers, y'know. Show us a shovel and we fall to pieces."

"Thank you," for the brew and puts it down untasted on the fridge.

Gavin is quite slim these days with the interesting look of a Romeo rampant. If ever a man were obsessed, body, mind and soul, with a woman, here is that man. He sits with elaborate care, knees apart, elbows on them, hands hanging between them in a pose of glistening hell that would put to shame the sculpture of the past. The eyes lifting to Dan, portals of betrayal, are the eyes of a man peering from a cavern of racks. A soul staring out through two barred windows from authentic hell itself. He speaks in this soft smoldering voice, "I might lose my job over this. All the time I take off over my family. I know why she wrote this note. Borg has told her that he repeated to me what she said, 'There's hope for me yet.' Borg said she was so furious she wouldn't speak to him. I can imagine Tarl," with considerable pride, "white hot with fury. Rage. And now here are divorce proceedings in the blundering hands of her lawyer."

"Him? He couldn't divorce a couple of fantails, let alone a couple of Prackets."

The smile, white teeth and the silver at the back. A sweet smile like Dessida's.

Much later, rising to go, "By the way, the kiddies have decided," not, We have decided, "to go in the boat each day with the islanders' kiddies to the school at the Bay. Ben says he's more likely to be paced there than with the Maori kiddies here." Along the hall, "So will you break the news to Ric about the kiddies not coming back?" So courteously spoken, so crass a rudeness. "I won't have time to see him before school reopens." So public à wound for Ric.

"No," as courteously replied. "You make your own explanation to the Head's face."

No answer as he retreats in the darkness and a new soft rain, and Dan calls after him, "I didn't mean to hurt you, Gavin."

"No one can hurt me any more."

He re-emerges from the enclosing rain, dripping, a specter

173

haunting the night. A terrible spectacle of a man who has lost his love, and hope with it. The nadir of agony. "I'll cut my cleaning in town tonight. I'll go to the island and see her. I don't know how. I've missed the ferry. I must keep her out of court. I'll do anything at all to keep her out of court. It's not the talk of divorce . . . she can't do that. It's the court I can't face again. I'll even give her my savings for the home. She can go for a long holiday . . . the six months she's always calling for."

Dan is about to say that the whole thing seems an inflated price to pay for one small boy's not going to school, but the specter has already dissolved in the now ponderously falling rain, in the broken-hearted darkness—not to his cleaning up in town as usual but to his cleaning up on the island. Alas . . . prisoned hope. As if any large staff of servants, much less Gavin on his own, could ever hope to clean up after Tarl.

But the rain, like nature, soon forgets and gathers momentum and volume on the roof, pondering on something else, possibly on how to ruin Rod's hay or how to hold up the bulldozing on the land, when Dan sits down to his paper again. There he finds the large area of the mind his creatures inhabited no longer inhabited. It's a citadel sacked by the enemy. Only dead bodies lying about in pools of shiny blood. Staring at the printed page, the printed words mean nothing to him. Just random remarks somebody made. Some kind of ancient Chinese language or Egyptian hieroglyphic. He lays the page in the box with the others at the corner of the table, picks up the entire neat stack grown over a couple of years, the poor corpse, and, following Gavin's footsteps through the rain beneath the trees, he buries it in the compost. The book that it almost became, just one more casualty from the collision with reality, and the best of him rots away with it.

SEVEN

. . . the casual week
that filters away relentlessly as sand
in the lady's hour-glass . . .

—LOUIS JOHNSON

⚜ COME ALL CHILDREN, call the bells the length and breadth of the land. Come and receive education. Education to understand, to sort out the good from the evil, the truth from propaganda, and to preserve the heritage of the past. In order that the land you love may not deteriorate into desert and rock, the people following suit as, when one generation failed to teach the next, befell other cultures. Come ye wild ones, call the bells, and learn the true freedom of the spirit, to be found only within the framework of discipline and order. When is enslavement more bitter than under the rule of whim? Freedom is not a change of address; boredom can follow anywhere. "I am bored," sigh the free, the last *cri de coeur* of the prisoned.

It is autumn by the feel of it, if not by the look of it. The cathedral stillness abroad, the absence of ambitious growth and of pelting exciting events. There's nothing new to see in the morning as there always is in spring. The same blooms as yesterday, exactly the same number, all thinking the same thoughts as yesterday. Neither is there anything to be planted in a hurry down in the vegetable garden as there is in spring; only stalks left to dry away like last year's passions. A state of mind in which Dan is comfortably and legitimately on all sides in anything.

The morning is wet from last night's rain. Word has got round of the book in the compost and no bird speaks, neither is there sound from the trees. Anyway, where is Tui* these days with his tongue and his bird exhibitionism? You'd think these berries on the umbrella tree would be sure to bring him back, not to mention the grapes down there. Has he too fallen backwards into the mood of the landscape, immobilized and mute? Even the voices of the children arriving for the first day of school are wonderingly subdued. Over the dahlias and beneath the gum tree he sees a few of them, little boys peeling the leaves from the hedge cuttings left last Saturday, leaving a tuft of green at the tip and waving them about. Always doing something, these children, brown and white, in continuous creativity. That disputed word "doing."

Another of these critical Monday mornings with the local bell ringing in and out of the trees and down the road to the corner. What does it hope to achieve? To the wild ones it is not a call to free the laboring spirit but a toll for the death of the spirit; not a peal to allure but a knell to be gone. At this very moment maybe Tarl is packing the sleeping bags with a few of the children's possessions and Ramona weeping on hand. Shangri-La suffers without her weeping, and the bells calling all round.

She has not returned next door. No one will come flocking silent, barefoot beneath the expectant trees, dark eyes peeping from the veranda in smiling advance guard. True, that is Gavin hurrying down the lane to college . . . he must still occupy the tall quiet rooms echoing with their voices but what of the rest of his family? Has Blondie hunted them down to the island, lassoed young Benjamin and thrown him in some alien classroom? Will these Monday mornings of school reopening never be clear of tension? Has Benjamin actually gone to school at the Bay in the boat with island children? But nothing of this Dan mentions to the Head to spoil his entranced morning, to dilute the glamour of his new shirt and tie bought for opening day.

"Daniel—?"

Swirls in on one of these do-or-die, hit-or-miss crests of emotion, blind to any reaction. Her white hollow-cheeked face is browned and filled out from lashes of island "just-rightness." And she actually wears a dress. What is so familiar about this dress? Print with flowers on it. He's got a feeling he's seen it before. There's a grandeur about her, possibly from the six

---

* *the emblem bird of New Zealand*

island weeks with Borg, not to say with Gavin's savings in her pocket, and an aura of temporary victory. An authority in place of the humbleness. Neither does she gasp and hold her head though she does resume center stage.

"Daniel, I want you to drive us all down to the Lakes now. Right *now*. And set us up there. You said once you knew the Lakes. You can spare a couple of days, can't you?" With Tarl, to want is to do, expecting her desires to materialize with tropical effusion.

Dan actually stands. "How pleasant to see you again, Tarl. How are you?"

"I thought you might have just happened to be going down there."

Neither does she crash spread-eagled on the bed but for a short time at least before huddling on the step, sits on the chair . . . miracle . . . one leg folded over the other leg in an orderly manner that would please the Head and the magistrate. Just like a woman.

"I'll make you some coffee. We'll have to have it on the veranda. The berries on the umbrella tree, they draw the birds. And you know what birds do eating. Full birds. The table under the tree, it's . . . un-sit-at-able. Really, birds can be indecent."

"Will you take us or not?"

"Tell me, how are you keeping? You do look well. Aren't the children brown! Was it you who left that twig of purple leaves here during the holidays? I found it on the veranda when I came back. It . . ."

"You're not, then?"

"I must scrub that table. I don't know what Angela would . . . and the chairs too. Sickening, the habits of birds."

"So you won't?"

"As for the *Lakes* . . ." He sits and rolls a smoke.

In the kitchen, "We came to an agreement for once which *is* progress. He flew over to see me last night in all that rain." Gratified, "He chartered a whole plane for himself. And we had one of our three-hour barrages. But no more of that anger and saying I'm cruel. I'm *not* cruel. He has agreed—*agreed!*" staring at the floor profoundly, "for me to go away. I'm not used to being *allowed* to go away. Now that I've got my freedom and money I don't know what to do with it." Thoughtfully, "I don't know if I'll even be going now. I don't know what I want to do. That's what I love . . . moment by moment. The Nothing. The magnificent unfolding of the Now."

Later still on the veranda, "How are you keeping, Daniel?"

Astounded silence.

"You look tired. Gavin said you were not very well. You've lost weight."

"You've put it on."

"I missed you very much. I did come over in the ferry to see you one day but you were 'not here.'" Dan bursts out laughing. "And I rang once, twice, but no answer."

She even mentions, for the first time he has known her, his work. Even in appreciation; but it turns out that some overseas tourists on the island had pointed it out to her. Doleful but miraculous . . . all of it.

At the bottom of the steps with Homer on hip, towards lunch time when the Head comes this way, "What a lovely year you'll have without us next door." Adds with rue, "Peace." Then with swift ominous change looking up at him, "I wonder if I'll be going. I feel better already." Dessida coiling round the veranda post like a saucy little snake, "Mummie, don't go. I want to stay here."

"Now steady. Don't take my name in vain," from Dan.

They cluster off, not furtively beneath the trees to the fence to avoid the Head but down the playground through the children, blatantly displaying Benjamin before the school. No . . . merely absent-mindedly, he thinks. As he watches them wistfully he confirms that she's put on weight. The wispy romantic look is in jeopardy. "Come on, Bennie," her victory call.

At five when the Head passes through, "You won't believe this, Ric. Y'know what she wanted? To drive them . . ." and so on. "Me . . . mind you. Who practically am the school. Can you believe it?"

"She must be mad." Then reflects a moment, "Was that boy in my home again?"

"Cheerfully."

He writes in his memorandum notebook.

Dan breaks out, "She'll lose that boy yet. She'll go so far she'll hang herself and him."

"He's still on my roll till I hear to the contrary."

But Dan cannot bring himself to carry out Gavin's instructions of the night before to "break the news" to the Head, as he puts it, of the children going in the boat to the Bay school. By evening he can no longer deceive him and out comes the hurtful thing.

"She's doing a lot of harm to the school. Really, if I knew, if you rang me and told me she was here in my house again during school hours I'd . . ." accelerating, "I'd have the chance to come up and order her out of the house. Off the grounds altogether."

"I've just about got to that stage myself."

With his door open upon the evening and the outside light pointing its rays here and there among the trees looking for his little flock of ibex, its light-fingers pulling aside the foliage peering into the dell beneath the grapes and under the chestnut tree . . . are they here? Or here? Maybe they're up the camphor tree . . . an unsteady conclusion comes to him. Tarl is improving, by Western standards, that is. Later when he returns to the house for supper another thought arrives: even after six weeks with Borg on the island with everything "just right" for her . . . reading, children, surf, lover, pulses, freedom and all, six weeks of unadulterated Shangri-La, unpolluted Now . . . she still returned to his place. At which rears again a long-buried thought: is *he* her Shangri-La? A third conclusion does not arrive until he has slept on the former two and opens his eyes upon it: he must free himself. With Tarl upon him he cannot work and without work he is doomed. Only two eventualities can save him . . . either she goes away under her own power or he sends her away himself.

Yet, over toast and tea, how can a man drive away a soft-footed, large-eyed, trusting, appealing pathetic animal from its one water hole? With its young dependent upon it? Only the vicious hunter does that. Yet if he does not, he himself is destroyed. Indeed, in destroying him, Tarl destroys herself. Whether he rejects her or not she loses. The only way out is the hope that in her slight "improvement" she may recover her own source of water in time. At the moment he is on his own side.

Until he sees the Head upset the following Monday morning, when he swings to the Head's side. "I can't understand it," from Ric. "No boy, no word from two allegedly intelligent parents. Gavin is supposed to be an educated man. It's beyond believing."

"He can't face you again, Ric, that's why. It's all too futile, trying to reconstruct goodwill. She puts her knife through it all at once."

"The child is still my responsibility. So is Ramona. Where are they now, do you know?"

"No. They might be at the Lakes. They might be still on the island."

"All this goodwill in the school for the boy, and the desire to help him. They've . . ."

"They teach everyone to hate him. Right down to the dentist. I hate the kid myself. The only child I've ever hated in my life. I didn't know the thing was possible. I hate all her children, including her. I . . ."

"By God, Gavin's weak."

"I don't agree. Even a strong man could be weak with a woman like her. If we can use the term 'woman.' I'm as weak as water myself. Or have been. She's not a woman as I know women, tender, concerned women. She has not one thought in her head for anyone else. She doesn't mean to be a woman. She tries, actually tries to be an animal. But she's a poor advertisement for them. I don't know why she doesn't make off to the fields with the sheep and cattle instead of begging civilization. If she wants company why not eat grass with them, pick up a few virtues from them, instead of hounding me. After all, what can I, a human, give her? She favors the doctrine of 'no-mind.' Very nice, very nice, jolly bloody nice. But I like minds myself."

"I repeat: he's *weak*."

"If she turned up now with her monster kid it'd be I . . . *I!* who'd do the ordering out. She's no longer a parent of ours. Her children are no longer our children. Let her set her tentacles upon some other school. I'm sick of the whole bloody lot of them." This rage she so often leaves in her wake and manages to escape herself.

"This whole Pracket business disgusts me." He sets off down the path, the enchantment of going to school in the morning, ever a joyful occasion, confronted by disillusion. Then he turns, "But here we are criticizing somebody. We've got to stop it."

Dan follows down the steps, "We mustn't let this thing upset us. If for no other reason that that she'd love it. She'd read it as a score to herself."

"No, no you're right. I've risen above much worse than this." He looks a moment at the dahlias which his wife tends. His voice comes down and softens and the keys in his pockets are silent. "But you're wrong in saying she's no longer a parent of ours. As long as Ramona and the boy remain enrolled here the Prackets remain our family." It was that look at the dahlias and the thought of his wife and the thought of his own young family. The concept of "family" as such, which he loves. A hallowed word to a teacher.

Dan gives away Tarl's two earlier pictures that she brought in from the garden and sold him, to Doctor Bob. "If she wants them back as she said she did I'll send her along to your place." Goodbye, Doctor Bob. Bad luck. He liked him. But he does look funny walking off through the trees with those two framed paintings slung over his shoulder like carrying off his Pracket troubles. Like Tarl herself, her pictures come and go in strange ways. He watches him from the veranda. If only he could cart off his dead imagery too . . . decomposing, dehydrating. Never mind. Now whom among the people who interrupt him would he prefer to get rid of? Here's a potential in Tarl not to be overlooked.

"I've come to say goodbye."

"Tarl."

"I saw the light on."

"I thought you'd gone."

"I hope you don't mind."

"I thought you had well gone. The end of the Pracket story." In the music room in the evening before seven he has put down his paper and trundled up the hall to the door. Good heavens, her face is made up. A woman from the night. What basically is a woman's function but to receive the imprint of a man, to receive the signature of his work? Not a sign of a child with her. His resolution to dismiss her dissolves like darkness at morning bird call. Like moths before the sun. "Come in."

Still the print teen-age dress and the scarf on her head but for once her black hair is brushed like Ramona's and neatly tied behind. She has a new yellow cardigan. She sits in the big chair. What with the powder and lipstick and the way her legs are no longer apart in that unwomanly way but folded one upon the other, the thighs chastely clasped within the skirt . . . by God she's all but civilized. With the low reading lamp behind her the enshadowed eyes have mystery. Within his male recesses he trembles at what she could be to him, this woman from the night. He could sign himself upon her. Man . . . you traitor to yourself.

"We're all in at Auntie's tonight. Gavin too. Just for tonight. The children and I are going away tomorrow. To the Lakes. We're all badly in need of a holiday. Six months. Gavin is executing all the orders I give him. You *can* do anything you like in this life." A pause of doubt, bewilderment. "A whole six months."

After wine and coffee, "Those last two years here. The loneliness, the time dragging, the boredom." Hand over eyes. "People say, 'You *should* work. You *should* paint. You owe it to the children to be interesting.'" Remembering, "I've been an exile for seven years. I've had no friends and there's been no joy. But here I was reminded of it all. The overseas magazines, the music, poetry, talk, all that culture . . . it wakened me again."

"I thought I'd failed."

"It brought back everything to me, the kind of life I once knew. I'm beginning to make more coffee lately. I drink it stronger now. I feel now I want to get out into the world again and find a place that is just right for me so that I can paint and understand music. I want to meet people . . . y'know, really *nice* people. I want to live now."

"Didn't you find Borg company at all?"

Swift hand to cheek, "Oh how can I say I've had no friends after knowing Borg?" But even one question makes her restless and she continues with impatience, "Once I'm living the kind of life I know . . . *know!* is right for me I'll be able to do all these things." Thunderstruck, "I'm allowed to now. Gavin no longer argues."

The evening deepens. "No dreadful day-long rows any more. Poor old Gavin," rueful gratification, "he's humbled now, Daniel. Y'know, really *humbled*. He sits quite still all the time. Just staring ahead of him, silent." Her inner eye dwells on this image, satisfied.

"I have as much regard for Gavin as I have for the rest of you. I've had him here in terrible agony."

A groan, covers her face, rises restlessly, "I must get back to the children. I don't know how he's getting on putting them to bed."

"They'll be all right with their father." But she takes her cup to the kitchen in silence and he adds, "What a lovely sentence that: 'They'll be all right with their father.'"

"The coffee is still on, Daniel."

"Is it?"

"Shall I turn it off?"

"No. Good. We'll both have another cup." He goes to the keyboard in response to the wine, a spurious effort from a spurious impulse engendering a spurious reaction. He knows he fails to reach her and is reminded of the fatality of trying to recapture. There's a shift in the relation between them: from "beggar and giver" in its perfect form to something less extraordinary. "We'll take this coffee to another scene. The library."

"Ramona is grieving to get back to this school. She adored Mr. Richmond."

"He is broken-hearted to lose Ramona. And not only her, he appreciated the family. He told me he felt you had a great potential. He said once, 'If ever they put all that imagination of theirs into the bloodstream of the school—their originality, their force. The school would be enriched for them. A school does need the support of its families. The families make a school.' However . . . children come and go, neighbors come and go, resolutions come and go and pictures come and go. It hardly pays to spend from the heart."

She savors this. Tarl alone, triumphant, while the rest of them lick their wounds. But the rue in her face is no more than rue. In Tarl are no such offenses against wholeness as the trivia of remorse, regret. "I must get back to the children. But what I really came for . . ." Rises with purpose, walks firmly along the veranda into the house, he so foolishly following, down the hall to the music room again. She unhooks the portrait of Angela, "I'll take this back to town. Auntie wants it because people are still talking about it."

Thunder is rumbling from the mountains, ruminatingly, at times savagely in one of these hot autumn stormless sky-storms with no rain or gale to show for it, no uprooting of trees, no action. Like Dan doing nothing, making no protest, when someone takes from him the portrait of his heart. "As I say," a shrug, "pictures come and go."

For the first time ever he accompanies her across the darkness of the playground to the gate as if she were a real woman truly come to see him. As if she had said, "But what I really came for . . . to see you, Daniel." He opens the gate for her like the gentleman he'll never be.

"By the way," from Tarl, "you don't happen to know anyone at the Lakes I could ring, do you? About some place to live?"

"Lemme see now." Whom has he had enough of down there? What about Brandon . . . has he returned Dan's books? Come to that, what about the way he lent his presentation copy? Gross indiscretion. In order to exploit his knowing Dan. He's not interested in Dan's work but when it came to receiving from Dan a presentation copy, he lent it fast enough, saying casually, "Daniel Francis, a friend of mine . . ." He didn't even read it himself.

"Y'know that man you met here once on the veranda, an engineer. Brandon Just. You told him all that you felt about education and he told you what he thought—the exact furious opposite. Now he's got houses. He organizes these public works camps in the back blocks on big jobs. He can put his finger on shacks in the most remote places. He's your man. D'you want his number?"

Opening the door of the car, "I took these projected departures of yours seriously once."

She slides in evasively behind the wheel, her face unreadable in the gloom. "Oh I'll be back in a week." And returns to the night whence she came.

Looking at the blank on the wall where Angela's sweet face had been for months he feels an upheaval in him. Jealousy bursts to the surface again, the impulse to destroy her. . . .

"That parent of yours."

It is Brandon. And here on the phone is one of those blue rages familiar in anyone in the path of Tarl. "The one I met at your place. Madly against schooling. The 'legal duress' expert. She rang me this morning. She asked me . . . *me!* knowing what I think about the necessity of education. She asked me to give her one of my houses down here. I said, I said, 'Out of reach of school, I presume?' And she said, 'Yes. I'm enrolling the children at the Correspondence School.' She had the temerity to . . ."

"Now hang on, Brandon. This parent . . ."

". . . the temerity to ring *me,* with twenty thousand others in the borough. You know why? *I* know why. She knew I'd respond emotionally. This blazing compulsion of hers to—to . . ." splutter, splutter, "to repeatedly remind us of her rampant . . . yes I say rampant . . . her rampant defiance. Sensation at all costs for Mrs. Pracket. This parent of yours has a very real horror of anonymity. She has a coarse talent for . . ."

"Hold it. Hold it. This . . ."

". . . for infuriating us. If she's an animal she hardly does them credit. She's the most . . ."

"Shut up. You're abusing one of our parents. This awkward and valuable woman has abilities that would leave the likes of you out of sight. At least she's bloody well got the courage to stagger round with her convictions, to commit herself publicly and not, as you do, slink . . ."

"She's mad in any language."

"For Christ's sake go to hell."

Attaboy, Tarl.

❧ RAINSTORMS FOR A WEEK and as he leans on the veranda post late afternoon watching nature so exposing herself, "When like a lid the heavy low sky weighs Upon the soul that moans for weariness, And from the whole horizon's circled space Pours light sad as the night of the abyss; . . . And when, like endless prison bars, the rain's enormous curtain has begun to spin . . ." he hears the sea pounding as it comes to high tide, exposing itself also, pounding out its tale of time. In mind he sees this same tide up north both delighting and frightening me. Waves behind waves behind waves rearing far out at sea to climb upon each other. Gray the sea in the rain, that time, and dull white the foam. Always he fears for me when he hears the sea pounding, banging on the shore like Fate on our lives. As the gale bangs these trees, bangs their heads together till they cry for mercy and until the birds complain of headache. But he's fearing a lifetime late. "I hate the sea! thy tumult and commotion Are my own soul's. The sobs of conquered men, Their bitter mocking mirth, I hear again, In the enormous laughter of the ocean." But all he says to the Head appearing beneath his large umbrella after school, smiling his easy smile, is, "You can hear the ocean booming all those miles away." And Mrs. Ric, tying up the dahlias in bare feet, all she says is, "It is refreshing, the rain, isn't it?"

A further week of the same thing and branches come down outside. Hardly Shangri-La weather. There is little that a man alone does not learn about the darker side of nature's soul. What would the magistrate do with nature in the dock? Try to make her go to school? He'd be adjourning the case until the word "adjournment" wore right out and fell from the legal vocabulary. Even so he'd probably do a better job in disciplining nature than he has so far with Tarl.

True, it is on the understanding that she enrolls the children at the Correspondence School that Blondie let her go, in his incurable trust in people and his professional horror of force. But honestly now—can anyone see Tarl conducting correspondence lessons in the face of the God Whim and returning them in time by post? Moreover, does the man or woman breathe who can get Benjamin to work, least of all his mother? "Will you go down to the gate, Bennie," she said here once, "and get my book from the car?"

"No," he said.

Ah well . . . they can do with a joke.

The weeks turn over page by page as a plot turns over in mind, unfolding his brave new work. Once more, in the peace from next door, he knows the moving experience of enrolling candidates in the imagination. I.Q. tests, auditions, physical-fitness tests, the excitement of getting to know his new creatures, his own body trembling. Once more a girl in swinging skirt covered in deathless flowers, the re-enacted me. Yet he still works in damaging unease beneath the sword of Damocles in case his time is short. In case of that soundless step on his veranda again, those eyes of liquid pathos, the humble request . . . break again what he has made again. This hovering threat in the future, whereas a writer at work wants to know no future, even of beneficence. Nothing at end of day, nothing next morning; no next week, next month, next year. No appointment in reality whatever, malignant or benign. He needs to forget the walls about him, the house, the district, the country, the entire era he is in. He doesn't want to know he lives. Time and place are the worst of his enemies, above all a publisher's date. Yet Tarl is In Charge of Dan. On the whims of Tarl depends his work.

But all he says to Angela is, "I'm just afraid she'll be lonely. I think she'll be back again. They hardly supply the action in which Tarl flourishes, these deceptive Shangri-Las. The flights and returns, the defeats, triumphs, the exercise of three-hour barrages. It's not her favorable habitat. Where among the sleepy Lakes will she find occasion for defiance, exhibitionism? There's not much of an audience beyond the buses. No one to fight, no one to escape, none to shock and enrage. And, which is worse, none to beg from. Not forgetting no one's agonies. Excepting, of course, Ramona's. By now that child's tears could have swollen to a flood that may well flow on forever."

"Oh I understand, Daddy. I understand it all. But I can't get worked up about it."

The Head usually wears a smile when he comes up from school, the contagious smile he catches from the children should they pass near, rubbing shoulders with them in the gateway or slowing down through the juniors where the five-year-olds take his hand . . . but today he arrives without it. "That father," he says, "he rang me today. He wanted to know if I knew where his family were. The Education Board, apparently, wants to know why neither Benjamin nor Ramona are enrolled anywhere else in the country."

"What?"

"They're not . . ."

"Aren't they enrolled at the Correspondence School?"

"I repeat, they're still not enrolled anywhere else but here. In which case they remain my family. And my responsibility. Gavin said he thought they were at the far end of the South Island, as she used to have friends there. He said . . ."

"They're not at the Lakes? All those storms . . . I . . . Were they never there anyway? Was it all a big hoax to . . . ?"

"D'you mind if I finish, Dan? He received a wire from his wife from there asking for more money. Blondie said . . ."

"More money?" Strikes the veranda rail. "The whole deposit gone?"

"I'll continue when you're ready."

"So sorry, so sorry."

"Blondie said he'd have to rope them in in time, but for the moment he plans to give her her head. Playing the long line. He was speaking to me on the phone after school."

"By God, Blondie'll have to look out for his job, won't he? Two years now . . ."

"He's a . . ."

". . . isn't it, he's been trying to get Benjamin to school?"

"He's a humane man, as you know. He hates force too."

"He trusted her and she tricked him." Pulls out his smokes and puts them away. All this glorious sensation again even from the distance of the length of the country. "Not the police now, is it?"

"He'll manage without the police."

"The joke is, once she gets back, the minute she gets back she'll be calling for a home." Pause, "Again."

With deliberation, "I won't have them back at this school whether they are enrolled here or not. I'm not putting my staff through all that again. And I'm not going through it myself."

"Neither am I. In any case I do not have the mathematical endowments required to follow intelligently the sequences." But this is far longer than the Head can stand on this subject and he glances about him impatiently. "Your grass is a bit long, isn't it?"

"No longer than my beard."

"How's the mower going?"

"It's a dreaful thing. I'd get more cut on my knees with a pair of nail scissors." Back comes his smile, thank heaven.

189

Months turn over like chapters.

With temporary peace however, as it often is in absence, one forgets the irritation of another and remembers much to appreciate, so that, released from the rages Tarl provokes in him, he's able to admire more the variation she plays on the old human theme. Indeed could she manage to stay away from him forever she could well take on in his mind the proportions of a martyr, if not a minor messiah, in her battle for the freedom of children. Besides one does miss the pelting supply of sensation. When you are geared to these flights and returns and crises their absence leaves rather a hollow. And it is round about now at the end of the autumn term with winter making sign language that Angela says one Saturday, "What I mean is . . . all those paintings, Daddy, they must be of some value, don't you think? Like . . . I don't want you to think I'm thinking things or anything like that but . . . I mean if I had time from the babies . . . I don't get a *minute* to do a *thing* that I'd like to. I—I'd collect them. I'd round them up. She'll lose them. I can't remember one single solitary time when she's even mentioned them. I think it's a shame, don't you, that they should be lost? I'm not trying to say that I know anything about art or . . . or . . . anything like that. I . . ."

When she has gone, and in this more favorable mood, Dan brings himself in a high degree of furtiveness to look over the large package of paintings Tarl dumped firmly in the blue room one day. Not that he, either, claims to know a thing about art but what her brushes—his brushes to be correct—have had to say on the intricate nuances of nature is much what his own words would have said had he her vision. But it is at great cost to himself, to his pride in particular, that he decides to do what Angela wants, collect them, and only because she wants it. Cleaning up again after Tarl, which is what it amounts to. But whatever Angela wants of him, even this, is the only remaining law of love in his life.

"In any case she'll be back," to Angela tending the new Macushla on the bed. "Any time now, Ange, you'll see. Holidays coming. She's got to come back to base. Winter coming, children young. And whatever she thinks of Gavin she won't find anyone else with such a passion to help shelter them. No one could care as he does unless it is Blondie himself, Archenemy Number One. The Someone In Charge. Besides . . . Ramona. She must be putting on the pressure by now to get on with her schooling. And here's a point: not only has the deposit run out but so have her supplies of audience. Who at the far end of the farthest island is going to react emotionally? She'll be back, mark my words. If for no other reason than to be on the spot *after* the autumn holidays in order to run when the bells start calling. That's something never to be missed in the lifetime of Tarl."

"Oh I'm sorry for her, Daddy. When I think of those little ones . . . give me that safety pin, Brucey, please. I dunno . . . Rod said he would let me take them all in."

"*You?* That means when I go down and collect you each Saturday I'd be collecting Prackets too? Do you want me to choke before my time? Your heart runs away with you."

"They're really lovely children, Daddy. They'd be a very good influence let loose among mine."

"I . . . I'm choking *now*."

Her face lights up, her blue eyes so full of life and love and hope and trust in life, all so missing in Tarl so often. "There are a lot of paintings left at my place. Things she did down there. Benjamin, Paddy Tu, whitebait fishing . . . I don't know where I'd put them, I mean hang them, but I could hold them in one place. Y'know, preserve them. Some day the children might come back looking for them. It's terribly *good* of you, Daddy, to . . . I mean . . ."

⚜ "Tarl? Hah. It's you."

He is among the leaves with a rake. The autumn afternoon is radiant with color as she walks up the path with the two younger ones. Where's that thing she wears round her head? Good Lord, her hair is cut. Combed, parted with care, and her face is powdered, her mouth painted. Heavens, her shoes are new. But she still wears Angela's dress. And she's lost that extra weight and the island suntan and she's wistful and wan again. Very much so. He bursts with effervescence. "You *do* look nice."

"Do I?"

"How most interesting to see you. Hullo, Dessida. Hullo, Homer. I didn't know it was you, I looked up and I thought it was someone else. My word," to Tarl, "you must have some good stories for me."

"No."

"Ah. Here you all are back again. I guessed," it escapes, "you couldn't do without me."

Puzzled, hand to cheek, "No."

"I thought you'd be back about now. I said to Angela only last week, I said, 'You'll see, Ange, Tarl will be back again soon.' " Is that a cloud forming over toward the mountains in the bright sky? The lit garden seems to be darkening. The bubbles of his effervescence begin breaking in sixes and sevens. Then he stops his gushing and sinks out of sight into the depths of these incomparable eyes gazing up at him, their brown a brooding gray with a sensation of violet in them, set in the flawless white. He sees in them the whole of the autumn reflected heavily.

"I brought you these."

"Me? You brought *me* . . . ?"

"You like feegoas, don't you?"

"*You* brought *me* something?"

"And these biscuits I made this morning. They won't be any good. You don't have to eat them. Give them to Angela's children."

"Look at that now," a phrase of the Head. "Just look at that. You brought me something. Look, Dessida, Homer, your lovely mother has brought me something."

Her eyes do not waver from him. Low and sweet, "What a wonderful, wonderful welcome."

Suddenly she comes to life and strides past him and up the steps, down the dim hall and into the twilight of the music room from where he hears sighs and groans like a swimmer reaching the bank. Like a wanderer reaching home.

The umbrella tree is loaded down now almost to the ground with red berries which every bird from here to the mountains, from here to the sea—every man jack of them—is acutely aware of. But by now he carefully keeps the table out of range of their droppings out on the grass. He loads his little flock of ibexes with Angela's sponge and tea. "Have some of this?"

"Oh no. I must watch my weight." Then in a moment takes a slab.

"Have you any plans, dear?"

"No. Just my refuge . . . do nothing."

"You haven't done any work . . . painting . . . I suppose."

"No. Only some sketches. It all comes with too much facility and there's too much bitterness in it. I know I'll have to work it all out of me before I do anything worth while. Before I can break through to the infinity beyond reality." Ruefully, "I went round the doors of houses down south trying to sell them but," wistfully, "nobody wanted them." It is true about that distant cloud toward the mountain; it has spread over darkly now and the trees no longer look radiant but gloomy and doomed. "I've been to see the friends of my youth." A fleeting joy. "We've been right down south, you know." He does. But the light goes out at once. "I was so disappointed in them, you've no idea. How they've changed! People we've thrashed out with years ago the ideal bringing up of children. In the theory stage. Letters for years, and I go down there . . . it was as though there had never been anything." .

Eyes on the grass, "There they were in those little suburban boxes. Those dreadful suburban front rooms. Little stuffed chesterfields, patterns on the carpet, venetian blinds pulled down . . . ugh! But their attitude to my children, Daniel. The asides . . . y'know? About children still being up after ten o'clock. '*We* get rid of our kids at half-past seven. We're entitled to a bit of evening to ourselves.' And about my cutting the crusts off their bread and peeling their apples. And *Daniel* . . . all this sitting up at the table. Oh-h-h . . ." Shuddering moan in the grand old manner. "*Manners*. Think of it. 'Now don't reach past like that.' " Excellent mimicking. " 'Ask for it.' And—and . . . *well*. As I came away I said to myself, I'll go home and have *five more children*." Which would suit Gavin, no doubt, but the magistrate would have to put on more staff. "I'm very disappointed in New Zealand. We might have made a mistake in returning home. If ever I got away again . . ." the eyes lift and roll with wonderful visions of freedom, "I'd never come back." Reaches for more sponge cake. "And if ever I got the money . . . I'd leave the country."

Restlessly, "I've got to meet the two o'clock ferry. I must send a message to Borg. All that stuff of ours we left on the island . . . we need it. We've left our things all over the country. If only we had a home. I've been married for *ten years* . . ."

"Twelve?" almost inaudibly.

Both hands to face, "Oh, is it that? And Gavin has never given us a home. The children keep asking where their things are. Ramona said, 'Where's that little blue notebook I put on the window sill three places back?' And we've been sleeping on the floor at Auntie's ever since we got back but the children need warm beds these winter nights. I'm worried about Bennie. He doesn't seem well lately." School coming up? "And Ramona's asthma. I do *need* a home for the children."

"What about Borg's cottage on the island?"

"There's not a stick of furniture in it. Besides it's empty only in the holidays."

"What about the house just down the road across the intersection? The one I told you about; the lady's gone to England for six months. Trees, privacy . . . pretty as this. A dear little concentrated Shangri-La."

"Didn't I tell you about that? Last year at this school Ramona was entering her diary and she put in, 'Mummie took Daddy down to see the house across the intersection but Daddy said five pounds a week was too much. And Mummie said, You could afford it all right if you put us there. You wouldn't have all the expense of our running round in the car for freedom and having to buy cream buns and tinned food and fish and chips. Then Mummie threw the baby at Daddy and said, *You* look after him if you won't let me.' All that in her diary for the teacher to read. I had to go down the next morning and see the teacher and I said to her, 'I didn't *throw* the baby at Gavin. I only *thrust* the baby at him.' " Smile behind a hand.

"What about the deposit Gavin earned for the house overlooking the estuary, Suldoon's?"

Vague moan, fingertips to face, "I don't know." Silence while the last flick of sun blots out behind the cloud. "There's no more to say between Gavin and me. It's all been said. There's nothing left to analyze. He just looks at me with abuse in his eyes and says nothing. He believes I've let him down and I believe he's let me down. There's only bleakness between us now." From nearby the infants pour out to play, caroling, carousing joyously.

"What have you been reading lately?" and "Did you meet anyone who reads the same subject as you?" These questions are dangerous and careless if not disguised aggression. The last, gently, "Did you fall in love?"

She thinks, her features concentrated, her face brooding downward. She looks wholly lovely for the first time known to him. Interesting, suffering, glamorous as she examines the secrets of herself. The light filtering through the high foliage about them touches her tenderly. Her skin is so white again and the shadows have returned to her cheeks. The bottom lip, seeming before too thin, now, outlined in red, shows a quite classical fullness, and the gemlike eyes pouring thought hold the intense mystery. Mystery beneath the lowered lids in spite of the constant revelation of herself. There's still much of her she compulsively hides. Furtively he watches her shadowily outlined where she sits withdrawn upon herself, searching, exploring what she is. And now he sees her, not as Tarl, not as what she could be to him, but as a woman laboring from the burden of her kind upon her. In her humility he perceives the enslavement of the mind of humanity by the steam-rolling weight of tradition, militarism in schools and the regimentation of children . . . all dragging down her spirit and her fine-boned body, immobilizing the small hands. In this text of poetry rather than of the practical and in the light about her there's a messianic quality. In her humbled pose there's an immemorial beauty and he's non-man enough to respect it.

Forcefully, unannounced and with clarity the thought flashes to him as it has before that Tarl is luminously good and considerably truer than the rest of them.

"I believe in my own inner goodness and purity," she once told him, but must purity ever trudge arm in arm with bitterness? "And hearses, without music, without drums, File slowly through her soul, while Hope, nigh dead, Lies weeping there; and Pain the Despot comes And plants his black flag on her bended head."

His respect breaks to the surface fully, at last, uncomplicated, unqualified by the law and society. At length she answers him but to the leaves at her feet. "No." A little uncertain, then with conviction, "No."

She stands restlessly and takes a few urgent steps, "I must catch the two o'clock ferry." Hand to cheek, "I feel upset about something. Churned, oppressed . . ."

"You've been talking about yourself. You always hate it afterwards."

"Yes . . . yes." Returns and sits down.

"My questions."

Annoyed, "Yes, the questions."

She makes a touching attempt to clean up after the children which doesn't make much difference and gives the tray with the crystal and hot teapot to Dessida. She always did allow the children incredible responsibility. Halfway across the grass, however, he can't stand it and takes it from the child. But Tarl doesn't see it. "I'm going to make a wonderful dish of chop suey tonight. I've got it all planned and prepared." Does he hear aright? "Now . . . back to the loneliness and bleakness." A few sad steps. "No one ever asks me out."

"A metaphorical statement. I asked you over last spring to see the snowball blossom."

"How could I forget that?"

"They came back," from the Head in the evening, "because Blondie had to engage the police after all."

"You knew it. You didn't tell me."

"I knew it would upset you. It's all over now and no harm done."

"Benjamin wasn't here."

Evenly, "That no longer matters. I had notices this morning that both he and Ramona were enrolled in town. They're no longer my responsibility." Very evenly indeed, too much so.

"No word from the parents," he tells Angela. "No thank you, no regret. Just 'not here.' Even an animal might have looked back over its shaggy shoulder in regret and affection upon those who cared for it. But there would be no place for our wounds in her Everlasting Now."

"All right then, let someone else try getting him to school."

"By the way, Ange, couldn't you give her another dress? I'm tired of that one."

"Let her have the lot. I'm pregnant again."

Topographically at least the storm has rolled over and away from Dan's vulnerable work. The need to dismiss Tarl may not arise. But when he recalls that deep breathing of hers in his music room after months of absence, the earlier, recurring question remains: Is it he or what he's got that she wants? Is he her Shangri-La? Anxiety endures on the countenance of life.

⚜ To DAN'S ASTONISHMENT, during the holiday respite from the sport of How to Get Benjamin to School, letters from the two Prackets begin appearing in the local press taking on surprised correspondents who have inadvertently offended them, fighting on two different fronts with the same wholehearted and imaginative fervor with which they fought each other. Gavin defends all teachers in general against the accusation that their hours are too short and their pay too long, writing forcefully above his own name. And Dan has no difficulty whatever in recognizing Tarl under the pseudonym "Freedom," who, often in the same issue, takes on the whole country on the moral point of militarism in schools. And even had she not used the pseudonym, the number of times the words "individual," "rights," "conforming," "should," and above all "freedom" occur spells only one pen to him.

In this double counterattack echoes the incorrigible compulsion in them to point out to all how *wrong* they are, as indeed they all are, and to prove how dead right they are themselves. Surely there's another court case round the corner to draw off the Prackets and relieve the exhausted defenders? But the newspaper action is soon over. In a matter of only a few letters Gavin so utterly routs the foe that Dan can't help laughing. They don't know Gavin Pracket as he does; that not only is he always right, and can prove it scientifically, but that he stakes his life on the very last word. While Tarl, living up to legend, backs out at the height of the fray and is suddenly "not here." No one can say they don't supply Benjamin with powerful reading material; that boy's vocabulary by now . . . it would qualify him for anything. For the law at the very least.

As he reads these letters from the speculative comfort of his chair by the fire he ponders, How could two such live together? On the other hand how could two such not live together? How could one survive without the exercise of the other? Plainly they delighted in disputation for its own sake and feel deprived of it living in silence together with the little Auntie. If only this admirable drive in Tarl could be harnessed she'd have them all revert to animalism in a matter of weeks, where there'd be an end to all disputation forever . . . material, educational, military or atomic in the grandest of all Everlasting Nows. Her whole impassioned involuntary effort makes him think he should continue to support her though he is anything but martyr material. He has a personal distaste for martyrdom and a considerable boredom with it.

No blood will be drawn over Benjamin, he concludes. It's the meaning of life that's the issue. An artist married to a biologist. Poor old magistrate pitting man's laws against the unfolding of the Now.

"Daniel . . ."

A new post-holiday do-or-die Monday morning looming up but centered this time in town. The school bell in town calls Benjamin so innocently, so confidently, it never crossing its clanging mind that Benjamin could resist it.

"I have a request, Daniel," on the phone. "I'm wondering if you'll buy this portrait of Ramona. It'll be in the exhibition this week. I hope you don't think I'm awful but I remembered your remark about meaning to buy another picture. If it were you who bought it I'd know it was safe and I could buy it back some time with my Child Allowance. I desperately need the money."

"You shouldn't be selling a painting of one of the family at all."

"Say no if you need to."

"How much is it?"

"Twenty guineas." Then, "I need the money for food."

"Well, go and do twenty guineas worth of starving and keep the picture."

"Oh-h-h, how lovely. All right."

"How are you?"

"Oh, I'm living a dreadful *dreadful* life."

"Why don't you come and tell me about it? I always look forward to seeing you."

"I'll have to go now. I'll burst into tears." She does.

"Daniel . . . !"

"Where are you ringing from?"

"The island. Say no if you need to. Could I and the children come to your place," shock, "on Friday? A headquarters for house hunting." But there's no Tarl on Friday, no children, no word, in true Pracket style. He'd bought extra food too and the coffee sponge she likes, not to mention fetching Angela all those miles to act as buffer between them. God bloody damn it. She probably took exception to his remark, "Certainly. As long as you take the children with you. I'll be working." He feels such a fool to Angela.

"It's you she wants, Daddy."

"She's far too young for me."

"Too young? Is that all? Is that the only reason? You mean . . . ?"

"Daniel."

"A masterpiece."

The portrait of Ramona. In the doorway of the library she draws it out from behind her. He writes out a check for twenty guineas on the spot although he doesn't believe for a moment it's for food. They'd live on clover heads from the roadside before they spent freedom money on food.

"Celebrate," he demands. A wave of exhilaration sweeps them all to the kitchen. A new winter dress that is not one of Angela's, slinky fashion. He's sure it is not Angela's, it fits her so well. Angela's are too long for Tarl whereas this, sheathing her thighs, shows bare knees. Frightfully smart. And he hears about an expensive flat in a posh suburb Gavin has rented . . . by God the same suburb as his land . . . where unfortunately there is every amenity she both cries for and denounces, even to comfortable beds. "We've a wonderful record player. Music . . . a wonderful habit. Another I got from you. Did you know they were talking about you on the radio last night?" Radio too? Culture at the turn of a civilized knob. No piano or lessons or anything that stank of effort. "It's the best place we've ever had but for its situation. The pavement underfoot instead of grass or sand. Respectable suffocating suburbia. And the rooftops . . . ugh." Closed eyes.

What about the bell calling in town next week? Here's Benjamin drawing on the blackboard in the red room while Homer cracks nuts. Dan says, "I saw a very good painting once of rooftops. The view from an artist's window." School or else, do or die in town? What's that got to do with Tarl? Luxuriating in wine and scones.

"It's what goes on under the roofs."

"No different from what goes on under a tree." All sitting round at ease in the warmth of his fire . . . doing exactly nothing. And Dan sitting round too, painfully idling, minding Gavin Pracket's children. "Man remains man whatever he's under."

"He shouldn't be under anything."

"I can't win."

He stands and starts pacing, "What," to Benjamin, "were they saying about me on the radio last night?"

He curls his knees to his chin like his mother and giggles. He's deteriorating, this boy. "I don't know."

The Now unfolding, unfolding . . .

"How's Borg?"

"Oh, he's been in once or twice lately. He came in the other night and I just had to say, 'Look, Borg, I'm feeling too bleak. You'll have to go away.' And he said, 'That's real communication,' and went. I think his life is hard." The one man she speaks of with charity. "The other fishermen are a bit concept-ridden."

In the library he takes up the forgotten check and says with pomp, "Come, Benjamin, I'm going to decorate your mother." And walks respectfully to her and pins the check on her dress. She is serious and humble as he recites formally as the Governor-General at Investitures, "Congratulations, Mrs. Pracket." Benjamin watches absorbed then runs out and calls, "Look. He's decorated Mum." And in run all the others.

"There have been times," she replies softly, "when I could

see no hope at all but now I have a little. Since I've come here ... a little sense of future."

He hears how she has been trying to write to—and failed— "Your friend."

"His name is Mr. Richmond."

"I can't bring myself to use it." To say how she regretted taking the children away without any word. Can he believe his ears? And it is astoundingly new that she should sit in the armchair of her own will, her legs no longer starkly astride but one closed mysteriously upon the other, the slight knees bared and the autumn from the window in her eyes. Also the children seem to want to be near him and Tarl follows Dan with her eyes so that he thinks they regret the school they've thrown over, miss it, and recall the care they were given, not to say the attention.

"I've got to get back to work. You people don't have to go. Put some more wood on the fire for yourselves. Make the tea. Plenty of stuff to read. You'll have to excuse me."

"All right then," peaceably.

All of which could be called "improvement," but it occurs to him that this improvement could be the result of, if not the reason for, the defeat of her spirit whereas he can't stand to see a battler beaten whatever his cause. Above all he can't stand to see a dream unfulfilled whatever its content. That's his life's work, nurturing dreams to their shaky realization. Along with the friends of her youth down south she may yet end up in comfortable banality as an escape from the no longer tolerable status of a "peculiar person," leaving him to mourn his ibex.

Yet her labored concern for him gives her an extra dimension, the missing dimension; and the suspicion that a little charity, a whiff of tolerance has somehow got through to that iron-barred heart makes him glad of the fearful sacrifice he has made in not sending her away. And again he has this fleeting conception of what she could be to him. Now she reminds him of a woman rather than an animal and he is dangerously touched.

❧ WAS THERE EVER a weekend before school reopening without Tarl raptly planning? I doubt if any Pracket child could approach a school now without the exhilarating preliminaries. With the ease of exhaustive practice all members of the cast take up their roles and play the lines impromptu: father, mother, children, Welfare officer Blondie, magistrate, current headmaster in town and with Borg standing in for Dan. On Sunday when he comes over the harbor in his little boat with its one sail Borg is delighted with his promotion; his school-or-else, do-or-die, bell-on-Monday, court-on-Wednesday crisis at the dead center of the action. At last life is not passing him by.

"Tarl did a bunk from the flat on Friday and turned up at my door on the island. She begged me to hide Ben from Gavin. I said I refused to deceive Gavin but if anyone spent the night in the fish shed I'd know nothing about it. But in the morning Gavin appeared at my door and told me he'd found her the night before. She was in the empty cottage. That frosty night, remember? Ben was hiding under the cottage." A reminiscent smile. "They ding-donged till eleven in the room above him." Puzzled, "But I'm in doubt about my position. Pregnancy would complicate matters. I may have to reject this particular aspect of my relationship with Tarl. I see no reason why our relationship should not remain a good one."

"You don't?"

"It wouldn't do if Gavin found himself in the position where he could extricate himself from legal responsibility."

"Wouldn't it?"

It's the same thing all over again but with the male lead changed. But then in a few days Dan receives a cheerful note from Borg following up the Pracket drama: "When I returned to the island on Sunday night Tarl had taken off to an unknown destination. Gavin came looking for them on Monday morning . . ." and so on . . . and thinking of the little boy under the house for six hours on a white frosty night while his parents barraged in shelter above him, he writes Borg a note withdrawing his invitation to his winter lectures and dismissing him, "for some years anyway until the tide of strife sweeping about you at present has receded." The coward's escape by note. But he'd said goodbye to Borg a year ago anyway, the day he sent him to Tarl.

"Hello there, Dan," on the phone from the victorious tongue of Gavin after the court on Wednesday. "Blondie has lost custody of Ben to me. He is now legally mine. If Tarl takes off with him now I can send the police after her myself. With me In Charge she can't take flight as she constantly did with Blondie. We had a ding-dong go in court today, Blondie and I.

He showed his teeth and we stood up to each other before the learned judge. I pointed out to His Honor how for over a year this welfare officer failed to get my son to school. I proved him hopelessly incapable."

"But you know he was playing her gently. You appreciated it at the time. That wasn't incapacity but humanity. Your own subject. You were playing for time yourself then. And you're using that to discredit him?"

"Yes, I am. He's too soft for Tarl. I'm the only one can deal with Tarl. I'm using everything to hold my son."

"Even Blondie's career?"

"He can look after himself. I'm looking after Ben. He'll go to school every day now that I'm In Charge. I'll deliver and collect him twice a day through the headmaster's office. No one will get my son from me." Then with vast pride in his wife, "She cried for five hours with rage."

"Daniel."

The crest of the five-hour rage. His students are due and his door wide open. In whirls Tarl from the black of the night in a glamorous white coat but red-lidded, wan, exhausted. "Look, I wonder if Ric would let me use his school phone. I've got an urgent, very private . . . *private!* . . . toll call to make." Any number of private phone boxes at the post office in town.

"Use my phone, dear. Just close the door." The playground is alive with cars.

Trying to lecture, however, with her voice laboring through the walls he constantly loses his line of thought and often returns to the house. The first time she is in the doorway feverishly turning over the pages of the phone book and in order to get past her he lays his great hands on her white-coated hips. Another time she is pacing the music room, hand to cheek in thought, and he passes her wine. "Drink this, dear. I'm fearfully busy. I've got to go." And another time she is standing beneath the eleventh-century masterpiece, hands clasped, imploring, "St. Francis." Later he hears her soft closing of the front door, her creeping steps over the veranda and knows she is weaving her way through the cars to return to the night. But his lecture is an exciting failure.

"Daniel."

Collapse on chair by fridge with Dessida's arms round her legs. "I had to come. I've got to talk. I've got two things to ask you. Just let me know if you've had enough of my asking for this and that. Could you let me have the air fares for myself and the children to Tahiti? I feel I could live there. I've always said I would never fly. But now . . . yes I think I could. Yes," with conviction, "I would fly."

Yes, he will. But not just yet. The time has not quite come. He blames his accountant again. He hasn't the gift of speaking straight as Tarl has, among his many faces.

"All right then. D'you know a place I could go . . . y'know . . . to *live?*"

"You've used up all my places."

On rising to go much later . . . taking with her some stale scones she sees on the bench . . . the cushion from her chair falls to the floor but she walks upon it and past it quite unseeing and unknowing and so exactly does Dessida behind her, neither feeling anything under their feet, nor caring if they did, possibly, let alone stop and pick it up. It is Dan who does that. Passing the children's bookcase with the set of ten huge encyclopedias, "Can I have those?"

"They're to go down to school."

It seems that he never gives her anything, but as a matter of fact he does. He gives her his precious time, which means his work. Which in turn means himself, his life. Like Gavin. As the Head has given his reputation. Like Blondie's career. But he doesn't think she knows all this.

Quite sunnily on the phone at the end of the week, you'd never dream of the recent five hours' rage, "Which of my paintings shall I send to the exhibition? I shouldn't be asking advice I suppose."

"No. Are you well?" Are you pregnant, is what he means.

"Oh . . . no." But no paintings reach the exhibition.

Almost radiantly on his sunny step on her own in the weekend, "Gavin realizes now that his educational theories are no more than theories and that they won't work. Faced with the law they've failed." Outright gratification. "I was feeling quite warm toward him recently, quite warm, and I showed him some of my paintings in an effort to establish contact but he said, '*You* can paint because you never work. You just sit in the sun while I work. I could paint too if I lived your life.' But I'm not lazy, Daniel. Looking after four children is a full-time job."

"I think," from Angela another day, "she's relieved to have Bennie off her hands at school. She seems to be much happier."

One morning in the weekend he says, "Don't blame Gavin for everything. I have a regard for him. His warm personality."

"You wouldn't say that if you saw him standing in the middle of the flat shouting at us all."

"His rage itself is warm. Anyway it's good to see a man roaring from the middle of the house. You women need discipline."

"Don't you praise Gavin. I came out this morning to stop you. You were speaking well of him last time." They are walking together across the empty playground to the gate this benign autumn morning. The children are seldom with her these days. He says, "These metal slogans you use, the two of you. They've torn to pieces the feeling between you." As she puts in the clutch of the dusty little car she lifts her autumn eyes to him, but they don't say, I love you, Daniel. "Please say something unpsychological."

"I never say anything else."

Rage and repose, despair and hope alternating like the moods of the autumn weather, yet how can one seeing the overall picture not register an impression of a general all-round "improvement"? An increasing adjustment to what society must be, a long-drawn-out realization? Soon it will be time for her to walk without him, he hopes . . . he fears. And if she can't, well, give her the money to leave the country.

Not that he can follow the complicated plot of the action clearly, if at all, but he's following himself a bit better. As his new work lurches and gasps for breath the conviction strengthens within him that before he is very much older he's going to dismiss his flock; drive them away from the water hole on the assumption and hope that they've found their own. Yet a wrongly timed action might undo the whole and she might fall back into the awful night of the "seven years' service," never to emerge again and the blood of her soul would be on his hands. Often enough in mind he writes the note trying to phrase it without too much hurt but it never gets to paper.

Until one late afternoon in town after a rough passage with his accountant over absolutely extraordinary taxes . . . "I simply refuse to pay this astronomical sum. You can write to the Government and tell them from me that I refuse. Let them send me to jail. I've never been to jail. I'm a writer and I should have been. I'd be glad of the experience. I consider no man has matured until he has known a breakdown, a jail sentence and expulsion from the library for overdue books. I've only been expelled from the library. I refuse to . . ."

"The Government will sell you up. Send the bailiffs in."

In the street before the picture theater he hears in the crowds,

"Hullo Daniel," in tones of surprise and joy. And here she is all expensive in this white padded coat, brushed sleek hair, dramatic make-up and with the children frolicking about her in and out of the people, smartly dressed too, in the very latest. He just cannot recognize in her the woman who arrives at his door. Is that what she's really like between her visits? Glamorous, beautiful and even happy? Yet she looks so small in the bustling crowd and seems so much, so very much, woman that he can't help touching her shoulder, "Come 'Down Under' and have some coffee. I've had a dreadful time with taxes."

"Oh-h-h . . ." breathed. All of herself in the loveliest face that has ever lifted to him. Her eyes reach up into his like encircling arms. The two of them isolated a moment in the crowds, isolated in the storms that pelt about her. Ruefully, "But I'm taking the children to this Dickens film." Then eagerly, joyfully, not unlike Dessida, "I'll come out soon. I'll come to see you soon."

All of which brings him to think that it is quite safe now to dismiss her and the very next morning in a rage of jealousy of her seeming independence of him, the cheek of her to be quite happy and successful in town without him, swept in a surge of revenge for all she has taken from him, he actually writes this note, using the phrase "Forget your way to my place," and such. But is it his doing that Ric forgets to pick it up on his way to church? When he looks on the stool in the hall later he finds it still there. How can he deny this to be a sign that it should not be posted? He puts it in the flames at once. Then strides to the bathroom to wash his hands and the marks come off quite easily. Asking her to join him in town while planning to dismiss her anyway. Traitor. No one is so weak as the man with many faces.

Yet very seldom is he not glad to see her. She's such an interesting person. Almost always the pleasure when he hears her calling him, calling him expectantly with a lift of joy in her voice. This marvelous capacity of hers to *come*. Always coming. Arriving. Being. Never demanding that he return her calls. Coming, coming, a woman who comes. Increasingly groomed these days in her one new dress, warm for the winter, a tweed of the latest cut. "I've got a question to ask you. Oh well," heroically, "I can see you don't want me." She takes rebuffs so philosophically, never grieving or sulking at him. Like a child. "D'you mind if I read in the garden awhile?" So fond of books too. "I do need a rest from the children." Practically everything she says flows from her inner being, so that her utterances, however divorced from logic, are so worth while. Dan seldom questions others, Tarl in particular, feeling that answers are not important. Only the thing spoken from an inner compulsion is worth the saying, and worth the listening to. One day when he mentioned this to her she replied, "So long as we think logic final we are chained. We have no freedom of the spirit." Now he says to her poised in the doorway, tentative, as though she might vanish on the wings of a moth, "You've got a lovely smile for me. You'd better make me a cup of tea."

Sincere joy, "Yes."

"I *am* glad to see you. There are times when I'm not but today I am."

Halts, joy arrested. Ponders, eyes to floor, one heel forward, "I know there are times when you're not but . . ."

"Are you well?"

"I'm quite all right." Pause, "But I had to come. I'm always better when I get home for awhile, then . . ." a glance at him. This messaging without words, electric.

On these weekend visits with Gavin to mind the children he finds himself relaying to her his lecture of the Wednesday before. Pencil and paper appear now from the white raincoat pocket. "I was inclined to forget last time." He'd invited her to attend these lectures where she certainly would have met the "really nice people, y'know?" she was calling for recently but she chooses, characteristically, to have her own private lectures at a time that suits her, not him, and quite overlooking his having to give them twice. Sometimes he thinks the reason she tore out that night, the five-hours-crying night . . . was to find out what these lectures were like and decided there were too many cars. Now, "I don't know what you mean."—"You will in time." —"I'll think about it. I'll find out." She makes an excellent student. As she is excellent at anything she means to do, when she puts her hand to it, as with the children's sewing. "What does 'profligacy' mean?" "How do you spell it?" "Will you say that again, please?" "What does 'exorcise' mean?" "What is the interpretation of those metaphors you used?"—"You'll have to find out."—"I'll look them up at home."—"Gavin will tell you." —"Don't mention *him*." And in these intimate undisturbed discussions she often teaches him: "The soul is always crying for freedom." "Any answer is satisfactory if it flows from one's inner being." "When facts are handled as facts without any intermediary they are generally rude things."—the best of her reading and thinking coming out in these sessions. "Logic is the bane of humanity." "To explain is to apologize and why should we apologize for living?" "Freedom from artificialities," and "We are like those who die of hunger while sitting beside the rice bag." So that his own series, "The Pen and the Shovel," appear piffling by comparison and he can hardly continue, "Wherever you are in life however—youth, late youth, middle years or late years—the motives for writing are . . ."

"Of course there's no youth, middle years, or age."

"If you say so . . . let it be that way. I don't argue."

"There's only time." Trust a Pracket on the last word. "I can't absorb any more. And I've left the children with my aunt." Finish. Because she chooses, not he.

As a result of all this there comes to be something vital missing from his lectures the following Wednesday so that he feels it is time Tarl herself were missing. How can he afford the mindspace to give lectures twice a week? It is time Tarl joined his memories to become no longer a beneficiary of his imagery, but an ingredient of it. Yet when a week or two has passed it is his class he dismisses, not Tarl. He's brokenhearted about it and tells Tarl, "I was beginning to listen for their steps and to love them."

Stares downward in thought, "I . . . no I haven't. I haven't loved anyone. Ever."

So it's true.

"The children of course."

"You teach me much. The two of you."

"Don't you praise Gavin."

"All right, I won't praise Gavin. But sometimes I wonder whether you are great . . . or not. I've got to be careful in case you are."

Serious consideration of this. She is standing on the veranda before she returns. She looks lovely among the autumn colors. "All you want now, Tarl, is stockings and . . ."

"*Stockings?* The next thing I'd know I'd be walking round with gloves and a handbag." She returns to the earlier issue, "I get all . . . *all!* . . . from Nature. All I think or do. It's my source, nature. My water hole."

"You may be one of these originals with the effrontery and bad taste to change the character of society."

"Must she," from Ric at noon, "always leave her car bang in front of the gate blocking the passage of hundreds of children, with the rest of the whole road vacant?"

He does not voice his thought to Ric: She doesn't want me,

Ric, but what I've got. She helping herself to my mind now, and I'm fool enough to give it.

A howling rainstorm takes over the day arranged for the bulldozer on the land, hauling out old stumps and heaving them to a heap, even removing three whole trees, three of the many he planted before he married me, for us to enjoy in later life. And here's the later life, such as it is. Seeing Gavin pull up on the side of the road he leaves Rod a moment and goes out to him. Not that he needs to; it's this compulsive magnetism the Prackets radiate. Sensation does draw. In his little battered car Gavin is coatless and shivering but still radiant with his legal victory over Blondie. "I'm just on my way to look at a section near here. Balliol Street. Round that next corner."

"Round that next corner?" His sou'wester dripping with rain.

"Tarl said she'd agree to that although my wife is not suburban material. But we've been in the country three years now and can capitalize on the Family Benefit. Put up a house any time." Then with tremendous pride in his son, "Ben has hepatitis. He's off school for several weeks. Doctor's certificate too."

"You're putting up a house just round that next corner?"

"Mind you, he did attend for a while. *I* saw to that. Ay? Yes. Just round that corner."

From Gavin again in town weeks later, on the eve of the spring holidays, "I've been having a bash with the boys." Laughing all over. "I've got three kiddies at school now."

"How did you get Dessida there?"

"She followed Ben."

"Of course, of course. We can have a blind eye, can't we? Of course she'd follow Benjamin. You've lost weight, haven't you?"

"You're wrong, Dan."

Dan bursts out laughing, "Of course."

"Well," with a marvelous show of normality, "I must get home to dinner." Home to dinner? Gavin? What's wrong with his hearing these days?

"I'm thinking," he tells Tarl over some lager in the library one workless morning, "of selling my land and going to live in America. I've been offered a lectureship there. Several. Indiana University. I might as well live there. My taxes have practically bought that country."

Hand to cheek, eyes to floor, heel forward, concentrated

thought, then, "Yes I think I could live in America. Yes, yes . . . yes I'd *like* to live in America."

It actually is true.

"But what I really came for . . . could I have that Byron up there?"

He reaches to the shelf he never lends from and passes her the leatherbound volume. "It belonged to my great-grandfather."

"*Tha-a-ank* you. Now I must get back to the children. I feel much better these days." He doesn't walk to the gate with her this time across the green playground. It's too far. Too much is likely to be said walking side by side in the isolation of its emptiness. Besides she must try to walk on her own.

"It's you she's after, Daddy. She hinted to me that she meant to stay near you for the rest of her life."

"Daniel!"
The way her face lights up round his door.
"I had to come. Do you mind? I . . ."

"Daniel . . ."
Looking lovely, fresh, without the children.
"I have more sense of future. I feel better, I . . ."

"Daniel . . ."
These convulsions of the dying spirit.
"This is a Desperate Situation. Could you . . . ?"

"Daniel!"
Hope defeating pain in her face.

"Daniel . . ."

"I've written this note again, Ric. It has taken me two years."

"I had been on the point of speaking to her myself, asking her to refrain from disturbing your work."

"I almost asked you. But it's my own problem and had to be dealt with within myself." And this time when he looks on the stool after he has gone the letter is no longer there. But he doesn't bother going to the bathroom as he knows he'll never get the stain off his hands.

EIGHT

❁❁❁❁❁❁

...this rapt act.

—Louis Johnson

❧ THAT WAS AUTUMN. Winter goes by. Now it is spring. The apple blossoms a year ago missed the spring storms and held to the tree for weeks. They stood beneath them the day he called them over to see the snowball tree. This year's are lost in the recent spring storms. They were not so lucky. But the leaves have taken their place, brief, fluffy green, for it is November now. And the umbrella tree Dan sees from the library window in the mild warmth of the morning has enlarged itself with a complete set of new and paler green leaves; it's time that thing was cut back. It hasn't a thought in its trunk for the other bushes about it, as is the way with nature.

The snowball blossoms he called them over to see a year ago are just going off, he thinks. Yes, the large frothy white balls are tarnished. That series of spring storms came at the wrong time for some trees, better they had been earlier. Before the blossoms were exposed. Which is a thing about spring, the way youth exposes itself, both in trees and people. It would have been better luck had the storms come after the blossoms were pollinated, when they would have gone off anyway, it being the time to do so. Nature herself, apparently, is not above timing an action erroneously, let alone a clumsy man.

Opening the mail an hour later he comes upon a letter addressed in a hand he seems to recognize . . .

. . . My fan mail, he brags to himself later to still the thrill in

213

him, is not without its lighter side. A man could dine out on a letter like this, did a man dine out. Then tries to get on with what he was writing about the power of the memory of a person over a living person but he no longer seems able to say it, or anything else for that matter. He excuses himself and goes to the blue room and checks on that package of paintings there, then he gets out his posh car that everyone looks at and goes to town and drives past the little aunt's house where he knows the portrait of Angela hangs. He even manages to draw up on the grass verge but the place has no one there. Back home again however he can't bring himself to look at the paintings again in the blue room but shuts the door firmly upon them. Two rooms now with two doors shut upon the memories of two women. Only memories for a man like him.

And there they stay until one wet day a few weeks later in the crowds in a bookshop he runs into Tarl herself and her startled gaze is so full of sorrow, old clothes again so redolent of sadness, hair streaking as it used to and face unpowdered, that he says, "Give me a smile, Tarl." Whereupon she nods vigorously in negation and cries and pushes her way out to the street. Only Homer is with her.

On Saturday morning however the rain has lifted and the sun takes a look out to see how things are going and tosses him down a whole lot of warmth from his surplus stock and some spare feeling too, so that he doesn't go and fetch Angela. In any case she's reluctant to come these days . . . "It's too much of an undertaking, Daddy, with all the babies. Getting them ready and that . . . home in time. They get cross and tired." And she hasn't pulled up yet from the loss of the fifth. "Isn't it funny? A baby that's not even formed and you haven't seen and you grieve when you've lost it. Everyone says, Doctor too, that it's better I lost it. Too near to the others but . . . I'd give anything to have kept it. I did try to keep it. But I couldn't lie down and keep my feet up with all the other little ones. It's a shame, you know what I mean? I'm always thinking of the little thing. I can't stop planning its little clothes. Mary was so sad too."

So he doesn't get Angela. She's becoming more and more embedded in her own life and doesn't seem to need him as she once did. It's all Rod said this and Rod said that. So he really has no women now. Only the phantom of me. He spends the entire morning and much of the afternoon examining Tarl's work. The large abstract "Freedom" he pins on the music-room wall where it can be seen from the distance up the hall. Conceivably it calls for distance. It is the first thing to be seen when coming in the front door from the veranda as it is the first thing to be seen when coming to know Tarl, its author of visionary distances.

"The Quarry," "Escape," and "Whitebait." Angela didn't like giving up "Whitebait" even temporarily. "Yknow, Daddy, I mean ... what I'm trying to say is that I didn't like them much at first but ... I haven't seen Tarl for months and months and months now, I mean I can sort of see the pictures apart from her. For what they are themselves and what they mean. Does that sound silly? I haven't got your words to express myself or anything like that. But it's that little canvas about catching whitebait, oh ..." a willing blue tear and a touch ... "The little children in the water and the ... Daddy, look how the light comes in behind them."

"She was always wonderful on light."

"Pipi," "River Song" and "Reflections." "Decisions." And here's the poetic portrait of Ramona. Holding it for the first time closely in his hands he realizes what it is. He remembers when she first showed it to him in the doorway of the library. He remembers when she rang up about it and can hear her soft pleading voice, "I have a request, Daniel. I'm wondering if you'll buy this painting of Ramona. I desperately need the money." And he told her to go and do twenty guineas' worth of starving and keep the picture. Is this the one he decorated her with a check over, pinning it on her dress, and the children came running in? He examines each detail of the features, the liquid poignancy of the eyes of Ramona whenever she was pirated from school as the bells were calling her. So Tarl saw all that after all and recorded it sacredly. His big lonely fingers move on the frames as they would on Tarl's slight thighs and as they have already moved on the contours of her mind rousing it to respond to him. He cannot part with it and he hangs it back on the wall. Her handling of light on a face ... but all that is past. All that vitality, all that happening quality in her transferred from reality to join his imagery.

And he keeps the portrait of Benjamin. In his eyes speaks the same compassion as when he held a monarch butterfly in Dan's garden before he'd let it go, unbruised, and when he brought a white hen to him once in the filth of Hallibut's fowl run. This wonderful look of sympathy for, and identification with, inarticulate animals, right down to the spiders at his feet.

The best of the essence of Tarl, fruit of her frightful sufferings, which she never valued herself. She was forever coming back to get them but never did. Once they were finished they might as well have been thrown in the estuary round the corner for all the thought she gave them. Never mentioned them again. Yet seen in their unity, seen apart from Tarl and at a distance in time, perceived with the needle-pointed vision of the inner eye polished fine by regret . . . *felt* . . . they appear to represent a fortune.

For no reason that he can possibly put a finger on he takes down the portrait of me in my wrought-gilt frame and hangs it on the wall in the library facing the window. Well, he should have done that years ago so that I could watch the changing of the seasons.

Then he takes the entire collection down to Angela's keeping and goes to town and opens an account at the bank which he calls his "T" account. And pays into it a sum which he considers her work is worth. And not a penny more.

But he still hasn't got the portrait of Angela and early in the morning he gets out the car again with purpose. He means to have this picture if he's got to drive over a cliff into the harbor in the attempt. They're back with Auntie, he hears, the flat only another address in the past. This time he drives twice round the block before he pulls up on the grass alongside the Pracket car. How will her permissiveness stand up to this?

"Look, there he is," from the children.

"Daniel, Daniel!" Two small hands wave desperately through the top of a window, the rest of her invisible. "Oh Daniel . . . Daniel . . ."

And there is Angela on the wall. All that fair hair tossing and the blue eyes sparkling and the plain indication of a tear, right on top of a smile. The tremendously ready capacity for a laugh . . .

"Make the tea, Tarl, please."

"Are you going to buy it?" Children palpitating. All the freedom in the value of that picture.

"What about Gavin. Didn't he want it?"

"I could have sold it," with fire, "time and time again but he wouldn't let it go."

"It's going this time."

So joyously, "I've been crying all the morning." Proudly. "I have to buy Ramona a uniform for school. Black. And black shoes and socks. *Black.* On *Ramona.*"

Here is Benjamin still in the most fascinating state of Do-Nothingness, his identification with all nature's children, her wild ones, intact on his face. The children are still all smiles

216

and brown legs and joy. No dashing round the country after Shangri-Las has changed any of them, nor the uniforms at school, while Tarl does not take her eyes off him. Surely this is affection.

Some old skirt on her, far too long, handed down from some-one . . . Hey! Those flowers are Angela's. Faded now. Bare legs and feet, hair defiantly untidy and her eyes red-lidded. As he undoes his fountain pen to write the check the children eddy and flutter near him like insects round his outside light in the spring. About him, the great Giver of Freedom. Right down to young Homer they watch the marks of the ink on paper spelling out to them in a fine reading lesson visions of imminent freedoms: bubbling creeks in hidden forests, whitebait fishing in limpid waters, soft blue mountains.

Neither he nor Tarl sees fit to mention the note he wrote to her, nor the note she wrote to him: "I desperately need five hundred pounds for freedom, to escape from the country to some place where I can lead the life I believe in." Both trivia of the past, forgotten. The check he writes with the cup of tea on the table beside him remains no more than the twenty guineas she asks for while the large sum he paid into his "T" account remains untold. Trivia of the future. As he writes and blots it and gives it to her he is aware that in the palm of his hand, in the ink of his pen, he holds the fate of his flock of ibex. It all but bursts the seams of his mind but fate does not yet move him to lift a hand about it.

"I feel better now," from Tarl as she and her brood follow him to his car standing a little aloofly alongside the Pracket one. "I feel I can hang on a little longer. I feel I can face it . . . buying the black clothes for Ramona. The day has recovered . . . it was very ill. Do you have to go, Daniel? Please don't go. Can't you stay? Goodbye, Daniel."

An hour or so or more later he runs into them all again in front of the theater in the loveliest freshly bought new clothes, Tarl painted and groomed in the queue at the box office and the children gamboling and frolicking in the crowds. As for the black clothes for Ramona . . . she wears now an outfit with every color represented, no more than an hour old. School . . . *school?* Never heard the word.

217

NINE

*In the distance
did the cowbells ring for a freedom you could not have?*
— CHARLES DOYLE

❧ THE SEASONS turn over year after year, a great wheel revolving through time. I never saw a season wait for me until my mood had caught up with it, or pause while my life caught up with it. Tide and season wait for no man . . . they didn't wait for me.

Yet there have been times when Dan would shout to the seasons to stop. His heart when he was young would run out madly into the weather to stop them himself. To cut off the buds in spring, slay the flowers in summer, fix back the leaves on the trees in autumn bowed with superfluous fruit, and on the stark boughs in winter. Anything to stop the rolling wheel leaving me behind him, the mindless wheel of the seasons. To stop, to halt time.

To anchor time to a picture a lifetime behind when I wild-heartedly loved him. Full-mindedly, full-bodiedly loved him. There, just there . . . stop there, time. Stop before that hour on a hot afternoon way up north when he came in from the lawns of a hospital and through the window doors upon the carpet of my room into the scent of flowers and anesthetic. And my eyes filled with tears to see him, in place of the words I could not speak.

And he said, "I'll do your living for you. I'll carry you with me till I die, too. I promise your death will be deathless." And the two tears I had did not fall. In all these years since, through all the rolling of the wheel of the seasons . . . my two tears never fell.

That's the time to stop, he'd shout. Before that came. But the wheel went rolling on its way season after season. Autumns after summers, summers after springs and springs after many winters.

Here is a winter after an autumn, after another summer and spring. June in another winter. All this noise of thunder and rain and high-water-marking rivers. "Is that bridge down too? Fancy."

"Daniel."

"Is that you, Tarl?"

"Yes."

"I hardly picked your voice. How are you?"

"Good, thanks."

"I'm glad to hear that."

"I thought I'd come out to see you. I thought I'd like to see the portraits of Ramona and Angela. Are you too busy?"

"Well of course I'm always . . . I'm engaged on some work at the moment but afterwards . . ."

"Are you sure?"

"About three. Do come afterwards. After three."

"All right then. I only want to see my paintings. I get lonely for them. Just the ones of Angela and Ramona, and have you got Benjamin?"

"I'll see you at three then, Tarl."

"All right then. 'Bye."

Phone again. "Oh by the way, I won't be coming. I've remembered something else I have to do."

"I expected that."

"Oh . . . did you?"

"But I did put more wood on the fire. A lovely big fire especially for you."

"Is it?"

"Leaping up the chimney."

"Oh . . ." heroically. "Anyway I won't be coming."

"Never mind. Another time."

Gone again.

Knock on the door about four. A pale green silk scarf frames her face and is tied behind her chin. Three of the children clustering behind. He gasps at the beauty of her and touches both white-coated shoulders and kisses her briefly on top of the scarf. A moth's touch. The children giggle. "I expected you."

"Did you?"

"Hullo Dessida, Homer, Benjamin. Haven't seen you for a long time. You've all got taller."

Tarl, "We came in a hired car."

In the kitchen, "I haven't come to tell you a lot of stories about my troubles."

"Why not?"

"Why not?"

"It's all good clean sport."

Later speaking of the children, "It's their spirit that's the joy. Yes . . . spirit. And joy. That's all I can call it; joy."

"Where are you living now?"

"In a motel at the moment. I'm not living with Gavin now as you probably know."

"No. I don't know anything."

A considerable silence.

"I'll make you some tea, Tarl."

"Oh don't bother."

"*What?*"

"Only if you're making yourself some."

"I'm always making myself some. I make it on the hour. I can make it with both hands tied behind my back, blindfold, and thinking of something else. Of course I'm making myself some."

"I feel better away from all that. It was so . . . he . . . but no. I won't bring all that up."

"I understand."

"I just live from day to day."

"Yes."

"It's wonderful when I wake up in the morning . . . away from him. It's not there . . . all that. My mind when I wake up . . . I'm so grateful for my *mind* when I wake. The things that drop into it . . . that happen. Yes," profoundly, "grateful. I'm *grateful* to my mind."

"I understand."

Her impassioned vision crystallizes into one gem of light giving to her countenance a staggering beauty. The soft green silk frames it incomparably. In the pale face her eyes when they turn to the light have this violet-blue shadow which, when

223

pondering downward, changes to a mystical hazel. "The tumult of my existence . . ."

"The benefits of a stormy existence are not immediately obvious."

"I still remember the things you say."

"I'll come and see you."

Silence.

"Where did you say that motel was?"

"I don't know."

Benjamin, "It's on the corner of Allenborough Road and Winter Street."

"Oh yes, I know that place."

"The beds are lovely," from Tarl. "It is lovely waking in the morning there."

"And how are you keeping?"

"Oh, very well. But I'll never be happy till I get out of this city. The implications here, the obligations. They smother me like . . . like religion. Benjamin legally Gavin's and all which that means. Only money could free me."

She moves back to the music room. "But what I really came for," and stands beneath the portraits of Angela, Ramona and Benjamin, "I wonder if I could have these back for a few days."

"They're mine. I've paid for them."

"Just to hang for a few days. Just to look at them."

"No. I won't let them go. They've grown into the blood stream of the house."

"All right then."

Walks up the hall to the door with the children trailing, "Only money can free me."

The very next morning he dresses with care, early, and drives into the city and pulls up before the motel. The proprietor is on the lawn, a smiling fellow. "Where are the Prackets? At the back?"

"She's not here."

"Not here?"

"No."

"She was yesterday."

"She was," smiles. "But she came early this morning and booked out."

"Do you know where she went?"

"No."

"You don't know where she went? You've no idea?"

"No idea whatever." Smiles again.

Not here . . . "Not here."

"I ran into Gavin in town," from Ric a month later. "He had a great story. He told me he'd just got the arrangements completed for building a new home. Capitalization of the Family Benefit and loans came through from the state advances. He was on the point of building when one day . . . he was at college . . . Tarl walked into the offices and canceled the lot. He said she had taken Benjamin from him, taken both Benjamin and Dessida from school, he said she's forging his checks right and left, hiring cars and living all over the country in expensive motels. She's definitely left him." There's silence from his pocket where his fingers lie idle. "He said he'd just come from his lawyer who had burst into a rage and called him a fool and told him to get hold of the children in a house and lock her outside till she came to her senses. He said, 'Have you ever tried smacking her bottom?' And Gavin said, 'Three times. But not till she'd smacked my face.' But oh, that's not the treatment for her. Then Gavin said 'I'm broke, Ric. She's driving me crazy, Ric.' "

"The state will take Benjamin now?"

"It's hard to say what they'll do. The state appears to be doing its utmost not to take the boy from his mother. I give them credit for that."

"She told me years ago that she'd rather the state took Benjamin than that Gavin should have him."

"To think it has come to this."

"Daniel."

"Who's that?"

"It's Tarl here."

"Hullo Tarl. How are you?"

"Good, thanks."

"How lovely to hear your voice."

"Look . . . I want you to drive me down to Angela's right now. I've . . ."

"I was down there yesterday."

"Were you? I've got no car. I had a hired car but the salesman strode out into the street as I was driving past and took it from me. I protested and told him I had to get back to the children but he . . . it was dreadful. *Dreadful.*"

"I couldn't go again today."

"Oh . . . you couldn't?"

"I'm up to my neck in work. I've got a date to keep with my publisher . . . He . . ." Pause.

No answer on the phone.

"I haven't seen you for a long time, dear. Are you well?"

"Yes. Good."

"How are the children?"

"Fine." Stop. "So you can't then?"

"But I'm sure Angela would be pleased to see you. She'd love to see the children. You should see her Macushla June. And little Reuben. I was down there yesterday afternoon. Reuben's only two and he spends most of the day at the keyboard. He put C and E together and said to me, 'That feels a lubberly color.' Baby June walks up and down the keyboard . . . that's her music. She . . ."

"I'm not in the mood for conversation."

"Well, come and see me sometime. I'm always delighted."

Pause, "All right." Pause again, "Yes I will, sometime. 'Bye."

A pose would have cracked up long ago. The freedom business must be genuine. This is a Tuesday.

Angela speaks swiftly, tensely. "Gavin turned up at our place last Tuesday night, as it was getting dark. He left his car way down at the road gate and walked soundlessly up the lane to the house. I was just feeding Macushla June and I looked up and I saw him at the door. I got such a shock. Isn't he thin now? Sort of, y'know? lean? And he said, he said, 'Come on Angela, where is she?' and I said, 'Who?'

"And he said, 'You know. Tarl.'

"I said, 'She's not here.'

"And he smiled and he said, 'Yes she is. Come on. Give her up.'

"I said, I said, 'She isn't, Gavin,' I said.

"Then I said, 'I haven't seen Tarl . . . well I haven't seen her for months and months and months.'

"And he said, 'I know she's here, Angela. You can save yourself the trouble of trying to hide her. She left word with the travel agency that if they wanted to get in touch with her she'd be here. You've got to give her up, Angela. She's run off with Benjamin and the . . . and if I can't find him this time, and soon, Ben will be taken from me too. They've had enough, the state. We'll never see Ben again.'

"I said, 'Look, Gavin Pracket, you can search the house and grounds. Search the whole farm anywhere. You can look in every single solitary corner. Go up into the bush on the ranges. You won't find her.'

"He said, 'Won't I?'

226

"And I said, 'Look here, Gavin, I don't go in for lies. I've got something better to do.'

"It took me ages to convince him, Daddy, that she wasn't here. Then he got onto the phone and rang up simply *everywhere*. He was in a *terrible* state. He hadn't had a thing to eat since . . . so I made him a cup of tea and gave him some bacon-and-egg pie. I hadn't even finished feeding Macushla and Reuben was still in the bath and Rod had not come in."

"He's still madly in love with Tarl."

"Oh no, he's not, he's not. He said, he said, 'It's not *her* I want, Angela. I don't want her any more. It's my son I want. I don't want the state to take my elder son.' That's what he said.

"And then he said, 'I wish I had met you in time, Angela.' But Daddy, don't you tell anyone he said that. Rod or anyone. Although I might as well tell you here and now that this is the nearest I've come to falling in love with somebody else since I married Rod."

"What did you say?"

"I just said . . . well I just said, 'It's a bit late to talk like that.'

"And he said, 'Eight children too late.' "

Angela pauses for breath then tosses back her hair and goes on.

"At the door as he was going he told me, 'I'm not going to try to protect her any more, Angela. I've decided between them at last. I tried to keep them both for years; then I knew I could only have one. It's my son. I'm determined to go to any lengths now to keep my son.'

"I followed him to the little gate near the house and I said to him, I said, 'I think you still love Tarl.' And he said, 'No. My love for her broke between the fourth and seventh court case.' And I said, 'But what if she came right again?' And he said, 'Oh I'd love her again then.' I said, I said to him, 'Well that means, Gavin Pracket, that you do still love her.' But he didn't say anything and just looked away to the mountains. They were black against the evening sky.

"Then he turned to go away down the lane and he touched my arm, but when he said 'Goodbye, my love,' I wasn't fooled. I knew it wasn't to me. I knew it was to his wife."

"It's true, Ange. He's still madly in love with her."

The local Ancient Mariner buttonholes Dan in the street one late afternoon in town. "I made the mistake of thrashing her, Dan." Both are shivering in a sudden burst of viciousness from

227

the antarctic. Gavin is an exceedingly handsome Ancient Mariner in the full virility of man's zenith, with a wonderfully alarming way of looking you in the eye. His own never wavers, like his purpose, like his passion for his wife. Swiftly, tensely, "The police brought them back to me at school. The constable appeared at the door of my classroom and handed over Ben. I said, 'Can't you hold him, Constable, till I've finished here? It's nearly three o'clock.' But no, I had to take delivery. Those were his orders. So I handed over my class to the rector again and went out to the car and said to Tarl, 'Move over.' And she said, 'I'll cheat you to the death.' I drove them to the flat and as we walked up the path she said, 'Don't think that because the police brought us back . . . that I'm finished. I'll take Bennie away again tomorrow morning.' And I thrashed her, Dan. I thrashed her till she could only crawl. She crawled to all the neighbors and showed them the marks of my hand on her bottom for future evidence against me. Then she got to the doctor and showed him too. That was my mistake." Shivering, but burning with pride in his wife. "Then she grabbed the kiddies and tore down to the wharf to take off to the island but the ferry had gone. So she chartered a whole boat from the Harbor Board to take them over. And booked the cost to me."

The fingers tighten on Dan's lapel and the face comes closer, with the crowds in the street passing by as though they were phantoms only. As though only here in his words was reality, and in the images in his hot mind. "But I thrashed her again, Dan, soon after. She was lying on the couch by the window and as I reached across her to collect her dishes from the sill to wash them I laid a friendly hand on her thigh. She swung her elbow into my genitals and I dragged her up and thrashed her again but this time she was beyond crawling to the neighbors. But did this discipline Tarl? She continues to strike me with anything near her. She hit me with the egg-beater. She throws food and easels at me. Yet on two occasions I've put my arm round her shoulders and said, 'Let's forget all this.' But she said 'Get away. I loathe you.' "

❧ THE MUSIC ROOM after dinner, the window open behind him on a cold blue evening. As blue as the eyes of the new Macushla who grows more like me every day. Life has its own rough justice and makes her own casual replacements. Miracles happen every day.

A dry blue evening before Christmas with holidays coming up, waving to them all from the beaches, the forests, the lakes, the bays and from the blurred blue mountains. Dan opens his evening paper. He reads two whole columns of it down to the last paragraph. "He convicted Pracket and ordered her to come up for sentence if called upon any time in the next twelve months. His Honor said that if Pracket appeared before the court again on similar charges she would go to prison for seven years as she would have deliberately flouted the law."

"I hear," Doctor Bob tells Dan, "that the kiddies are back at school, the mother is back with the father and that all is sweet again."

"No."

"See? That's the way it's done. That's the stuff to give the troops. That's the way to handle rebels like Mrs. Pracket. Give her a *real* fright. That has brought her to reason."

"Would they truly put her in prison, Borg?"

Mosquitos and moths are out for the evening as well as Borg. The old-time roses curl high round the veranda posts. The outside light draws their shadows on the veranda, static and two-dimensional. Their outlines are not fluid and changing as when drawn by the sun.

Borg strokes his chin uneasily, "Oh yes." He's much shorter on this subject these days than he used to be. Then adds, "She's already been there. I ran into her in the street on Christmas Eve and she said, 'I've had two nights in the cells.' They locked her up between catching her and the hearing. She was laughing about it. She said, 'As one old lag to another . . .'" He laughs briefly himself but without mirth.

"I hear she's back with Gavin and that all is sweet again."

He laughs with more true mirth, "I've heard that too often before."

"They're in a house together. I saw it. A smashing house, large, modern. How could they afford it? Wonderful outlook on the inner harbor. I saw Benjamin and Homer playing out on the street on the way to the land. D'you know where it is?"

"No." Finish.

"She was laughing about it," he repeats to Angela when he goes down to see her.

"Oh."

"Y'see, it's not a . . . she doesn't see it as a disgrace or punishment or correction as the rest of us do. Apart from the Prackets never going in for pride . . . when you go to jail on principle it's not a disgrace. Many of the great have had a go behind the bars at some time or other in their careers. It's a kind of prerequisite. It's almost sought after. To—to prove the validity of their argument. I seek it myself. I'd go to jail myself for not paying my tax except that the rotters would sell me up. I'm not great enough to be locked up. Rather than a disgrace, it's an ornament for people like that. An ornament. Something to wear like a decoration on the breast. A jewel in the hair."

A brilliant blue tear, "I see."

"Nothing to cry about. *I* think she'd like to go to prison for seven years. She's used to being enslaved for seven years. She called it the 'seven years' service.' This could be what she's been angling for all this time. There's nothing like a prison term to prove yourself right. And think of the sensation value. Tarl would never overlook that. She knows we'd all simply love it. I doubt if she really cares whether or not Benjamin goes to school as long as Gavin doesn't get him. She needs to make her point about freedom. She's out to prove Gavin wrong as well as the rest of us if it costs her the rest of her life in prison."

"You don't think she'd run off with Bennie again, do you?"

"I think that anyone who gave her the occasion, the means . . . the money we'll say . . . to abduct him again—they'd be doing her a service." But Angela doesn't know about the "T" account.

"Tarl . . . behind bars . . ."

"Ange. She was always behind bars. Black iron bars. There's nothing so black and iron as the bars of whim."

Summer passes, autumn follows, winter follows autumn and now spring will soon follow winter in the endless revolving of the wheel of the seasons. The spring holidays will be here in a few weeks.

One late afternoon when Dan is in the city paying for a packet of pork sausages and a bag of coffee beans from Madagascar he drops his checkbook on the floor by the counter and a small boy picks it up. Dan takes it from a small brown shapely hand. "Thanks so much." And looks into the face of Benjamin. In his eyes is the luminosity of wide horizons, far-stretching beaches with the tide out and unforgettable streams.

"It's you, Benjamin. How are you?"

"All right, thank you." No toss of the horse's head. After all, a checkbook and Mr. Francis are a profitable combination. Through the door Dan sees Gavin sitting in his car at the curb waiting for Benjamin, peaceably reading his paper. Domestically and normally. He gets the sharp impression that the turbulent Pracket family has settled down.

"And where are you going for the holidays?"

"I don't know."

A pause. Benjamin doesn't look up at him soulfully with the begging-bowl technique. He looks away and out upon the summer street with the traffic low-gearing by. One long slim brown leg curls round the other long slim brown leg. Hair long over forehead, silky, well washed in every wild water place from here to the dreaming mountains. He waits courteously to be dismissed. A graceful, gentle-hearted child never built for a desk. Something comes up in Dan that is not altruism. It's something that has reared from the depths to the surface only once or twice in his time with Tarl. Jealousy, resentment, rage at their brilliant talent for life. Of them as a family. Of their freedom from conformity. Of Tarl's rejection of him as a man every step of the way. Of her utter lack of reverence for his fame. She never ever bowed her head to him as women should. She never shaved her legs, wore silk stockings or put on a brassiere for him. And now she was settling happily, domestically, without a thought for him. *Leaving him out.* As life had left him out. As reality had left him out.

Is fate at last moving his hand? Don't tell me. He takes out his pen from an inner pocket. After all, it *is* her own money. He does hold all her work at Angela's. How can he blame himself? As for his motive . . . at least he knows it and, to the extent that a man recognizes his motives, does he justify himself.

She never did want from him other than what he had. She never had other than used him. It was always what he'd got she was after: his time, his civilization and, in the end, his mind. And from beginning to end of the drama . . . his money. She wants what I've got, he reflects. All right, here's what I've got.

A few moments later, "I say, Benjamin. I've got something for your mother."

"All right then."

"Got a pocket?"

"Yes."

"There's no need to show your father."

"No."

Benjamin goes out and Dan pays for his sausages and beans, quite a lot, too—but nothing like as much as he has just paid for the destruction of a woman . . . Tarl.

The wheel of the seasons turns full circle and here is the spring once more. School reopens tomorrow. No boy again, of course, at any school whatever.

A worn wan Romeo rampant leans back in the chair of the weary in the quiet of the library. With the loss in bodily weight and the gain in heart weight he is handsome indeed. No wonder a mistress has got him. Nevertheless it is the same Gavin who first sat in this chair, how many years ago now? With exactly the same words.

"Where's my family?"

"I don't know."

"Don't you know where they've gone, Dan?"

"No."

"I should have read the signs. She'd been different to me before she left. For months. I thought the threat of imprisonment had made her change her mind. She seemed to warm toward me in that lovely big house I rented, after a while. I chose a house with trees and flowers and a view across the harbor. Knowing she was not suburban material. I thought the house pleased her too. She stopped crying all the time. She even . . ." a star rises in the night of his eyes, "spoke to me of her own volition. But . . ." the star sets again . . . falls, rather, sweeping with a tragic trail of light into the cosmic darkness . . . "but all the time she was deceiving me." Stares downward clean through the floor to the very core of the earth as though he might find her there.

"Three of the kiddies were attending school. That might have been her undoing. She was never alive without her children. Besides, with Dessida away, no Dessy to occupy Homer, she had the baby on her all the time. She had even less time to herself with one than she had with the four. These spring holidays were coming up. Unknown to me she must have borrowed some money from someone, I don't know how much. I'll have to repay it some day. She bought the kiddies a whole swag of modern clothes and took off for a holiday. I took a job at the Public Works as usual, in addition to a night job at a bakery. And as you know I've begun building them a home and I need the money since she canceled the loans.

"Suddenly I got wind she meant to leave the country. I went to Travel Headquarters and asked them to alert all agencies not to issue a passport without the signatures of myself and a witness. They replied it was too late. She had forged my name and the witness's too. She'd left the country. She's driving me crazy, Dan." Then the same old question like the chorus coming in, "Where do you think they are, Dan?"

"Shangri-La for certain."

 ❧ BENJAMIN, DESSIDA, HOMER, call the bells the follow-ing morning, come to school and learn. Learn how to keep the apples on the apple trees sweet and how to take care of the grapes. Learn about the preservation of the fine black soils that distinguish God's Own Country. Come and receive the culture of the preceding generations as I've said so often before; hold it to yourselves for a while, then pass it down to the generations to come. The sound of a tracking pencil, the fascination of paper, the intricacies of your native language . . . these are yours for the learning. Your teachers are geared to another term's work refreshed from the rhythm of rest. There's the tremble of thousands and thousands of steps as the children are arriving, and the sound of thousands of voices, the length and breadth of the country.

Benjamin, Dessida, Homer . . . ring, ring, a-ring!

"They'll be back, of course," Gavin says between two holiday jobs. "And that's where I come in. I've spent the last years try-ing to keep her in the country. That was the crisis . . . to keep her in. But now, with the law as it stands, how can I keep her out? Poor foolish little girl. When she comes back . . . and if I know my wife, she will . . . if for no other reason than to chal-lenge the law, to spit in its clichéd face . . . she'll walk straight into prison."

Dan leans back and lifts his eyes to the portrait of me on the wall, serenely surveying the seasons. "Your mistress came to see me the other day."

"She's a very very sweet woman."

"As long as you know where your real heart is. I told her you loved your wife."

233

"I'm longing for affection. I'm a hungry lonely man . . . for warmth. I've had none for years."

"A little light color for the next court case."

"She went to Tarl and asked if she minded. Tarl replied, 'Take the great oaf away. I *loathe* him.' "

Silence in the library.

He adds, "She told me, when I showed her the plans of our house, that she'd never live in it. She said it was 'a house designed by a baker.' Because of my bakery job at night in order to build in the first place. 'A house designed by a baker.' "

More silence in the library.

Then Gavin, "But I'll never shut the door on Tarl."

"La grande passion."

"She'll be back, Daddy." In Angela there is the access to instinct of the female breeding, in and out of childbirth, in the ruthless primeval rhythm of creating life, underlined by death. "She'll be back, I know it."

She is walking down the lane with him to his car at the road. She takes one of Macushla June's hands and Mary takes the other. Her other hand takes Reuben's, and Brucey takes Reuben's second hand. An uneven line of them, the smallest each side of the parent and the taller farther out. Her dress is tightening on her girl's body with another pregnancy. The newest and smallest within. "I can't tell you why I know but I do. She always did come back to base however far she'd been. Didn't matter what was waiting for her. It's summer now, Daddy, then it will be autumn, and she always got back before winter. I can't work out why I know these things but I just do. All I'm saying is . . . I haven't got your words or anything . . . Tarl will be back this year."

"I know she will. Her life is 'on the road.' There are no more beautiful highways on earth than in this country. She knew every stone of them. She said to me once, 'I am Nature. I get everything I am from Nature.' And Nature in person abides in New Zealand."

He slides in behind the wheel and Angela and the children mount the bank here in order to see him as he drives away. And as he looks back he sees them, silhouetted against the mountains, with the late sun touching them, and the wind from the Tasman lifting their hair. The unborn inside her, Macushla in her arms, Reuben at her knees, Brucey a step away and Mary on her own. Waving, all waving to him. And smiling. Smaller and smaller the group as he drives away ... smaller, blurred ... but still the primeval shape of the family backgrounded by the mountains. A vital cell of humanity.

⚜ ANYONE THESE DAYS driving round the estuary near the school can see a man building alone. Very alone indeed. What could be a lonelier sight than a father building a house for a family who have no further use for him? Where are his sons, helping him with the concreting? Where are his daughters, making him tea to break the piling man-hours? Where, for that matter, is his wife, interested in the design? "Cupboards here, my dear. Not too high where I can't reach them. This room for the boys and this for the girls. And this will be ours overlooking the water. Nice wide windows, my dear."

Where are they? They're not here. Only ghosts are here. Ghost boys playing on the shingle heap, ghosts girls on the balcony. And a phantom wife building with him a phantom dream for a life that may not be. Yet a man is unable not to build either dreams or houses. A man must have faith in his dreams and house ... they are himself. Even a phantom house inhabited by ghosts alone. He must believe invisible hands, inaudible clustering voices, or drown himself in an estuary.

Anyone can see him building there after school or during the empty weekends, with an apron on at times, his head down in concentration, feverishly making a home. Stirring hope into the concrete mixture, painting the walls with memories. But never is self-pity used. Proudly to Dan, "I'll guarantee I'm the only man in the country building without a loan. But I couldn't do without the job at the bakery at night." A man alone, building. If only "a house designed by a baker."

Yet not wholly alone. I myself often see another man there sweating his sweat along with Gavin. A man in old khaki trousers, a gray open shirt with sleeves rolled up and large clumsy boots. His hair jerking in the tufted gusts of wind from the sea in the winter, flat and wet in the rains in the spring. He shares Gavin's sweat on Saturdays in place of sharing his dreams. He's jolly good with a hammer and nail and a saw, from what I can see, and takes enormous pride in his concreting, smoothing it with a little tool—I don't know its name—the way he strokes

235

the head of a child. It took even me some time to recognize the elegant headmaster of our school. "I don't know," he confesses to Dan, the grand master of receiving confidences, "why I do it. I haven't got the time. He's not even one of my parents now, his children no longer ours. But there's something about it that touches me. It may be . . . just children in general. Families."

"Y-yes . . . I sort of see."

"Unless it's when I'm slogging away there in all sorts of weather, rain and so on—there's quite a biting gale off the water at times, especially towards evening—I find myself thinking of Ramona. Gavin's got his ghosts but I've got mine. His ghosts play on the shingle heap and on the unfinished balcony. But my ghost is in a schoolroom. During the week I see her there, a phantom at a desk. I see phantom work on the wall. A phantom not strong enough for sport on Friday, reading in the library. I'd give her odd jobs to do for me. Counting out change and . . . Or sorting out office cards and . . . I liked Ramona near."

A man building a home. To Dan at night, "When I've finished I'll put all my children in it. Supposing I see them again."

"Supposing you see them again."

"And if she wants to see them, here she'll find them. I'll never shut the door on her."

"No."

"I like building, Dan. Work with the hands doesn't hurt a man. It enriches him. You can think when the hands are busy. Besides . . . when I'm building for them I hear her saying, 'This will be our room, dear, overlooking the water.' Whereas, when I'm not building, all I hear is, 'Take the great oaf away. I loathe him.' "

The Head tells Dan, "I can't believe it. I don't know how he keeps going."

"I do. His heart believes it is all for her whatever the evidence to the contrary. I never saw a real heart take account of evidence. The heart is the source of all action, the imagery flashing in it. Which is my life-work's subject: 'The Movements of the Heart.' I know Gavin's heart because his is mine, just as I know Tarl's. Which is the infirmity of a man who writes. I wish I could be spared it. I have no heart exclusively of my own because mine is everybody's. Gavin's heart is certain he is building for her. And so often the heart is right, with all manner of miraculous foreknowledge."

Yet no amount of words can encompass and contain the full sum of human feeling in this building that I witness, this exercise in the entire range of a man. It takes something much more simple. Angela records the entire thing over the kitchen table at her place with the babies all over and round her. With consummate ease to Dan one morning: two silent blue tears.

A man alone building a home for phantoms. Anyone can see him there.

TEN

*Will you savour again and again
the few brief moments you felt yourself expand
to meet the air's real freedom, as
you count the stony minutes of the years?*

—CHARLES DOYLE

❧ A QUARTET of seasons turns full circle. I see them myself from the library as I gaze from my aging portrait. I see an evening in another summer, the moths using the open doorway. They use it as a freeway, a skyway, as many others do; why not?

The moon is high and the evening still, the very conditions that draw me. With the ease of miracle I take phantom shape in the shadows of the veranda; I am about to speak his name, Daniel . . . when there's a footfall on the steps behind me, a footfall of reality, and a mortal voice speaks what I would . . .

"Daniel."

Can the dead compete with the living? I vanish.

But he doesn't look up, thinking it's I.

"Daniel," the voice again.

He does look up. "It's Tarl."

Fashionable green stripes slashed obliquely across the top of her like shadows across the flank of an animal gliding through the jungle. Tight short white skirt. Silk stockings. Great God! . . . and high-heeled shoes. Hair built up high on her head with a reflecting gem set in it.

"I had to come."

"But you're still in the shadows."

Steps in the doorway. "I survive the light."

"Tarl."

"Only Tarl."

"I prefer 'Only Tarl.' "

"Do you? Oh, how wonderful."

"How are you?"

"Fine."

"What did you say?"

"Fine."

"Oh 'Fine.' That what you said. I see."

A moth from the evening settles upon his hand on his paper. "That's the same moth."

"What's that?"

"This moth is the same one. It came before."

"I'll only stay one minute."

"I can't stand up as a gentleman should. I might disturb it."

"Oh well then, I can see I'm disturbing you."

"Oh . . . no."

"All right then. I can see you still don't want me."

"It's you that says it."

"D'you mind if I read awhile in the music room? A book . . . I . . ."

"You're not disturbing me. It's this moth on my hand. I can't stand up. I might frighten it. Crush it . . . might damage it in some way. Its delicate antennae—look at them . . . like the touch of one mind upon another's. Like intuition, like sensibility."

"What I really came for . . . I hope you don't mind."

"At least you come."

"The very last request of all."

No answer.

Heroically, "Say no if you need to."

"Yes."

Defiantly, "Well, what are we going to do about it?"

"About what?"

"About you and me."

"You ought to sit down, Tarl."

No answer.

"Do."

"Oh . . . all right then."

She does, crossing her legs chastely, the silk knees exposed.

"I wonder why this vulnerable and exquisite creature doesn't spread its wings and fly back to the night? Escape while there's time. It immobilizes me. I believe it is the female. I could blow it away but it could easily return. I could brush it away but I'm afraid of what its touch would do to me. I might inadvertently hurt it, accidentally kill it, whereas I've killed enough as it is. I might even . . ."

Hit-or-miss, do-or-die voice. School or else. "There's only one more thing I want before they get me. You know of course," casually, "that I'm going to prison." A step or two. "Of course the moment I come out I'll take Bennie again."

"Look how this thing sways. Indecision."

"Say no, if you need to."

"Isn't it hot? Not enough air in here."

"You."

A long long silence in the library.

"I do, Tarl, recall all that you could have been to me."

Stands, "All right then," bravely. "D'you mind if I walk in the garden? I need a rest from the children." Her eyes are upon him. Gems, like the gem in her hair. Nocturnelike. "I said I survived the light. I like those words of mine. I'll remember them. But I'll survive the darkness too. I can survive anything. Nothing can ever really harm me in the Everlasting Now."

The moth takes flight at last and he stands. Turns over his work and removes his new glasses. "You stay here and rest."

"It doesn't matter in the least, of course, but I meant to say this some time or other. Just *one more thing* I've got to say. D'you mind?"

"There's not enough air in here. Even with the door and window open."

"You are my Shangri-La."

He walks to the door, passing her. "No, Tarl. I've got too much to forgive you." It's he in the doorway now.

"Forgive *me?*"

"You've done too much for me. You've given me far too much."

Astounded, "I didn't know that."

"The armfuls and armfuls of life you've tossed into this room. Explosive stuff."

Incredulity. Hand to cheek, heel forward, staring downward.

"You've simply wrenched me back to reality. I'm stinging all over. I'm absolutely sore with it. I can't stand reality. I belong to the realms of imagery. My own life. The life I've created for myself . . . creatures . . . phantoms. I . . ."

"Oh I'm sorry. I'm dreadfully *sorry*."

"And you've taught me far more about this freedom you're always raving about. This freedom. More than I ever wanted to know about it. I'll never be at peace again. I *feel*. I'll never forgive you that."

"No, no, no, I mustn't apologize. I can't apologize for life. Or freedom. I can't apologize for freedom."

He turns back to the night outside. "Anyway, anyway, Tarl, I've . . . not for me the tortures of Gavin or the upended Borg."

"No," heroically, "I can't apologize."

"I've served my time in heartbreak a lifetime ago. And that is man's wages, any man's, when he touches you."

"You've served your time in heartbreak." Then the light of revelation, "That's why."

"I don't know what you mean."

"That's why you're my Shangri-La."

The dew is heavy.

Across the grass to the umbrella tree where he can see the light in the library. He's come without his smokes. He begins making his way back to the house to slip round the side to the back in order that he might not have to witness Tarl's terrible crying. But she's not crying. Through the door he sees her standing exactly as he has left her; poised on back foot, one heel forward, one hand on hip, one to cheek, concentrating downward.

He walks in the morning to children's voices and the buses already arriving, and the bells calling all children. He walks back through the wet grass to the steps, along the veranda to the open door. The light is still on. But Tarl is "not here."

Only the portrait of me serenely surveying the morning, watching the seasons revolving.

❧ DAN NEVER quite knows why everything is brought to him in his quiet room on the veranda. He never goes out for it and never does anything about it. I'm a sort of grand conscience, he thinks. They don't think of me as a man.

"I've got the children in the house," from Gavin, his voice on the phone at World Theatre pitch.

"Oh, congratulations, Gavin."

"We've been here the whole weekend."

"The whole four?"

"Well, no. Not Dessy. She's not very well and she stayed with the little auntie."

"I think you're wonderful."

"No furniture or anything like that. Nothing in the cupboards. I'm trying to get a housekeeper. A liver-in. This getting the children off to school in the morning, and myself. Breakfast, dishes, cutting lunches. And the meal at night, I . . ."

" 'Course, children take a lot of washing and ironing, don't they?"

"I've always done that myself anyway. And in the evenings, you see, I've got commitments. But this is the first time, Dan, I've ever been under my own roof."

"Oh, congratulations. I am most touched. And good luck."

"Thank you. That is warming."

From Angela, "Dessy's all right, Daddy. It's she who was the one who caught all the hate. Always had her arms round her mother's legs. She was terrified of her father."

"I did say, I admit," from the Head, "I did say in the past that I definitely would not have the Pracket family back at this school but . . ." outspread hands . . . "with Gavin and family just round the corner, a family with no mother with them, I don't know, I'm sure. I venture to say that . . ."

"They always liked this school, Ric. And whether they did or not, it doesn't matter now which school they attend. Their serenity is established. Forever. Tarl saw to that. Gavin too. The two of them knew what they were doing whatever it cost them. The villain in their story is the social law."

"By gee, I'm looking forward to seeing Ramona again."

"As I was saying, their serenity is established forever."

From Gavin again, impassioned, "I said to her, 'When you come out of prison I'll bring all the children to meet you at the gate. I'll never shut the door on you.' But she replied that when that time comes she'll immediately sue me for custody of all the children and occupation of the house—this 'house designed by a baker'—with a demand that I move out. Using as evidence all those thrashings I gave her and, of course, my mistress. She'll win it. I always knew I was building the home for her . . . my heart said so. I see myself roofless again, a wanderer. The Wandering Minstrel, the Ancient Mariner forever telling my story. On the outside looking in. Painfully looking in on my family."

"Stop it. I can't stand it."

With increased zest, "She promises to have every one subpoenaed to give evidence, you included. It was a mistake, those thrashings. I always said I should never let anger guide me.

She's suing me for assault." Also, perplexed, "Failure to maintain."

"Failure to maintain?" Dan roars with laughter. In a moment Gavin does too.

"She also plans to name my 'very sweet woman.' Not for anything so obvious and trivial as adultery, as anyone else would—in her reckoning that's nothing—but for keeping me away from the children. Can you believe it? The very thing she's suing me for in the first place . . . *in order* to keep me away from the children."

"Pure Tarlism."

"She claims my affair takes the car from her. It's the occasional absence of the car that's important to her. Not me."

"Do forgive this awful laughing."

Later, "If you ever married V. S.—sorry, Very Sweet—would she . . . I mean . . ."

"*Never*. I'll never shut the door on my wife."

❧ I DON'T REVISIT my Daniel now, appearing on the veranda in the shadows when the moon is high and the evening still. Eternity has loneliness enough without looking for it on earth. That which I lost in dying early is what I seek in the living . . . laughter, love and the real.

I transfer my haunting to Angela's place, where you see things like the mother plunging across the paddock like a shooting star to chase the turkeys from the garden; like a shooting star, Angela, with a tail of following children. Mary dashing after, Brucey next, Reuben trailing in line and baby Macushla last, the whole tapering line of them in strict comet formation, waving a tail of squealing kittens.

And where you hear things like "I saw the Pracket children, Daddy. They were at the Sapphire Springs. They were saying goodbye to Gavin, who had left them there for the day. They were standing together on this hill with the wind blowing across them. They were all waving in the one direction to Gavin and all of them were laughing. Different sizes they were. They all had marvelous colored shorts, bought in the islands, I think. And their legs, Daddy. Their legs were so long, like antelope or deer. Ramona was absolutely stunning. Her hair was cut short to the line of her head. She was erect, she was utterly slender.

246

And Dessida's long curls were flowing in the wind like some kind of shining flag. And Homer . . . he was jumping up and down between his brother and sisters. And Benjamin . . .

"Then all at once they ran away, careering down the hill. Waving back and laughing. All together . . . a unit. Wild they were . . . superb."

FREE CATALOG
of over 650 Bantam Books